BLAME IT ON THE MISTLETOE

BETH GARROD

Internal design by Ashley Holstrom/Sourcebooks

Published by Sourcebooks Fire, an imprint of Sourcebooks
P.O. Box 4410, Naperville, Illinois 60567-4410
(630) 961-3900
sourcebooks.com

Originally published as *All I Want for Christmas* in 2020 in the UK by Scholastic Children's Books, an imprint of Scholastic Inc.

Library of Congress Cataloging-in-Publication Data

Names: Garrod, Beth, author.
Title: Blame it on the mistletoe / Beth Garrod.
Other titles: All I want for Christmas
Description: Naperville, Illinois : Sourcebooks Fire, [2021] | Originally published in the United Kingdom by Scholastic Children's Books in 2020 under title: All I want for Christmas. | Audience: Ages 14. | Audience: Grades 10-12. | Summary: A teenaged social media star living in New York and a sixteen-year-old girl living in the English village of Little Marsh swap places in an attempt to have the perfect Christmases.
Identifiers: LCCN 2021028971 (print) | LCCN 2021028972 (ebook)
Subjects: CYAC: Christmas--Fiction. | Love--Fiction. | Internet personalities--Fiction. | London (England)--Fiction. | England--Fiction. | New York (N.Y.)--Fiction. | LCGFT: Novels.
Classification: LCC PZ7.1.G3767 Al 2021 (print) | LCC PZ7.1.G3767 (ebook) | DDC [Fic]--dc23
LC record available at https://lccn.loc.gov/2021028971
LC ebook record available at https://lccn.loc.gov/2021028972

Printed and bound in the United States of America.
SB 10 9 8 7 6 5 4 3 2

For Moomin, who made sure Christmas was—and always will be—magical for all of us.

FORTY-TWO DAYS TILL CHRISTMAS

Is it so wrong to put a Santa hat on a shriveled pumpkin? I did it anyway and pulled on my elf onesie. It must have had an incident in the dryer, because it only reached my calves and the H on the front was half dangling off.

But who cared? Not me. It was November 14, my Christmas playlist was on, and everything was going to plan. Freezing ankles weren't going to get in the way of tradition (unless the tradition was woolly socks).

I sat on the edge of my bed and reached underneath. Bingo. I pulled out the battered shoebox, blew off the dust, and peeled back the tape.

I loved this moment. Every. Single. Year.

And there it was, waiting for me. A Christmas card, some paper folded inside. I snapped off a piece of chocolate (actually two, but they seemed so happy together, why separate them?), and opened the envelope.

Happy Christmas, Holly!

If you're reading this, it means only one thing. It's Chriiiiiiistmas. Well, the start of it anyway. Well done, you, on getting through the other less pointful ten months of the year. Is it snowing? I hope for the sake of all that is festive and cinnamon-scented, it is.

IN FACT. STOP. Are you sipping on something gingerbread flavoured rn? If not, SORT IT OUT before reading another word—because this is about to get biiiig.

What you're holding in your hand is not just a Christmas card. Oh no. It's a time traveling gift from the Best Christmas Ever. Honestly, this year was IT.

And no detail must be forgotten. EVER. (In case you're not getting the hint, this is your reminder to make notes starting...now.) Treat this card like a priceless relic. Like the... er...Mona Lisa. But BETTER. Because she doesn't have Malteser Reindeers.

Or maybe she does...and that's why she's smiling?? So lemme break it down...

OF COURSE, Carol singing was amazing. As in Carol, Mum's friend, who NEVER lets us down at the village

Christmas Eve singalong round the tree. Serious question—has she genuinely never heard of any of the songs DESPITE THEM BEING THE SAME ONES EVERY YEAR AND ALSO THE SAME ONES SINCE CHRISTMAS WAS INVENTED?? As usual, she sang the wrong words. And the wrong tunes. Iconic.

Then we all headed to ours for the legendary Christmas Eve party. After we'd stood around pretending mince pies are nice (and me telling everyone they used to be oblong, like the nativity crib), Naomi and I competitive speed-ate all the pink Quality Street without getting spotted (Mum genuinely thinks they just don't put as many in the tin?! Bahahaha), and I herded everyone into the garden. Mum, her new boyf, the twins, my sister, Ruby, Fred—everyone.

And, HELLO, best-ever surprise! I'd snuck back early and pegged up matching onesies—one for everyone, each with their initial on. They'd taken weeks! Sure, I do agree with Fred, that on reflection, seven full-length body shapes swaying in the dark garden was kind of creepy. BUT after I'd persuaded the twins to stop screaming and come back out, everyone was dead impressed and pulled them on. Not to blow my own Christmas trumpet here, but we looked A-May-Zing. I really nailed my yearly "Christmas Cracker" surprise. The group photo was perfection. (Mum has already put it on the fridge—over the one of Naomi passing her driving test. Hahaha.) The only one not in it was Colin. I'd crafted his onesie from an old jumper but had sort of forgotten dogs had four legs...and a head. So, basically, I'd made him an elaborate giant sock.

ANYWAY.

Mum and New Boyfriend drank mulled wine and chatted loudly about the heat burning off the alcohol (clearly a LIE, due to the volume at which they were talking about it), and Ruby, Fred, and I escaped up to my room for the most sacred of festive traditions. Watching Elf. Saaantaaaaa!!!!! We are word perfect. This year, Ruby and Fred went next-level with their attempt at recreating the escalator scene. Rubes was, of course, amazing, and Fred was...well, Fred. I don't think he'll ever attempt the splits again—or maybe not even enjoy normal walking judging by how he hobbled out. We swapped presents—Fred's looked very much like two Toblerones end to end. (SPOILER ALERT: You can imagine how excited I was when it turned out to be...two Toblerones superglued end to end. My friends are THE BEST.) Then everyone left, and it was just Mum, me, and Nay. So we hung our stockings on the stairs and went to bed.

And OH. MY. JINGLE. BELLS.

Christmas Day went and got even better?!

I got up early (the incentive of pre-8 a.m. Toblerone is a powerful thing) to surprise Mum by doing Christmas breakfast, but she was already up. In full Ms. Santa dress!! I unveiled this year's Christmas playlist, and we danced around the kitchen as we waited for Naomi to get up (which took forever, despite me walking outside her door really loudly four times). Then it was opening stockings and selection boxes. Mum still acts surprised when she gets her big sports sock stuffed with things as if we haven't been doing that for years, but I guess that's part of the tradition now too!

As usual, I shoved on every single bit of makeup from my stocking, so I looked quite extra (a.k.a. scary) for 10 a.m., and put on all my new bits of clothing, even though none of it matched. We had to delay proper presents round the tree as I had an incident with my Cadbury's selection box (i.e., had eaten all of it except the Crunchie) and bending to pick up the presents and pass them out was making me feel a bit... volatile. But then genius Naomi opened our yearly box of posh chocolates from Dad, and weirdly, it turned out eating more was the solution. Who knew?!

Mum and Nay loved their pressie from me—tickets to a baking class with one of the Bake Off winners (pheeewwww—it cost ALL my savings). But Naomi went weird, and I had no idea why until I opened my pressie from her. A ticket for me to go too! Absolute result!!! She said it was older-taller-sister intuition. (Fred later accidentally revealed he'd tipped her off about how much I wouldn't stop talking about it.)

Ruby loved what I'd bought her—a personalized handheld

mirror that I'd had engraved with "And the winner of Best Actor goes to..." around the edge. It was to use before her auditions, because if I couldn't be there to remind her how awesome she was, maybe this would instead. Honestly, when Ruby, the girl I've never seen express an emotion in almost sixteen years, rang, she looked kind of...teary. In a good way. IT WAS TOO MUCH! Maybe that's why I had major eye leakage when I opened hers—a snow globe of the ice rink in Central Park that she'd also had personalized! (Related thought—me and Mum's new beige carpet can confirm my new eyeliner is NOT waterproof.) It really couldn't have been more perfect if it tried. It said...one sec, let me get it...

"Shake my snow, dream what you feel, make a Christmas wish, then watch it become real."

** Full disclosure, I've now done that 1,000 times but haven't YET had my wish granted and been teleported to New York. **

** Even fuller disclosure, I also shook it allll the way through Nay and me watching the Christmas Eve Snow Ball concert in Madison Square Garden, but still nothing. YET. **

Argh?! Did I mention the twins? How could I not?! Oh yes...because they spent the whole day running around with a box on their heads. One box, four legs. Each to their own. Being five must be a lot of fun. Even Colin was looking at them like they'd lost it, and his favourite hobby is licking the oven.

Which reminds me. The big thing. COLIN WENT MISSING!

Around 2 p.m. We rang everyone to ask if they'd seen him—even Carol, who turned up to look with a torch, even though the sun was still out.

But guess who eventually found him? ME. He was splatted out in the cupboard under the stairs, lying on some coats, looking like a balloon with four corks sticking out. He wasn't even blinking. Obviously, we all panicked. Carol rang 111 (who pointed out they didn't deal with dogs). But... Mum discovered a plate under the kitchen table. Yes, tiny old Chewbacca-resembling, Jack Russell poodle cross that he is, he'd somehow dragged the whole turkey off the table. And eaten it. The Christmas turkey. Every bit?! For real—it was bigger than him. No wonder he couldn't make all of his legs reach the floor at the same time—he'd effectively grounded himself from overeating. And I respected that. I mean, I had to. He'd totally seen what had happened with me and the selection box earlier. (And every single year before that.) (And probably next year too.) Mum was upset about the turkey, but we promised her the best bits of Christmas dinner were the accessories anyway and stuck some frozen hamburgers in the oven. If Colin had gone for the pigs in blankets, it would have been a different matter.

But then. THEN. It happened.

****** DRINK BREAK. DEEP BREATHS. Prepare to relive this. ******

An unexpected doorbell ring.

First thought: Carol coming back to tell us she'd rung an ambulance for Colin after all.

Second thought: Fred arriving early, because he'd got the time (or day) wrong.

But no. All kinds of no. IT WAS WOODY. As in, love-of-my-life Woody.

As in, Woody who makes me think deeply inappropriate thoughts, just from writing his name.

As in...

(Sorry, no, had to take a moment to think deeply inappropriate thoughts.)

When I opened the door, he said, "I thought my girlfriend deserved a surprise on Christmas Day." Like in a film!! And he was holding out a big, red Christmas plant thing. (Have since found out it was a poinsettia. KNOWLEDGE.)

And then, right on cue...snow started falling. Most. Perfect. Romantic. Christmas. Moment. Ever.

He suggested we take Colin for a quick walk (or carry, due to his tummy dimensions) and we went to the walkway by the village hall where we'd had our first-ever kiss (November 17, 8:23 p.m.). But this time there was mistletoe.

And, not to be graphic, but we stopped underneath it and... well... THERE'S NO OTHER WAY OF SAYING IT, WE HAD THE BEST KISS EVER. EVEREVEREVER.

*** PHEW, HAD TO PAUSE TO ACTUALLY FAN FACE ***

Genuinely, best of my life (not that there's much to compare it to, hahahaha). Woody gave me this look before and after that was all mwwhhhhwwhhhwhhhw (a.k.a. the sound of me melting) and told me how much he liked me.

Hot. Romantic. Christmassy. And in the snow! With a poinsettia! (No idea why I'd taken that with me.) But who cares! (Well, Carol did as she walked round the corner, almost straight into us, and was all flustered, and said "don't mind me" five times, which made me really mind her, and then she tripped over the plant and then over Colin.)

I had to have a quiet sit-down when I got back to process it all. Naomi kept asking why I was grinning like I was watching a new Harry Styles video.

Then Fred came round, and I introduced him to my plant (he named it Stemi Lovato). He was still wearing his onesie from the day before. I asked if he'd taken it off at any point and...well, he was vague to say the least. He loved his present (ten packets of Jaffa Cakes cunningly arranged in the shape of an X). Then it was the usual—sofa cushions on the floor and bundling up under my duvet, Mum and Nay under another one. We stuck on the old Gavin & Stacey Christmas special and played games and ate every edible present, even though we were already stuffed and, well...days just don't get better. (Even if the main game we played was trying to ignore the noises Colin made as he deflated.)

I'm still smiling now...ten days later.

I have never looked after ANYTHING like I have Stemi Lovato. Stemi is basically my and Woody's first child.

Which brings me to...QUESTIONS. Is Stemi still aliving? And thriving?

Did Woody let you keep his hoodie? Does it still smell of him? (A.k.a., heaven.)

Ruby—please tell me she made it into this year's pantomime?!

And finally...

I know every year, you say you're going to make Christmas better than the year before, but srsly, HOW IS THAT POSSIBLE?! You better have started planning already!

So...that's it. END OF THIS YEAR'S CARD.

Happy Christmas! Go give Mum a hug and tell her you love her, and then you know what to do...

PUT THIS UP AND OFFICIALLY LAUNCH CHRISTMAS. HAPPY HOLIDAAAAAAYS!!!

Holly (from last year) (a.k.a. Christmas past)

PS: Mum mentioned she'd always wanted a calendar with pics of the family on—present idea?!

PPS: Get more Twiglets. Or hide a box. Turns out Fred panic eats them when he can't figure out who he is in the Post-it game.

PPPS: Although Colin pretends to be lazy, he's surprisingly good at mountaineering up a table. PUT EDIBLE THINGS HIGHER.

PPPPS: Oh, and New Boyfriend doesn't seem to be loving the New Boyfriend name. He pointed out multiple times he's been with Mum for four years. Maybe this could be the year we start to call him by his actual name. Colin. And rename dog Colin to dog-Colin...? Nah, I'm picturing your face, and agree. TOO SOON. As you were.

PPPPPS: Last thing, promise. Don't forget to not forget the golden rules of Christmas... Never say no to a novelty hot drink. And never wimp out of the high notes of "All I Want for Christmas Is You." It's what Mariah wants (even if Colin x 2 don't).

CHAPTER ONE

Elle

Hold up, who knew we had a pro in the house?!

@OneElleOfATime how much to do mine?!

The reveal of my snowflake nails had gone well. Amazing what some well-placed Wite-Out can do. I'll never not be grateful for filters. And YouTube tutorials.

I stretched out against the life-size plastic Santa I was using as a backrest and replied.

For you?! Free! Next time you're in New Jersey, slide into my DMs 😉☃️

I meant it. I totally loved @_Beckywiththemediocrehair_, even though we'd never met. Though...never meeting had its perks—if she saw my nails, she'd realize what a hot mess they were in real life. A bit like me.

It could *not* be normal to spend your weekend hunched in the back of your parents' work van, parked in the best neighborhood in town, day two of running out of time to wash your hair, while legit sweating over a math assignment.

And this street was something else. Which figured. It was *always* the biggest houses that wanted their Christmas decorations and lights up first. Mom said normally, these families weren't even going to be at home for the holidays—they just wanted to make sure no one else got the best pick of the bunch. Ha. The true meaning of Christmas spirit.

And the house my family was barfing Christmas all over was a cross between the White House and...an even bigger White House.

Still, I wasn't here to decorate. I was here to get this math done.

Point (a,b) is on the function f(x)=2x x>... numberslettersnumberslines.

Could they mark me wrong if I just wrote, "Ask Google"?

I got back to my notifications.

Queeeeen. I still have half a pumpkin and a flaking-off skull on mine. Wanna swap?!

I replied.

😭😭😭 **half chewed is a look too!**

Truth was, I'd only finished mine last night, and half-chewed was already my look. But truth wasn't exactly the point of the internet. Still, the post had done its job. I now had 23,132 followers. Awesome. I was finally getting my numbers back up to what they'd been on my old account. And, even more awesome, I'd just got a like and follow from @realdeallogan. He had 125,000 followers and was the closest Alpine Peaks got to a celebrity. Though I would like to see what he looked like with a shirt *on* for a change, I kept the feedback to myself and followed him back. I wonder how he even knew I existed? I knew about him because he was on a local basketball team with my brother. Oh, and a girl in my class had a poster of him up in her locker, which I had a *lot* of questions about. Mainly, did he print them himself?

Nick stuck his head into the back of the van.

"You going to help, or are you just going to sit there?"

Nice to see you too, bro.

"Just sit there. Well, here." I fumbled for a book and held it up. "It's called an assignment."

"Oh, right..." He put a finger to his lips. "Because I *swear* I just saw you posting about your hashtag holiday nails?"

He didn't even follow me, he just occasionally checked in so he could tease me about it.

I smiled sweetly. "You're welcome." If he thought acting

like an extra parent was going to stop me, he was wrong. "Don't forget to like, okay?"

He rolled his eyes, slung a huge Styrofoam reindeer over his shoulder, and walked off. Normally I would laugh at the sight of a six-foot-one guy trying a moody march off as the hooves of a grinning reindeer whacked him in the ribs, but things with my little brother had started to feel weird. Weirder than me sitting in the middle of a herd of fake reindeer. So pretty damn weird. There was something up with him. I knew it. There had been ever since before we left Nashton. We used to be so close, but then he'd started disappearing all the time. And whenever I asked what was up or where he was going, he'd brush me off. Which is why I hadn't told him about what really went down with my old account, with Clara...not that I'd told anyone. Who did I even have to tell anymore? Plastic Santa?

Life was so easy for Nick—well, give or take the bruised ribs. When we moved here, he'd fallen right into being his usual perfect Nick self—picking up friends, getting on teams, even starting a new band. And me—I had zero. Except Mom and Dad fretting about why I was in my room so much and blaming themselves for maybe making a bad choice in moving here. Which meant a high risk of them deciding to move...again. Nick swerved all their interrogations by always running off to basketball practice or urgent band rehearsals in "The Playground," the dive of a studio by Blake's. He was a genius like that. Which left me.

That's when I'd made the decision. Even though my last account, @NoWayNoelle, had ended in disaster, this time I was going to make one work. On my own. Show everyone I was doing okay.

So, I'd launched @OneElleOfATime, and the months of effort were already paying off. I'd told any of my old followers who'd come back that I'd been on a "creative refresh." Which sounded a whole lot better than, "Oh, y'know, my life became a dumpster fire, and then we moved to Boringsville, USA."

This time I needed my followers to know I wasn't going anywhere—so I'd posted to say I was going to hit 30,000 followers by the end of the year. Even Mom and Dad seemed impressed and had *finally* stopped bugging me about if I was okay.

"Elly?" Oh crap. I threw my phone down and tried to look like I was deep in mathematical thought. Mom threw some empty boxes over my head. "Nick said you'd finished your work. Want to give us a hand?"

Well, this was a toughie. Mom would stress if I told her I'd still made zero progress with my assignment—so, if they needed a hand, maybe I should pretend I'd finished and do it in bed tonight on the d-low?

"Does it involve carrying large mammals?" I grinned and clapped my book shut. Evidence gone. "Because I picked up a strain in track and was *specifically* told to avoid carrying anything with hooves."

Mom smiled and lifted a huge box like it didn't weigh a ton

and she wasn't wearing three-inch heels and jeans that weren't built for bending.

It was no wonder people sometimes asked if we were sisters—it was like the aging process had just stopped with her at twenty-five. Dad had majorly lucked out—although Mom always said that she could never turn down someone who made waffles like he did.

"Luckily for you, it's just stringing some candy canes up the stairs. Think you can handle it?"

Mom's definition of *some* could be in the hundreds, but I guess that meant they really did need my help. I squeezed past a snowman that was bigger than Nick and wriggled my way out the back of the van.

"You know you guys don't have a normal job, right?"

Mom passed me a box of candy canes. *Hundreds* of candy canes. I knew her too well. "And since when has this family ever been normal?!"

She did have a point. We'd always been the slightly different ones. We'd moved to America from England when I was four, and since then we'd moved houses another five times, across four states. It was three years ago in Philadelphia that they'd started Good for Your Elf!, their Christmas tree rental and decoration business. It had been super successful in Nashton, so just over a year ago, they'd moved here, to Alpine Peaks in New Jersey, to "franchise and expand the business," a.k.a., work 24–7. Nick and

I had stayed with Grams, Dad's mom, to finish the school year, then moved to join them at the start of the summer.

I'd lost count of the times they'd said this move would be "for good." I didn't have the heart to remind them that's what they'd said about the other four.

I jumped out of the van. "Consider me reporting for duty, Mom."

"Honey..." She shook her head as she looked at me. "While I appreciate all the hands I can get, next time, remember we said 'presentable,' not 'stuck-at-home-with-strep chic'?"

I would feel insulted if she weren't entirely correct. I hadn't thought I was going to be leaving the house today, and when I committed to staying inside, I committed *hard*.

I looked a total mess. A hair-falling-out-of-bun, elasticated-pants, no-bra, half-of-yesterday's-mascara-under-my-eyes, Mom's-old-Blur-T-shirt-on mess.

"What?" I did a slow spin, my bun flopping down to just above my left ear. Nice touch. "You don't think I make it work?"

But Mom laughed with me. "You want me to take a photo so you can post it, huh?"

I rolled my eyes. "Don't want to break the internet, so I'mma hold off..."

She held out a box. "And you're still aiming for thirty thousand followers by Christmas?"

"Uh-huh." Show no weakness, that's how it worked in my

family—at least she was taking my account seriously. We walked up the path, my sneakers crunching the gravel. "No problem."

I mean, it was a huge problem, but what she didn't know couldn't hurt her.

Mom and Dad were happy thinking things were finally picking up for me, especially when I'd gotten the sponsorship offer from SnapGoGo last month. They were a travel company and had noticed I was always posting about my dream trips. Ha. That was another reason to get my followers up. Stop them from realizing I never actually made any of them happen.

How did Dove make it look so easy? She was in my grade, and I didn't *know* her, know her, but I didn't need to know her to know she was legendary status. I'd figured that out before I'd even been shown where the restrooms were. Dove Moore had everything: friends, followers, a family who didn't move every two years... Sure, I'd never heard anyone actually say anything nice about her, but someone like her didn't seem to care what anyone else thought.

Since I'd started in September, we'd spoken, let me count them, yeah, zero times. Not that I expected her to—just because I'd followed her for years didn't mean she would have any clue who a lesser mortal like me was. Rumor was that she'd earned enough from all her sponsorship to book Shawn Mendes to do an acoustic set for her next birthday. Ha—for mine I went bowling with Mom, Dad, Nick, and Grams. *So* similar.

But Shawn Mendes wasn't what everyone was talking about. Nah, for Dove, this kind of thing was no big deal. The big news was that she'd launched a side account with her best friend, Morgan—@thingsthepeakgirlsdo. She was always doing new accounts and getting them huge. This one was challenging each other to do funny stuff, and even though it had only been up a few months longer than mine, it was already at 50,000 followers. Not that I checked. Every hour. And they'd just announced they were planning some kind of big competition with it and had lined up four people to take part.

It had been a BIG surprise when I'd seen Dove's follow come in on @OneElleOfATime a few weeks back, and an even bigger one when she'd just liked my post.

"This way." Mom turned up a path, bringing me back to reality. "Oh, and did Nick tell you his band just got booked for some more gigs? Thought maybe we could check them out. Family trip?"

I tried not to laugh. How much would my brother like us all showing up? We'd all seen my dad dance, and that was something even Nick's social life couldn't recover from.

"Sounds good..." I kept it vague. As much as I was mad at Nick for never being around anymore, deep down I knew it hadn't been a totally smooth start for him either. Just after we'd arrived, Grams had gotten sick, and instead of living with us like we planned, she'd had to go into residential care. Nick had always been closest to her and had been the one who found her the day she had the fall. So, as much as things were weird between me and my little brother, I still had his back.

As we turned the corner, I saw what they'd been doing all day and couldn't help but whistle.

"Nice job!" The garden was dripping in decorations, and one of the neighbors was out taking pictures. I ducked to make sure my face was entirely behind this box of candy canes.

"We aim to please." Mom looked pretty proud.

"Was it like this when you were a kid?"

I loved asking her about when she was growing up back in England. She tilted her head to one side.

"In what way, bubs? We still had Santa Claus, if that's what you mean?" She laughed her gentle laugh as we stepped over a string of lights.

"Well, of course. But did you have all this stuff?" I nodded toward the illuminated nativity scene Dad was rigging up on the garage roof. Baby Jesus was as big as a cow. A really big cow.

Mom shook her head. "Nothing like it." She side-eyed Dad, who was now hammering what looked like baby Jesus's ear into a wall. She dropped her voice. "Probably a good thing...not that I'd say that to our clients!" She laughed but then looked at me, suddenly serious. "But it was just as magical. I promise."

"Well, don't leave me hanging! Tell me more." Even though we didn't do much stuff as a family anymore, I was obsessed with hearing about Christmas in England. It always seemed so adorable. "What about midnight mass?" We weren't religious, but they always looked totally cute in films. "All those little candles and furry hats and button-up coats?"

Mom laughed. "You know I was born in the eighties, not the eighteen hundreds, right?"

"All the same to me." I tried to keep a straight face, but she tickled me right in the ribs, and I couldn't even defend myself. "What about the other stuff? Did you hang stockings and watch movies?" My brain raced through all the traditions Mom and Dad used to have before the business pushed our family Christmas back to January. "Have eggnog lattes in holiday red cups?"

"Ha." Mom leaned on the front door to open it up, but it must have locked. "I don't think I even knew what a latte was until I was in my twenties." My mind flipped. She put down the box and got out her phone to search for something. "This"—she held out a picture that looked like a film set—"was home at Christmas."

Wow. It was a picture of a perfect little village, all cute, jumbled houses, a Christmas tree with simple lights in the middle of some untouched snow. I zoomed in as Mom fished out the door key.

"And you're sure you didn't just search 'cutest Christmas town ever'?"

"Would I?"

"Can you send it to me?"

"Sure—it was the year we got snowed in. We were on the national news and everything." She laughed to herself. "The poor woman who came to cover it got her car stuck and ended up having to stay in my best friend's house. I don't think she'd ever left London before!" She laughed even more. "Shouldn't laugh really..." But she was. And so was I.

"I'd love to visit one day." I said it quietly, as Mom always talked about going, but we all knew we didn't have the kind of money that could pay for a family trip, especially with Grams needing help here.

"One day." She nodded. "And back in reality—what about Christmas here? It's always a busy time, right?"

I didn't say anything, as I knew she was taking a scenic route to the point. "Reckon Alpine Peaks will be as good as Nashton for parties?"

What she meant was, was I going to get any invites?

Have any plans?

I slapped on my happy game face—it came so naturally these days.

"Guess we'll see. I'm sure there will be stuff going on." I wasn't—unless Nick took me somewhere with him, which seemed as unlikely as finding out Santa Claus was switching his sleigh for an Uber. Mom smiled, but I could tell I hadn't stopped her from worrying.

Crash. "ARGHHHHH!"

We looked at each other, and in perfect unison, said the exact same thing.

"Dad."

And we dropped our boxes to run.

But when we got to the front of the house, the only sign of him was some extreme cursing coming from behind Mary and Joseph, my brother doubled over laughing, and the nosy neighbor looking even less impressed than before.

I left Mom to deal with it and headed inside to set up at the bottom of the massive winding staircase.

Just me, myself, and one zillion candy canes.

Ninety minutes later, my hands smelled so strongly of peppermint, I could probably earn a decent wage as the world's first human air freshener. But shout-out to me: I'd done an awesome job. There wasn't an inch that didn't look red and white. Nice—if you liked that kind of thing.

I leaned back on the wall at the top of the stairs and snuck another look at my latest post—562 likes. No new followers.

But a noise downstairs made me freeze. A key in a lock...the front door opening.

Oh no! The family must be home, way before they should be.

And I looked like a hot mess. Mom and Dad were going to freak.

Could I get out of here without being seen?

Deep breath. Heart, calm the heck down. I needed a plan. Quickly.

But when I heard the voice of the person who walked in, my brain went to mush.

Here I was decorating for my Christmas dream, and I was seconds away from my Christmas nightmare.

CHAPTER TWO

Holly

I put my card from myself—to me—up on my desk, angling it so I couldn't quite see what I'd written. How could I be eating chocolate AND ticking off my Christmas Bedroom Decoration Plan and still feel so meh?! This wasn't how Christmas was meant to feel! Although it wasn't really a *how*, was it? I knew it was really all about the *who*.

Nope. Brain, don't go there.

I stuffed some more chocolate in my mouth, turned up "Santa Tell Me," and draped some of the bushiest tinsel over my photo collage of Ruby and Fred.

Yes! Things instantly felt a bit better. How can anyone feel rubbish when there's tinsel around?

I should do some crowdfunding. Year-round tinsel for days that sucked.

I tucked a gold bit in my hair tie for good measure. Was Colin looking at me with jealousy or alarm? I figured jealousy, so I added some to his collar too. So fierce. (The tinsel, not Colin. He was scared of rain.) I put out the other six cards I'd sent myself over the years and tried to focus on all the happy memories they contained instead of all the meh that I contained.

I loved Christmas. I couldn't let *anyone* ruin it. Not even *him*.

I mean, sure: break my heart and make me cry into some popcorn, but *hands off my Christmas*!

That was *not* part of the plan!

I rolled back onto my bed. Seems my brain was going there after all.

Woody did it six weeks ago, in a cinema, right before watching a film. *Before.* I thought we'd had another great day, right up until he put the popcorn in the armrest between us, leaned over as the "turn your phone off" bit began, and said, "It's starting to feel a bit normal, isn't it?" I thought he meant the VIP seats we'd sneaked our way into, so like an idiot, to appear more sophisticated, I nodded. But then he'd said, "A break would make it more exciting again, wouldn't it?" I didn't know if he was telling me or asking me. But he squeezed my hand, let it go, and hasn't held it ever since.

Why did he let me pick a rom-com? It felt like a personal attack.

Apparently he thought we'd become too "routine." *Routine?!*

How was that even an insult? Surely fun was even *better* when you could plan it?!

Fred said Woody was clearly deranged and that I deserved way better. And that he could have at least done it in the snack queue. Then I wouldn't have sat through an entire movie wondering if I could make our relationship more exciting and spontaneous if I ran up and down the aisles screaming "nooooooooo" and throwing Revels above my head. Ruby just said "I'm going to kill him" with such aggression, I told her Woody was on holiday for a week to be on the safe side. Although maybe I should have let that happen?!

When we'd left the cinema and Woody had asked how I felt, I just said, "Same. Total same!" instead of saying, "Oh, you know, like my heart has been pulled out and pureed in my sister's NutriBullet."

And for the last six weeks I'd been trying to figure out if this break was a break...or a breakup.

It sucked so hard. Woody thought I was boring, predictable. I thought he was so perfect, I'd once calculated how many hair follicles he had on his head. (101,105.)

Holly, get your mind away from Woody's irrelevant (but objectively gorgeous) hair and focus on your thirty-nine-point Christmas-decorating list.

I had a system, and every year I added more. I picked up the miniature polar bear with the cheery cardigan on and put it on my bedside table so its happy face would be the first thing I saw every morning. The New York snow globe Ruby bought me had earned instant pride of place alongside it. I recited the rhyme, shaking it as I did. *C'mon, snow globe, do your thing.*

After the year I'd had, this Christmas needed to be perfect—and if that was going to happen, I was going to need some serious Christmas magic. And it didn't get more Christmassy and magical than New York.

But in the disappointing absence of teleportation, I got on with decorating. The "sending my future self a card" thing was a tradition I'd picked up from Mum, who'd picked it up from her mum. They wrote one every year when they took the decorations down on the twelfth day of Christmas and packed it up ready to find when they opened them again the following year.

And I was so glad I did. My memory wasn't like a sieve exactly—more like a big doughnut. One big hole that useful things fell right through. So, opening the cards every year wasn't just a great way of making sure I could make every Christmas even better than the one before, it was also the nicest way of remembering all the memories that got packed away with the decorations. Well, every year except this year. I'd been *dreading* it.

I knew it was going to make me go one of two ways: Realize I was over Woody—and put me back on track to having a perfect Christmas after all. Or make the thought that prodded away at me even stronger—that if I could just make Woody see how spontaneous and fun we could be, then maybe things could get back to normal, just in time for Christmas.

I dropped my head back on to my pillow and faced the facts. I was wearing Woody's hoodie. In my room. Again. And yup. The smell of it still made me feel like I was eating an emotional sour cola bottle. It really hurt, and I hated it, but I also loved it, couldn't stop, and knew I'd do it again.

I looked at the polar bear. Even he knew.

There was NO WAY I was over Woody.

So, if I was going to make Christmas perfect, I needed a proper plan to get him back. Not that I'd tell Ruby and Fred, who were so team #getoverhim that it felt like a betrayal even thinking it in my own head.

I wriggled up and looked out of my window. Ahhhh, the perfect view of Woody's house.

It was hard not to yell, "WOODY, I WILL BE HERE UNTIL YOU REALIZE YOU'VE MADE A BIGGER MISTAKE THAN WHEN YOU BOUGHT THOSE GLOW-IN-THE-DARK TRAINERS!" But Colin-human (that was the New Boyfriend name compromise) was downstairs, and there was no way either of us wanted to have a conversation about feelings. Especially as it would start off with me having to explain what they are.

I got my frustration out by yelling for my sister instead.

"*Naomi!*"

Without fail, she always helped me put up my lights, mainly

because it gave her a chance to point out I was the genetic mutant in the family, at least four inches smaller than her and Mum.

But if I was going to wait for Naomi, I'd be a while, as she was approximately... I rolled over, picked up my phone and looked up her latest location. Yup. 6,068 miles away. Why did I look?! For the past two months, her feed had been pure torture. What's that, Naomi? Another picture of a white-sand beach and clear, blue water?

How were there more beaches left in Thailand for her to post about? How did the world have that much sand?!

I opened our chat.

This is not a drill! Christmas decorations have begun!

I sent her a picture of Colin and his tinsel collar. It was almost eleven p.m. her time, but she replied straightaway.

Did you ask Mum for a ladder so you could get those cards up on your desk?

I'm actually very tall now.

Was it weird that I enjoyed bickering with her, even from the other side of the world? It really was a most enjoyable hobby. The truth was, I couldn't wait for her to be back on December 23. I felt sick-excited about it. Mum had a countdown on the fridge, and it was an unspoken thing that Naomi getting back was going to be the unofficial early start to Christmas Day. Our annual Christmas Eve party was going to be extra big this year—and *I was here for it*! As long as I sorted the Woody stuff before then.

If you've got a second in your hectic schedule of lying on a beach, or idk, making friends with a dolphin, let me know if you need me to pick any stuff up for you. Am doing Christmas shopping next Saturday.

She replied with a picture of her hugging a baby turtle. Of course she did.

Hol. Please. You need to shake off that commercial pressure of capitalism.

Wow. Maybe she really had changed.

Although can you let Mum know I've broken my headphones and would love a new pair. ☺ Noise canceling.

Or not.

I added the idea to the present-idea-inspo notes on my phone I kept all year 'round and got back on plan. Some people thought mid-November was too early for Christmas decor. Some people were wrong. And by the time I'd hung every bauble, draped every bit of tinsel and dangled every random ornament, it was time for the big finish.

I turned off the lights and flicked on Penny. She looked amazing. In a life-size, one-eyed, one-winged, light-up penguin way.

Normally, this would be the point where I'd decorate the rest of the house with Mum and Nay, but this year, we hadn't gotten our tree yet. I think my sister not being here was throwing Mum off, which sucked.

I peered at Penny.

But my eyes knew the truth. I was cheating on her.

Peering at Woody's bedroom window. *Again.* I must stare at it for at least two and a half hours a day.

It was our secret, but Woody and I still waved if we spotted each other as we closed our curtains. Or opened them. (I just had to hope he never worked out that I opened and closed them multiple times every day to try and increase the chances.)

Surely curtain buddies meant there was hope?

But today there weren't any lights at his, no signs of life. Guess he must be out. Which meant he might be coming home soon. Which meant there was a chance of accidentally running into him.

I suddenly decided my decorating was done, and that maybe I urgently needed to pop to the shop. I looked in the mirror for the first time today, yanked the tinsel out of my hair, swapped my hoodie that he'd forgotten I had for my jumper with a giant Christmas bow on (the perfect seasonal start to my now-daily festive jumpers), slicked on some lip gloss, covered up the trilogy of chin acne that had popped up to wave hi (thank you, winter, for your dark evenings and lack of natural light) and headed downstairs. A delicious smell wafted up toward me. I used my slipper boots as stair skis and slid downstairs into the kitchen. Yes, I did almost flatten Colin, but he'd rather die than move unnecessarily. Fair enough. Anyway, he was fast asleep, full-on snoring, making contented whimpers. Probably dreaming of the time he ate more than his own body weight in bird.

"Serious question," I asked. Mum looked around, alarmed. "When is whatever you're making coming out of the oven? Because be warned—I am going to eat all of it." I leaned over the kitchen worktop. "ALL. OF. IT!"

Mum pointed to the corner by her radio. "It's a candle, love, but don't let me stop you..."

She was grinning, but it wasn't my fault someone had once decided to get Nay a plate of biscuits that were actually candles. And she didn't tell me, even as I was biting into the first one.

My phone buzzed. It's from Fred.

Genuinely not an exaggeration, but Ruby is about to change my life!!! You want in??

Okay. Well, scrap the shop—new plan was witnessing whatever *that* was. Fred only lived a few minutes away, so I could be there quickly. I dived into the cupboard under the stairs to retrieve my boots from the ever-growing shoe mountain. Weird. Mum had sorted them all into pairs, on racks. In fact...everywhere was tidy. *Alarmingly* tidy.

Had she tidied for the tree coming in?! Although, was a perfectly organized shoe cupboard really necessary for festive vibes? OMG. I bet this was Colin-human's influence!

He was an interior designer and had about three items on display in his house, and they were all shades of monochrome. Nay and I reckoned he encouraged his twins, Zai and Kai (yes, he actually thought that was a good idea), to like things like pandas and zebras just to keep with his aesthetic. What was he going to persuade them to like when they were older? Nuns and barcodes?

I mean, this is a man who Doesn't. Even. Own. A. Toaster.

But his approach wasn't going to work here. Christmas at ours was like a box of decorations collected since the seventies had exploded over our house.

Just how I loved it. Naomi would watch me decorate the whole house, sitting on the sofa saying, "Oh, that's not straight," after I'd pulled twelve muscles gluing something to the wall. Then she'd somehow make our ramshackle collection of tree decorations look good together. Nay joked our family was proof that if you put a loop on anything, it could be a tree decoration. Glittery gherkin, a furry ferret, even a replica model of the Leaning Tower of Pisa (which ultimately was straight in decoration form)—they all dangled from our tree. If anyone has ever looked at a terrible decoration and thought, "Who would buy that...?" the answer is "me, my sister, or my mum."

Which reminded me. The tree. Time to get to the bottom of this. I tightened up my laces.

"Muuuuum." It's amazing how long that word can take to say. I didn't want to nag. Although...I *did* want a tree. What was the difference between *interested question* and *nag* anyway? "Any idea on when we might be able to go to Enchanted Forest?"

"Is that a nag, Hol?" she called back from the kitchen. Maybe she'd forgotten what week it was—despite me writing it in massive letters on our family calendar. And underlining it in highlighter.

"It's an interested question, actually." I pulled out my scarf and hat. "You know ancient Egyptians were some of the first people to have a Christmas tree. Sort of. And they didn't even have cars."

She walked into the hall and leaned on the banister. "What's the name going to be this year?"

"Hmmm..." It wasn't something to be rushed. "We won't know until we see it." Get the hint, Mum—*when* are we going to see it?!

"Justin Tree-ber will be hard to beat." It still amused her. He was our tree last year because he had what looked like a floppy fringe that dangled down. She picked up the kettle and waved it in my direction.

"Tea?" Mum flicked the kettle on. "Just us."

I peeked out the window. Still no Woody sighting.

Maybe some more time here was a good idea.

I let Fred know I'd be a few minutes and said yes to a quick cuppa.

Mum was scribbling away in her battered notebook. I definitely got my list-making from her. (I know, as it's on my "list of things I got from Mum" list.)

"All right, nosy." She put her pen down. "I'm popping to Day and Night later. Want anything?"

"I refer you to the fridge." I'd already written the Christmas essentials up.

- ◊ Giant tin of Quality Street chocolates
- ◊ The Christmas edition of the Radio Times magazine
- ◊ Easy-peel oranges
- ◊ Anything normal that comes in a special Christmas variety (INCLUDING drinks with glitter in them and any novelty cereal)
- ◊ Any 99p Christmas accessory/homeware bargains

Mum looked over. "Noted."

"Oh." I tried to sound casual. "Unless they also sell Christmas trees?" Or massive boxes of huge hints?

She passed me my tea.

"Last time I checked between the air fresheners and beans... no." Excellent ignoring of the point there. She softened her voice. "Although, Hol, when we get back, there is something I need to speak to you about..." Well, this sounded ominous. Conversations that needed a pre-conversation were never good. Her voice went right back up again as she looked past me at the lights in the street. "Ooh, I do hope Sheila moves her car, she's blocking me right in!"

My heart stopped.

Sheila?! A.k.a. Woody's mum. Was outside. Our house. Well, probably her house, but there was only a twelve-meter difference.

Did that mean Woody was too?!

I picked up my tea and strolled to the sink. I needed to fully assess the situation, so I poured it away so I could stand and rinse it out.

"Didn't you say you wanted one?" Mum gave me a weird look as I washed up through potential third-degree burns.

AFFIRMATIVE. Woody was right there. Be still, my tinsely heart!

The tap was now running over my sleeve, but I didn't care.

Woody Theo Francis.

In his denim jacket with the sheepskin collar. He *knew* how much I liked that combo. And there he was, just carrying a shopping bag into his house all casual, like this wasn't pure torture for me. This must be how Colin feels when he sits in front of the oven watching a sausage with no idea of how to get through the glass.

"I...er...think I've gone off tea, actually. For today."

"Right," Mum said, like she definitely meant, *I wish your sister was here so I could ask her to have a talk and check everything's okay with you. In the sanity department.*

"And I don't want to leave Fred and Ruby waiting."

"And this has *nothing* to do with Woody being outside?" Mum's eyebrow was fully raised.

"Whaaaat? Is he *even* there?" Voice, why have you gone all weird? Whose side are you on?! "Col?" I patted my leg. "You coming?"

I needed moral support, even if it was from a Jackapoo. He loved walks—but only for ten seconds. As soon as he realized the UK still wasn't a tropical, sunny paradise, he would look like he'd been cruelly duped and try and head back in. If Colin hadn't been born a dog, he would have been born a cushion.

I clipped his leash on as Mum walked over and kissed me on the side of the head. "Love you, don't you forget that." Naomi being away had definitely made her more sentimental. "Oh, and take the bins with you?" Or maybe just extra good at emotional blackmail.

She thrust two massive bags into my hand, a gust of pure rot coming with them. Woody was going to smell me before he saw me. Was *that* exciting enough for you, Woody?! "And try and be back for six. Sunday-evening call with your sister, remember?"

How could I not? We used to have a proper dessert on a Sunday. Now we had a new tradition—Mum forcing us to ring Naomi before we could eat it. An hour of Nay talking solidly about how amazing her life was, some sea creatures she'd taken selfies with, and "how she never knew she could be this chilled," and me staring at the dessert in probably the same unrequited way I stared at Woody. Then, once that was over, Mum would talk about how amazing Naomi's life was and the sea creatures Naomi had taken selfies with—and only then was I was allowed to mourn my mess of a life in peace with crumble and custard.

But there was no time to think about dessert. Plan "Get Woody Back by Christmas" was on! I grabbed the bags and strutted out.

Straight into the eye line of Woody, who was pulling a bumper pack of cat litter off the back seat.

Brilliant. Terrifying. Awful. Amazing. Be cool, Holly. Be EXCITING. BREATHE.

Woody lifted his bag and did a silent "aren't we glam?" laugh and eye roll.

I did a very un-silent laugh back. In fact, so loud, his mum turned round.

Chill your boots, Sheilz?!? Not my fault your son looks fit clutching cat litter.

I smiled anyway, just in case we'd laugh about this moment when she was my mother-in-law.

I attempted the same ironic lift with my bin bags, but they were surprisingly heavy, and my arms gave up a little bit.

But. What?! Help.

He was walking toward me. Woody was incoming!

This wasn't meant to happen?!

Well, it was, but now that it was, I absolutely wasn't ready.

BREATHE. AND AGAIN.

Why had I rushed into this? I hadn't even checked my emergency list of conversation topics to remind him how spontaneous and exciting I was.

BLINK.

Woody leaned over our little metal gate—and grinned. How dare he come over here and lean over my gate and grin, like I was going to be able to manage conversation now?

Breathe. Swallow. Blink.

C'mon, Hol—what was in the "interesting conversation" brain folder?

Nope. All I could find was that the star of Bethlehem had probably just been Uranus. And I wasn't saying that. I stared at the sign on our gate, willing something good to land in my brain. "Welcome to the happy home of Sophie, Naomi, and Holly." Mum had had it made, and it had a symbol on it for each of us. And it was zero help. "Just a-doing the bins." *A-doing?!* Where had that come from?! "Bin having a great time."

Terrible. I. Am. Terrible.

"I bet. Looks like you've got Sunday in the bag." Woody smiled—his annoyingly brilliantly awful, cute, perfect smile—as he pulled his beanie off and back on. I laughed, mainly with relief that he'd joined me in terrible joke-ness. Being around him made me feel like a string of Christmas lights, all twinkling and happy.

Well, until I remembered that he might not feel the same way, and then I basically short-circuited and set fire to the imaginary Christmas tree I was on.

I gulped and tried to focus on what I was here for.

Other than to separate the recycling.

Being cool and spontaneous and Woody-getting-back. "So... good, erm...day?" Not exactly an award-winning start.

"Depends. Does helping my dad choose between five types of potato count as fun?" It did when he said it. Woody looked at me as if trying to work something out. "And is *now* the time we talk about how mid-November could be a liiittle early for a Christmas jumper?" He'd noticed my bow jumper. Wasn't noticing details a good sign?!

"We *could* do." Face, DO NOT smile as much as you want to. Permission NOT granted. "But I'd have to immediately point out this is actually my *semi*-festive jumper, so actually it's very time-appropriate." Hmmm, was knitwear scheduling conveying my inner wild child?! Better not mention the spreadsheet where I'd worked out a jumper rota for the rest of the forty-one days before Christmas. "And it beats football shorts."

Woody grinned. "Everything else was in the wash." What?!

I thought he'd actually been playing in them. It was minus a million degrees! He bent down and ruffled Colin's neck fur. Ahhhhh. There they were—all 101,105 glorious follicles. Colin eyeballed me—he was suspicious of Woody. Ruby had obviously been talking to him. Even Fred had said he wasn't sure I should be so obsessed with someone whose initials are WTF.

"You going out?"

Aha! Hello, perfect opportunity to remind him that I'm spontaneous and exciting and have all the fun and TODAY IS THE DAY TO STOP THIS RIDICULOUS BREAK NONSENSE.

"Yeah, totally. To...erm...somewhere I don't even know yet. Feeling pretty, y'know..." I tossed my head back, but my bobble hat just hit me in the eye on the way back up. "Unpredictable." Please let him not have seen that.

"Is your eye okay?" He'd seen.

"Of course!" I said, slightly too confidently, but spontaneous people probably didn't really experience pain. They certainly didn't admit there might be some fluff scratching their eyeball.

"Sweet." He stretched out. "Sounds like a good evening. No plans are the best plans, right?"

"Exactly!" I laughed, even though I had no idea what I was even talking about anymore. *Was this actually working?!*

"Although..." He started fiddling with the collar of his jacket. His nervous twiddle? "I was going to ask..." WHAT WAS HAPPENING? "...if you..."

Was this it?

The big moment!

But Woody never got to finish. Fred. Fred, who is meant to be my friend and at least have some clue about Massive Significant Conversations in My Life, chose this moment to appear.

I stared at Woody, blinking as if a force field could bounce Fred back in time by fifteen seconds and he could finish his sentence.

But Fred was hurrying—right up to my face. Too close to my face?! He leaned right in. "There you are. Whoa—is your eye okay?"

"Fine," I said, through gritted teeth (and fluffed eye).

What *was* Woody about to ask me? This was the first glimmer of hope in six weeks.

I just had to hope the reason Fred had run over was something super urgent that made me look even more spontaneous and exciting to seal the deal. And I could be in luck. He looked pumped.

"So, Hol." Fred's eyes were extra wide. "We were thinking. ANOTHER JENGA SUNDAY SHOWDOWN?!" No, Fred. *No.* "I've already done the snack run." He held up a blue plastic bag. "They had your fave. Ready-salted Pringles." Nooo—why had he chosen my least-exciting favorite flavor? Where were Chipsticks when I needed them? "Oh, and some caffeine-free Diet Coke." He held it out. I murmured a thank-you, trying not to sound ungrateful—or like I was actually wishing I could fall down a manhole. "I already opened it so it's not too fizzy for you."

Yes, Woody—that's right. I'm so fun and wild that I can't even handle bubbles.

I narrowed my left eye at Fred to hint that could he take that back and imply I was off to a pop-up rave instead?

But Fred just looked scared. "Hol...why are you looking at me like that?" Could I actually crawl back under the doormat? "Did you want salt and vinegar? I thought you only had salt and vinegar on Saturdays? *Ready-Salted Sunday*, isn't that what you say? And why are you holding bin bags?" I'd forgotten about those. "You *are* still coming, right?"

"Oh, yes." I smiled, my dignity slowly seeping into the bin bags I was still holding. Fred was the best human, even if he was the worst at hints. "Sorry...I'd totally forgotten. Been a hectic day."

"But I thought you said all you've done is shampoo your hairbrushes and finish your Christmas jumper spreadsheet?"

Sometimes I wish Fred wasn't such a pure, lovely human, and understood there's a reason for private messages being PRIVATE.

"Ah...yes. I'd forgotten that too." Out of the corner of my one working eye, I could see Woody trying not to laugh. This was a disaster. I plonked the bin bags down. "I'll, er...have to cancel my other plan. Of not having a plan..." Woody stood up. I swear his eyebrow had risen suspiciously in my direction. "Anyway, did I tell you?" Look out, emergency subject change. "Ruby's finding out tonight if she's got a part in the pantomime." I was talking extra quick, attempting a speed-conversation getaway. "Obvs, she's amazing and totally will, but still. Exciting, yes?"

Last year we all thought she was guaranteed a main part, but someone on the committee's sister got the role instead. Ruby said she didn't mind, but we knew she was gutted. She didn't put herself out there for auditions much, so when she did, it meant she really wanted it.

"Oh, wow." Woody sounded impressed. "Tell her good luck from me." I would, but I knew she'd just tell me to stop speaking to him. "Last year she was robbed. Anyways..."

He turned to go. *Was this the end?* WHAT was he going to ask me?! I needed to know!

"Woody. Wait... Weren't you about to ask me something?" I said it like I could barely remember, even though it was one minute ago—my acting was getting so good, I might get a part in the panto at this rate. "When Fred arrived?" *Remember, remember, remember.*

"Ah!" Woody grinned the cutest smile. The exact one he had in the photo of us I kept in my bedside table. "*That*. How about I come and call for you later? We can chat then." He looked back up at me. Man, those eyes could still do serious things to me. And when I say *things*, I mean... No... Thought process... Going... BRAIN JELLY ACTIVATED.

But he hadn't finished.

"I think we've got some catching up to do." Oh. My. Jingle. Bells.

It was all I could to nod.

"Sure," I said, smiling harder than I had in weeks. Plan Get Woody Back by Christmas was on.

CHAPTER THREE

Elle

I smoothed down my hair and tried to shake out my clothes, but I already knew this wasn't salvageable.

Had I even remembered deodorant?

I picked up my box of leftover twine, did a quick scrub underneath my eyes, and stepped down the stairs.

Ideal situation—sneak out of the house with absolutely no one seeing me.

But this wasn't a day for ideals. This was a day for the person you least wanted to see standing at the bottom of the staircase, throwing their hands to their face in shock.

My stomach clenched so hard, I almost missed a stair.

"Oh. My. Actual. Gee." Dove put her hands on her hips in that effortless way she had of making everything look like it was a perfected pose. Why did this have to be her house? "What are the chances?"

Okay, at least we were going down the knowing-each-other-exists route. Guess setting up camp in someone's house definitely moves a relationship along.

"Dovvvve?!" Yup, I managed "pleasantly surprised." Real me wanted to sprint the hell out of here, but if I wanted any chance of pulling this back, I needed to channel the only Elle Dove really knew—the online, confident one. "I had *no* clue you lived here."

I should have guessed though—I looked around the huge hall, Christmas tree stretching up, perfect square gifts already wrapped under the tree. Oh—and her family picture on the wall. Must strike *detective* off potential career ideas. "Your house is...incredible."

"Thanks." Dove tossed her ponytail as she walked up the stairs toward me. She looked like a real-life Anna from *Frozen*—but somehow even more perfect. I lifted my box higher to hide how much of a mess I was. "You and those guys outside have made it SO ready for the holidays. I had no idea you worked for that little company... *What was the name*? Good for Your Elf? Worst pun everrrr, right?"

"*Uh-huh.*" Why was I nodding? She was going to find out anyway, so I might as well own it. "It's my parents' business, actually." I winced, to show I felt the same as her.

Dove's big, blue eyes got even wider. "I am SO sorry. Like, no offense intended or anything."

"None taken. My little brother thought of it. I'll be sure to pass on your feedback on to him."

I laughed so she knew I was joking.

"And is this your hot brother who was outside doing something kinda weird with a reindeer?"

So she liked Nick—interesting. She didn't need to know that he was about as open to a relationship as he was to starring in one of my videos.

"The very same. Although not so much of the hot, IMO."

But she'd already gotten distracted—and had pointed her finger. Right. At. Me.

"Oh, I'm sorry." She'd definitely come from a fresh mani. "Is that...Blur?"

Was she impressed or disgusted at my vintage top?

"Uh-huh?" I left it open so I could go either way depending on what she said next.

"Greatest band EVER?!" She started to hum "Song 2"—Mom's favorite. Well, that was an unexpected result.

"My mom was obsessed." She always had music on in the house—probably what kicked off Nick's lifelong obsession with UK bands.

"Mine too." And something I'd never experienced before happened. Dove smiled. At me. "Guess that's where we get our good taste." *Our* good taste. "I used to have a fan account all about British stuff back in the day." She stopped suddenly as if it wasn't something she liked talking about. "Wait. Someone told me you're actually British?"

“Who?!” I asked way too quickly. But Dove had been talking about me. Me?! With someone who knew about my mom? I thought no one at school knew anything about me.

She shrugged. “Just people...”

“Well, they’re half right, I guess. My mom’s from there, and we lived there till I was four.”

“Literally the coolest.” She nodded in approval. “I HAVE to show you the pictures I got in London a few years back. Legit perfection.” So she was lining up another conversation? Mom, where were you when I needed you to witness something?! “Was the candy cane idea yours?”

“Can’t take credit, but I can say you’re all gonna smell great. For months.”

Dove laughed. I made Dove laugh. Weird—I always figured she’d be more frosty than funny. Maybe I’d gotten her all wrong.

“I bet your house is on point this time of year.” She sounded impressed, so I’d let her believe the dream—that I lived in a picture-perfect grotto—rather than the truth that my parents were so bored of Christmas that it might as well be April inside our front door. The outside still looked amazing, of course—Dad made sure they pulled out all the stops. Had to drum up business.

“Well, who doesn’t love the holidays?” I wasn’t a big fan of lying—I considered myself a semipro answer swerver instead.

“Speaking of great ideas.” She waved her phone. “That post this morning? INSPIRED.” I smiled as if it was no big deal, rather than it having taken all of yesterday, and hid the current state of my nails. "And I'm sorry, but commenting? @Realdeallogan must be *into* you!"

I hadn't thought it was *that* big a deal, but clearly it was from the way Dove was fanning her face.

And if she was impressed, maybe I could go bigger—maybe Dove could be the key to getting me the new followers I was after. "He threw in a follow too."

Her eyebrows shot up. "Wow, you *work* that!"

"Why, thanks." I laughed. "I mean, my account's tiny compared to yours." *Flattery, check.* "But I had to shut down my old one. @NoWayNoelle." And sympathy could never hurt. "Long story. Trolls, all that pathetic stuff. So now I'm all about getting followers up on this new one."

"ELLE? ELLLLLEEEE?"

It was Dad.

"Guess I better go..." I picked the box back up, but Dove was looking at me—like *really* looking at me.

"One sec." She put her hand on my arm. "Can I give you something to think about?"

I nodded—where was this going?

"You said you wanted followers, right?" I nodded some more. "I don't know if you've heard, but Morgan—you know her?" Uh-huh. *Everyone* knew her. "Sure. Well, we've been working on a competition. A challenge. To finish the year in style. We haven't figured what yet—but whoever wins will be the third member of one of our new accounts, @thingsthepeakgirlsdo." Wow, they were looking for a collaborator? That was *full* inner circle. "So..." She stopped and did a perfect raise of her left eyebrow. "Could @OneElleOfATime be in?"

Me? They wanted me, *my account* to be part of their competition that *everyone* was talking about? Luckily, I was leaning on the banister, or I could have collapsed down the stairs.

If I won, @OneElleOfATime would blow up. I'd hit 30k followers, no problem—probably way more.

Was I really ready to put myself back out there like this?

Two years ago, when I'd set up @NoWayNoelle, it had started off as just something to do. All I really wanted was to get free stuff, have some fun, but my best friend, Clara, wanted to be a proper influencer. But it was the first time we'd actually moved somewhere and I'd made a real friend, so I was happy to go along with it, and so we both started an account. I mainly did the filming anyway. But then Clara had an idea for a funny lip-synch video. She said it wasn't her vibe to star in that particular one, so she asked me to test it out. And that was when everything changed. I posted it on my account, and when it got featured on the home page, it ended up getting so much attention, my account got nominated for Lolonline Newbie of the Year. It was a public vote, and as much as I wasn't expecting it, I scooped first place, just beating the big favorite, @SpillMoreTea. At first it was great. I did loads of collabs, met loads of amazing people, like @_Beckywiththemediocrehair_, and was way more confident with my ideas than I'd ever been. But as my followers crept up to nearly 25,000, that's when the trolling started.

Clara and Nick were the only ones I told. Clara was completely amazing—every day she'd help me block and reply—but Nick? He'd started to never be around. It was like he didn't care anymore. Mom and Dad thought *something* might be up, but they were splitting their time between Nashton and here, trying to get the business up and running, so they didn't really have a clue, and I didn't want to stress them.

"So, is that a yes?" Dove was still looking at me, no idea about everything this was bringing back up. I tried to never think about it.

At first the comments had been normal stuff, but then it became DMs, and then it became personal. Stuff about me. About my brother.

Things a stranger wouldn't know. Things only Clara would know.

I'd been a wreck when I'd seen the notification on her phone and figured it out. And worst of all, I still had no idea why she'd done it. She said it was a joke, that she could explain, but it didn't feel like it. It felt like she'd hated my account being more successful and hated that it had been her idea that had kicked it all off. So I'd told her I didn't want to hear what she had to say—ever again—and closed my account. End of our friendship, end of @NoWayNoelle. I never told Nick I'd figured out it was her; he just thought the trolling had gotten too much, and I guess everyone just assumed me and Clara had grown apart because of the move.

One of the last things I'd told Clara was that I'd be back better than before, even though I hadn't believed it myself. But now it was all I wanted to do. That was one of the reasons I'd said I was going to hit 30k on my new account—she didn't follow me, but I knew she'd be watching. Just like I did with her. Lurking was a two-way street.

"Oh, and did I mention that the losers have to close their accounts?" Dove's words snapped me back into the room. "Tension, right?!"

Wait. What?! Talk about a mic drop.

So I'd either win and get all I wanted for Christmas, or crash and burn in front of everyone. In front of Clara.

Was it a risk I could really take?

"Absolutely." I heard myself saying it, before I even knew I'd decided. "Count me in." What was I doing?! "But be warned, I'll be in it to win it." And why was I digging myself in so deep?! "I'm aiming for 30k followers by Christmas."

Dove chewed her lip. "Interesting...you might just have given me an idea..."

But Mom and Dad had had enough of yelling and chose this moment to come and get me. Dove turned on the full parent-meeting charm, asking all about the UK, as my mind spun with what I'd just gotten myself into.

Mom and Dad chatted the whole way home about how lovely Dove's family was, and how nice it was to finally see me with one of my friends, as if I weren't even there. Nick had done his usual disappearing act, so he wasn't around to hear them finally sounding positive about my life here. When I told them I might be doing a project with Dove, they gave each other one of those looks, like I'd just lifted a weight off their shoulders. So that was that then—no going back.

And that night, as I lay in bed, the notification came through.

The notification that the challenge was on. And I was most definitely in it.

And it was going to be *way* tougher than I thought. #FestiveFifteen—a race to get 15,000 new followers first. All kicking off on the sixteenth of December. Dove would post totals as we went, and whichever out of the five competing accounts racked up 15,000 new followers the fastest would win the challenge and become a permanent member of @thingsthepeakgirlsdo.

Rules were all the posts had to be about the holidays, but we could do as many as we liked. And the losers, well, they'd have to close their accounts by Christmas.

What. Had. I. Done?

Fifteen thousand new followers?! I'd been freaking out about getting another seven, let alone more than double that.

I considered backing out. But instead, I replied to the post on Dove's actual grid, saying how "ready to go" I was.

I was such an idiot.

I was going to need quantity. And quality. And a minor miracle, unless I wanted to lose my account. I had the smallest following out of the five of us competing, so I'd have to think big. The biggest.

By two a.m. my bed was covered in bits of paper full of terrible ideas, and my eyes ached from searching YouTube for inspo. Guess my assignment was getting done in the morning.

But it was worth it. I'd had an idea.

Sure, Dove had been inspired by me, but that could work both ways. I'd had an idea so big, I didn't know if even I could pull it off.

So I did what I always did.

Put it online and told the world. There was no way back now.

CHAPTER FOUR

Holly

Feet in leaves.

Cat's feet in leaves.

Idyllic snowy Christmas village.

Color-coordinated lip gloss collection.

WAIT. Sorry, what?

I scrolled back up.

And zoomed in. And out. And in again.

That wasn't just *a* snowy Christmas village. It was *my* snowy Christmas village. Yup. The most glamorous influencer I knew had posted a picture of Little Marsh. As in, the actual place that I lived.

"One. Elle. Of. A. Time." I could hardly get my words out. "Knows where we live?!"

"And this is exciting...why?" Fred replied, confused, as he opened his front door.

"Not *you*, Fred. *Colin.*" I already knew Fred wouldn't have a clue who I was on about, but Colin, like the king he was, threw his tiny, furry head up, shaking the lead in what I took as a low-key celebration. He knew this was HUGE. Elle knowing where we lived was one step away from her knowing I existed. Which was basically almost best friends.

I'd followed @OneElleOfATime ever since Ruby showed me this amazing lip-synch video she'd done on her old account. It was Lewis-Capaldi-towel-and-sunglasses levels of funny.

I'd DMed her to say that I'd laughed so hard, a bit of crisp had come out of my nose. Weirdly, she'd never responded or followed me back. But she also hadn't blocked me, so that was something.

"The fire hazard has arrived!" Fred shouted upstairs to Ruby as I took off my many woolen accessories. To say his reaction to Elle's post was not exactly excited would be like saying Harry Styles had done a little bit okay for himself. Fred just didn't care.

When I walked in, Ruby narrowed her eyes at me. "*That* smile..." She said it like an accusation as she tucked her dyed platinum hair behind her ears. "You've seen Kit Kat Boy, haven't you?"

It was what she called Woody ever since the "break" convo. I couldn't look at her—I knew she could see into my soul, so I stared at Fred's only three posters. One giant one on each wall in tribute to his three great loves—*Brooklyn Nine-Nine*, Emma Watson, and sausage rolls. "Nooooommmaayyybbbeeeeesss?" So *that's* what happened when I tried to lie to Ruby.

She slammed down the purple rock she was holding on Fred's carpet. "DETAILS. All of them!"

"FINE." I took a deep breath and looked at Fred, who just shook his head. Okay, I'd keep him out of it. "Yes, we—I—just saw him."

"And...?" This was worse than a Mum and Naomi interrogation.

"And...hear me out. It was brilliant. Like old times? He had *that* jacket on." I inhaled with my eyes closed. "And the hat. And I was holding bin bags." I couldn't seem to stop. "And he wants to talk...to me." I crouched down and grabbed her leg. "Tonight." I didn't mean to. I just needed physical support. "I know what you're thinking, but, Rubes—this could be it!"

"I see," is all she said. We all knew what Ruby thought. That if Woody wasn't sure how he felt about me, I should be sure he didn't deserve me.

"And just to check. *Again.*" She leaned back. "You're *sure* you want to get back together?" She knew the answer, so I didn't bother replying. "Because you could literally do a billion times better. Or whatever is even more than that."

"Centillion," Fred said.

I sighed. I'd explained it before, but maybe it was worth one more try. "It's not about finding *someone*, Ruby. I don't need a someone. This is about being with him. Even if that makes no sense to anyone else." I wished they could understand how much I liked him. "It's literally all I want for Christmas."

"And the whole, erm, *compelling* thing?" Fred was too kind to say the word "*exciting*"; he knew it had been a trigger word since the cinema, so he had found thesaurus alternatives. "Are we over that?"

Well, no, but I didn't want them thinking I was a pushover. "I just need to show him that he was wrong. That's all. In fact, maybe I already have?"

Ruby laughed. "Says the girl who's already shared her suggested itinerary spreadsheet for every day of the Christmas holidays..."

"And?" I folded my arms.

"...And who once had the same cereal every day for a year?"

"I meant '*and what?*' Not '*and please tell me more, Rubes.*'" I threw a pillow at her. What was wrong with routine? And lists? And lists about routines?!

But Ruby threw the pillow straight back. "But that's the point, you nugget. We think you're the best, the actual best, exactly as you are."

Fred sat on the bed behind her. "Yup, we loved everything about this year's itinerary." He did a tiny cough. "All one hundred and twenty-four color-coordinated rows."

I huffed. Well, huffed and smiled. They knew I loved it when Ruby said stuff like that. And when anyone complimented my spreadsheet skills.

"Well..." I sat on the floor by Fred's feet and opened the Pringles. Ruby had gone back to checking her phone. "If we were all spontaneous Meeras, the world would be very dull." Meera had just started at our neighboring school, and literally every day, there was some new news about her. She just got a sponsor for her snowboarding! She ordered sushi in actual Japanese! She was interviewed on BBC News after crowd-surfing at a climate change protest! Quite frankly, it was exhausting even hearing about her.

But Meera could wait.

How had I only just noticed the Jenga was pushed to one side, and Ruby was surrounded by what looked like bits from Fred's garden path?

"Don't ask." Ruby saw my confused stare.

"They're powerful crystals." Fred bent down and picked one up. "Dad's magazine said they could make *stuff* happen."

"Oh yes." Ruby sounded entirely unconvinced. "*Especially* if they're from the spiritual site of your back garden." She picked one up and eyed it suspiciously before turning her attention back to me. Guess that was the life-changing development Fred had been excited about.

"Look, Hol." Ruby could tell I was dwelling. I always ate crisps when I was overthinking. "You know I just want you to be happy. He just better not be an idiot this time." She waved her hands over the mystic pebbles, murmuring something about "Kit Kats" and "personality transplant."

This time. Yes. Ruby was right! There was going to be a *this time*. And despite her wanting me to think twice (well, fifty-two-th), suddenly it felt real. Brilliantly, sickeningly real. Like Christmas Eve, but even better.

Woody and I *were* going to get back together. Have our second magical Christmas. Then travel the world. Open the world's first Shetland pony café.

Probably.

But I didn't just want me to have the perfect Christmas—I wanted Fred and Ruby to have theirs too. Although...maybe that was the perfect thing to put Ruby's newfound mystical skills to work for? "Rubes, while you're busy channeling good stuff, could you manifest a replacement for...Eve?"

Eve was Fred's ex whom he never got over. It had been three and a half years since they'd split up, and Ruby and I were at the point of wondering when an ex became just "someone from a long time ago," but we didn't want to rush him.

"Too soon, Hol." Fred pretended to sniff. "The only girl I'll ever love...and she left me to pursue her dreams."

"Fred." Ruby dropped her hands. "She left you because you were twelve and she wanted to spend more time at Guides."

He clutched his heart. "The wound is still raw." He sniffed again. "Anyway, what about you, Rubes? Who's on your Christmas list?"

"Nah," is all Ruby said. Subject closed, even though Fred and I knew Ruby only had eyes for one person—Temi. Temi, who she'd met back in September at the panto audition. Temi, who she'd stayed in touch with ever since. Who clearly liked Ruby as much as Ruby liked her. But neither of them had done anything about it. Yet.

"Fine." There was no point trying to make Ruby talk about her feelings, I'd been trying for years, and all I ever found out was I'd made her feel annoyed. "In that case, ask Fred's path to ask the universe to hurry up and call about the panto."

She made a sort of whimper. Nervous Ruby was a side we hardly ever saw. "Can we talk about something else?" But I did have something I could distract her with. "HOW COULD I FORGET THE ACTUAL NEWS?!" I opened @OneElleOfATime's feed. "Look, Rubes..." Ruby squinted at the picture of Little Marsh, all covered in snow. "We're basically famous."

Fred peered over my shoulder. "Remind me who @OneElleOfATime is again? And why she's posting about Little Marsh?" He'd have more of a clue if he had a single social media account.

"Elle is the one that made crisps come out of Holly's nose, remember?" Ruby was zooming in and out on the photo.

"Sadly I do. And believe me, I've tried to forget...a lot."

"And this is 1994. The year of 'the big snow'?" Ruby laughed—this village was so dull, people still spoke about that year like it was folklore.

I flicked to another picture. "Just look at her?"

Fred squinted at my phone. "Okay, in a totally neutral observer way, I can see that yes, she looks like a supermodel."

"But that's what her whole life is like." I mouthed *perfection.*

"I mean, it's clear she's a big fan of waffles. And nails. And nails that are holding waffles. But that didn't answer my question. Why is she posting about Little Marsh?"

"Erm." I actually didn't have an answer for him. In all the Woody excitement, I hadn't bothered reading the actual caption. I passed Fred my phone, and he read it out loud.

"'*Hey, guys!*'" He put on his best American accent. It was fair to say it was terrible. "'*First things first. Could this picture BE any cuter? And no need to reply in the comments—we all know the answer is no (although you know I always love your comments, so who am I to stop you?) So...we all know Christmas is a magical time, right?! Well, this year I've accepted the ultimate challenge from @DoveAllLove to see if I could pull off my own Christmas miracle, Vanessa Huggens style.*'"

"Hudgens," Ruby corrected. "Show some respect."

"Annnyywaaaaay," Fred continued. "'*I've been nominated in her #FestiveFifteen challenge—to try and be the first to get 15,000 new followers before Christmas, all kicking off when I do my first #FestiveFifteen post on December 16! Can I do it? Who knows?*'"

Fred physically did the emojis, although he struggled a little with the trees. '*(C'mon, who wouldn't want to see more of me in @thingsthepeakgirlsdo) So...I'm going BIG.*'

Fred paused.

"'*Dot dot dot dot dot. Can you feel the drama?! Cos I've got a question...*'"

He looked up from the screen. "She wrote that, by the way. That wasn't a tension ad-lib."

"'*Are any of my lovely UK followers—which is where this cute pic is from—up for a Christmas swap? Yup. You heard right. You come and hang in New Jersey, and I'll head to your side of the Atlantic? And, of course, I'll be sharing the whole thing right here...*'"

But I'd stopped listening. A Christmas swap with a random? Just because someone had tagged her into a challenge? Elle's life was ridiculous.

"Anyone thinking what I'm thinking?" I could feel a semi-impossible plan brewing.

Ruby scrunched her eyebrows. "This is your chance to go to New York?"

I loved Ruby, but I had to splutter with the hilariousness of her thinking that could ever happen.

"Hahahaahahahha very funny. Have you met my mother? No, I was thinking—we should slide into Elle's DMs, tell her that her photo's from here. Try and convince her to come to Little Marsh!"

Fred made a "hmmmm" noise. "Just so you know, having a supermodel spend Christmas here is definitely something I could get on board with."

I put my arm around him. "What a guy." Still, at least he wasn't talking about Eve—progress.

But there was no time to plot. Ruby's phone was ringing, and she looked like she might throw up. I squeezed her leg. "We love you! Good luck!"

With a very solemn hello, she answered the phone and walked out. I don't think Fred or I breathed until Ruby walked back in.

"Rubbbyyyyy?" Her face was giving nothing away. "Rubes?! Tell us!"

"Okay, okay..." She did a slow turn. "You are officially looking at...Mirabelle..." She took a deep breath in. "As in Snow White's mirror. Me. I got the part!"

SHE'D DONE IT! AND NOT JUST ANY PART, THE MAIN PART SHE WANTED! WITH THE ABSOLUTE MOST SASS!

Ruby crumpled on the floor, and we piled straight on top of her. Colin too.

"This is SO huge!" I was literally shaking with joy. "Rubes, you are officially not only a magical, pebble-waving witch, you are also going to be the best glass-coated-with-a-metal-amalgam the world has ever seen!" I'd been preparing that line for a while.

Fred sat back, a huge grin on his face. "How do we book tickets for every single night?" He wasn't joking; we'd already made a pact (plus I'd put it in the itinerary).

"First step, Little Marsh village pantomime. Next step, Lin-Manuel begging you to be in his new show." I tried to catch my breath. "And what about Temi? Any news?"

When Ruby had come back from the auditions, she'd spoken about Temi almost as much as she had about the part. Ruby might try and play it down, but the massive smile on her face gave everything away. "Maybe I'll drop her a message tonight to ask?"

Of course she would!

Ruby scrambled to her knees, her smile suddenly gone. "There is one thing though..." She chewed her lip. "They said it will mean rehearsals every night, and two performances for some of the days in Christmas week." Wow. Hardcore.

But I got exactly what she was saying. This year wasn't going to be like all the others. Our normal Christmas plans were now on pause. The itinerary would need some serious work.

But there was no way I was going to let her see me even the tiniest bit sad when she had such epic news.

I wiggled my eyebrows. "And that's why they make spreadsheets editable."

Fred gave me a high five in solidarity. "We'll be too busy fangirling to do other stuff anyway."

Ruby looked relieved. "I mean—there will ALWAYS be time for *Elf*, right?"

Never has a truer word been spoken. But I couldn't stay and celebrate. I'd missed three messages from Mum saying we were chatting to Naomi earlier than planned.

I was still buzzing about Ruby's news when I got home—but as soon as I stepped through the door, I knew something was up. Mum and Colin-human were sitting at the kitchen table, iPad set up—and Mum didn't look happy, even when I told her Ruby's amazing news. I studied Colin-human's face for any clues, but nothing. Maybe that's why he had a beard—a hiding place for all his secrets.

"Everything okay, Mum?" I flicked the kettle on. If in doubt, make her tea.

"Of course..." She rolled her shoulders as if trying to shake off whatever was on her mind. "You just missed Naomi, actually."

Oh great. I could have stayed at Fred's.

"She was in excellent form," Colin-human said, laughing like he was remembering that selfie she got with a crab that looked like Nicole Scherzinger.

Mum smiled. But it wasn't a proper smile from the inside, just a face one. "Have you spoken to her recently?"

"Not since she was showing us around the elephant sanctuary. Or wait, was it her whale-watching tour?" The dream life all blurred into one. "Oh, and I think she'd love some replacement headphones for Christmas."

Mum looked at Colin-human. Just a really quick glance, but it confirmed they knew something I didn't. I muttered "noise-canceling," got out the Christmas mugs I'd snuck into the cupboard, and pretended I hadn't noticed.

"Okay, so she hasn't told you her news?"

I shook my head.

Had something bad happened?

Had Naomi taken her elephant selfies too far and finally paid the price?! Surely Mum would be in tears if her eldest daughter was flattened?

I suddenly felt worried. Really worried.

"Okay, well, I might as well tell you then... There's been a change of plans. A change of tickets, really..."

"Dolphin tickets?" I didn't even know what they were, but everything Naomi did recently seemed to involve some sort of animal.

"Plane tickets." The kettle boiled, but I didn't move. "She's coming back on the twenty-sixth."

"Oh, amazing!" What was Mum's face about? This was *good* news! I looked at the countdown. "Less than two weeks!" As much as my sister was annoying, I still couldn't wait for her to get home. She might even bring airport Toblerone!

"No, Hol. The twenty-sixth of December."

Oh, RETRACT RETRACT. This wasn't good news.

This was terrible.

Almost on a level with the elephant-squash thing. Naomi wasn't going to be here for Christmas?

For the first time ever.

I leaned back against the cupboard. This was huge.

That's what Mum must have wanted to speak to me about. She sighed in that way she does when she's pretending to be okay about something. And despite my eyes prickling as I tried to stop the sadness bubbling up through the disappointment, I knew the last thing she needed was me making things worse. I walked over and put my arm around her.

"Well, it is what it is, Mum. We can still have an awesome time."

I wasn't sure how yet, but I wanted to be positive. I *needed* to be. The only thing that could mend my rubbish year was a perfect Christmas.

"I know, darling." She stroked a piece of hair back behind my ear—I couldn't be bothered to explain I'd spent ages getting that bit of hair out. "And there's something else. Something I wanted to speak to you about sooner."

Wait. So that *wasn't* the thing? There was something else?! "Do I need to sit down for this?"

"That's a good idea, actually." Colin-human's reply did the opposite of reassure me. "Why don't you come away from the window?"

But I didn't move.

"What is it? Is there a national shortage of Cadbury's selection boxes?" But I was the only one laughing. And as I turned to get my tea, I saw something outside.

Something I'd missed earlier.

Something that had arrived in our garden.

Something that meant Christmas—and life as I knew it—was officially canceled.

In our garden was a brand-new FOR SALE sign.

CHAPTER FIVE

Holly

My life was officially up for sale.

I looked around, suddenly aware of all the things I'd taken for granted and would soon be saying goodbye to. The cupboard that only opened if you shoved it with your knee! The sink that smelled of bin! The plug that gave you low-level electric shocks! How I loved thee!

"Does Naomi know?" It was the only reply I could think of that wasn't dangerously close to me saying how I really felt.

Mum nodded. "We told her today..." Colin-human put his hand on hers. "Col's already started packing up stuff at his to make room for us."

"So *that's* why she's not coming back?" No wonder.

Naomi wasn't going to fly all that way for a toaster-less house.

Mum shook her head. "No, Hol. Her flights had already been moved. She seemed really excited, actually."

Of course she did. She was probably going to relocate to the Maldives and become a hammerhead shark trainer.

"So how long might it be... Before we, y'know..."—I almost couldn't bring myself to say it—"move."

How long do house sales take? Hopefully at least twelve to two hundred years.

Colin-human smiled. I knew he was trying to be supportive, but really, I couldn't help wishing he'd leave us alone for a bit.

"Could be weeks, could be months." HOW COULD HE LOOK HAPPY AS HE SAID THIS?

Weeks?! That was basically days! Which was basically *hours*!

I steadied myself on the sink—the sink I was going to really miss. We were basically moving in with Colin-human and the twins in a matter of minutes.

"So I should start packing... What...now?"

Mum laughed, but this was no laughing matter. Especially as she was soon going to realize that I'd put up most of my photo frames with glue. And some of the tinsel earlier.

Hang on. Why was I even decorating?! "Is this why you haven't got our tree?" Mum nodded slowly.

"One of the reasons... The estate agent wants the house as tidy as possible for any viewings."

Tidy? That's the exact opposite of Christmas!

"But we can get one in our house, have Christmas Day over there," Colin-human said softly.

Christmas? At his house?!

So we were never having Christmas here again. Ever.

"I've already told your mum, I don't mind relaxing the no-tinsel rule."

I think my eyes did a boggle. Who has a no-tinsel rule? IT WAS A FESTIVE HUMAN RIGHT.

He could be such a wet wipe. I replied with a weak, "Great," but I needed to get up to my room. I needed space to deal with this without them both staring at me to see if I was okay. Spoiler alert: I wasn't.

"There is one other thing..." How could Mum have more? "That I'm hoping you'll be okay with." I muttered an "earhe-ghhh," which was as close to a yes as I could get. Never had a person in such a semi-festive jumper felt so un-semi-festive. "I've been put on the schedules to work on Christmas morning. But I'll be back by midday."

Right.

Stick a turkey thermometer in me—I was done.

My head dropped against the tea towels hanging on the back of the door (the door I was already missing).

I pictured the scene. Christmas morning.

Me, a confused Colin probably having turkey flashbacks, New Boyfriend (he'd been relegated to that again after the tinsel comment), and the twins, who, if I'm honest, I still had no idea which was which. And we wouldn't even be in our own house.

BUT WAIT.

There was one glimmer of hope. One Woody-shaped glimmer that I had just spotted behind the sign, walking out of his house. Was he walking right over here?

I WASN'T READY!

I had a ponytail my mum had ruffled at least ten times and absolutely no grip on a single one of my emotions.

I squinted again. Did he have something green and leafy in his hand?

Was it...mistletoe?!

Like the exact foliage we'd had our amazing kiss underneath last Christmas?

Was this all part of what he had planned for tonight?

BUZZZZZ.

My phone vibrated.

Give me an hour?

Oh. My. Sleigh bells!

This could be even better than I'd hoped!

I replied to Woody with a casual, "Sure," but had to put my phone in the fridge to stop me adding "IS THAT MISTLETOE FOR ME? I THINK I LOVE YOU!" and ran upstairs.

Mum then yelled that Woody had texted saying it "will be good to talk," if that meant anything? I told her to stop looking at my phone. She said it was hard when she was trying to reach the cheese. So I retrieved my phone and discovered the crucial detail she'd omitted. He'd sent *three* kisses. *Three!*

For a boy, that's basically a hundred. Actual evidence things were getting back on track!

I screenshot and shared immediately with Ruby and Fred.

But two hours later, and still no Woody.

My mouth felt like a freeze-dried Hula-Hoop even though I'd done three full electric toothbrush cycles.

And by eight thirty p.m., both my lip gloss and optimism had dwindled, and my Woody excitement had been replaced by the big FOR SALE sign outside. I'd been reduced to going around my room saying bye to the key items (walls, door, not windows in case Woody saw) and preparing them for my potential departure. I'd messaged Naomi to see how she felt about Christmas being a write-off, but she just went on about how warm it was going to be where she was.

Thanks for the solidarity, sister.

I needed a better distraction, so I got another decorations box out of the loft—but when I opened it up, I spotted something I hadn't seen before. A really old, really battered wooden box with "Soph" on it—my mum's name. When I opened it and saw the pile of envelopes, near-identical handwriting on each one, I knew exactly what it was. Mum's old Christmas letters. I took them downstairs, and the three of us picked through them, some of the frostiness between us thawing. That's how good Christmas is.

Reading them was like time-traveling with my mum, back to when she was my age.

"Too funny..." She held one out. "This was the year Jess and I ended up on the local news." The year of the big snow. She opened it up and started to read.

"'The green looked fit.'" Mum's voice was shaking with laughter, and we were only four words in. "'We've never had so much snow—and just before the big day! Radness! Even better than my new trainers with the zips in! (Best pressie EVA!).'" I tried not to react, although I wanted to on SO many levels. "'Jess had been crashing at mine when it started. That's when we had the idea! We set our alarms mega early and went out and did it. We stomped for ages. Probs three hours! In the pitch black too. Jess had Docs on, but my feet went numb in minutes. Absolutely minging! But we did it. A "HAPPY CHRISTMAS EVERYONE!" big enough to see from the houses. We were dead proud of ourselves—until Mr. Phillips yelled out of his window to ask why we'd written Happy Chritmas. He woke up the whole street. We totally creased! Absolute classic though. Jess said the spelling made it even better (yes, my best mate is a total dude) and never blamed me although it was totally my fault. When the news people came (yes, they came here!), they did their whole report in front of it. Actual FAME.'"

Wow—it was weird to think about Mum growing up here too. And saying the word *minging*. Apparently it meant gross.

"Honestly, Hol, it felt like we'd made Hollywood when the TV crew turned up." Mum was wiping tears from under her eyes. "I kept asking them if they'd film me walking past in my new trainers."

"Speaking of that year..." I got my phone out. "You know that girl I love? @OneElleOfATime? Did you see what she posted?"

When Mum saw it, her brow furrowed.

"Weird..." She leaned closer. "Can you make it any bigger?" She clicked on Elle's profile picture, and when it opened, she kept repeating the name *Elle* a lot, until she snapped her fingers.

"I think you're going to like this." She got her iPad and opened Facebook. "You know the Jess I was just talking about? Jess Miller?" I nodded. Mum went to her profile. It was picture upon picture of Jess...and Elle. @OneElleOfATime. On a beach. Putting up decorations. Smiling with a cute old grandma. "I reckon that Elle...or Noëlle, as I think it could be, might be Jess's daughter." She tilted the screen toward me. "I mean, they're identical, right?"

How could she nod calmly like this wasn't on a level with finding out Lizzo was your second cousin?!

"You can close your mouth, Hol—Noëlle's just like you." Erm, nope. "In fact, Jess was telling me she's been struggling to make friends."

Actual splutter. Parents could be so clueless.

"I think not, Mother?! She's an actual goddess!" I couldn't stop clicking through the family pictures of her. It was like getting behind the scenes. "And... You. Know. Her?"

As Mum went into it all, my mind was officially blown. TOO many revelations.

So many that I needed some fresh air to sort my head out. And to try and stop myself freaking out that there was still no sign of Woody. At least I knew Ruby was going to die when I told her the Elle news.

But as I walked, I had to face up to two things. The news about Elle wasn't making me feel happy like I should.

And I'd left my phone back in the fridge.

And both were Woody's fault. He'd made me feel rubbish. Again. And I hated myself for letting it happen. But my feet were feeling sappy and walked down the path toward the village hall. The spot where we had our first kiss. Our magical mistletoe moment.

But wait.

In the total dark of the cut-through, big walls either side, I could hear someone moving about. There was a shape in the shadow... A person-shaped shape. I stopped to be certain...but...

yes! There was definitely something strung up over the little wire that hung all year 'round.

Mistletoe?!

Someone *had* put some up extra early!

All my peering out of the window had trained me for this moment. I'd recognize that jacket anywhere.

It *had* to be Woody!

Yes! Well done, feet! I take it all back. Maybe he'd seen the FOR SALE sign and wanted to go extra big?

I put my finger to my lips, shushing Colin, and stepped forward as quietly as I could, fishing out some emergency chewing gum.

My heart was pounding. Was I going to be able to act the right level of surprised? Was I going to be any good at kissing after so long? Was I just going to faint and potentially squash Colin?!

Every bit of me was on hyperalert—even my knees knew something massive was about to happen.

At least I'd planned out some pretty excellent and exciting conversation topics.

But, no.

What was that?

Another figure had just turned into the alleyway.

I froze. Should I hang back until they'd gone? I didn't want anything ruining this moment.

But as they got nearer, Woody stepped back.

A slither of the streetlight lit up his face—he was smiling.

And right where I'd had the best kiss of my life, they started to have theirs.

With every second, my heart broke even more. "Holly?"

That's all he said. Like I was the one in the wrong for being here.

Colin had barked at the exact wrong moment.

And even though they'd both turned around, I couldn't do anything other than stand and stare.

I'd honestly thought we were getting back together. I'd thought today would be the day.

"What are *you* doing here?" Woody looked shocked to see me. The girl just looked confused. Gorgeous and confused.

I've never been too sad to cry before. Guess that's another first I can tick off today.

Woody wasn't just kissing someone else—he was doing it in our special place.

All I heard was Woody say, "Sorry, Meera."

Meera. Perfect Meera. First Woody broke my heart. Now he was pureeing it. Probably into a protein shot Meera would drink before winning Olympic gold in a sport she invented.

Woody and I were over. Properly over.

I had to get out of there. I couldn't let him see me cry.

But Woody was walking toward me, and my legs weren't doing a single thing I told them.

"Hol?!" He was almost shouting. "Why are you sneaking up on us?"

Sneaking?! *Us?!* How dare he sound cross?

"I was..." I swallowed. C'mon, Hol, breathe down the urge to cry. "...just taking Colin for a walk."

"Funny, 'cause right now it looks like you're just standing still." He looked back at Meera. "And staring..." Annoyingly, all I could do was stand and stare even more. "Did you follow me here?" He sounded disgusted.

All I could do was shake my head—not exactly the strong denial I knew I should be going for.

"Everything okay, babe?" Meera called out.

Babe.

This wasn't their first kiss, was it? I'd been waiting for us to get back together, loving his waves from the window, kisses on his messages...and him? He'd moved on long ago.

This wasn't just devastating. It was humiliating.

I had to get out of there, to the only place I could cry like I needed to. Under my duvet.

Everyone had been right about Woody—he didn't care after all. Maybe he never had?

He turned back to her. "Sorry, Meera, one sec." Wow. I was worth one second.

Maybe I was always just someone boring until someone better came along. "Hol, we've caught up now, right?"

Sick. I felt actually sick. The ground was spinning.

I wanted to call him out on everything—ask what he thought he was doing. How he dared be cross at me.

"I thought you were going to call?" was all I managed to say—I could hear how pathetic it sounded.

"I was. I wanted my hoodie back." Ouch. How had I let this happen?

I hadn't just let Woody break my heart once—I'd let him do it every day for months.

"I see." My voice was shaking. I had to leave.

"Oh, and I saw your big news. Well..." He actually laughed. "It was hard to miss when they put it up in your garden. I dread to think what that's going to do to your two-hundred-point Christmas plan!"

And something about the way he laughed as he said it, like I was so boring and predictable that my life being turned upside down was funny... It made something snap.

"Oh no. The plan's all changed this year." I felt weirdly calm. "Didn't I tell you?" I smiled. "I'm spending Christmas in America."

CHAPTER SIX

Elle

Thirty-Six Days till Christmas

I'd had tons of replies. Some funny, some creepy, but only a handful had been actual leads. Still, in better news, it had only been a week since Dove announced the challenge and I'd already picked up almost a hundred new followers. Shame one of them only had this to say:

> **@tooblessed2bstressedxx: I heard you can get a great deal on one-way flights xoxo**

Why was it that all the good comments disappeared as soon as a troll showed their face? Did they seriously have nothing better to do? I hadn't blocked. Yet. Because as annoying as it was, right now I was enjoying how people were jumping in to have my back. Even Dove. *Especially* Dove.

She had no idea how much I was going to go all out to win. I HAD to.

I knew it with every bone in my body as soon as I saw who I was up against—it was me, three randoms, and Clara.

My ex–best friend Clara. @CallMeClaraT.

It didn't surprise me she was on Dove's radar—she'd been creeping on her for years. But as soon as I saw her name, I knew this wasn't a challenge—it was war. She would stop at nothing to beat me, so I was just going to have to do the same.

We'd both followed each other. The standoff was on. I curled up on my bedroom chair and hugged my knees. This had all gotten so big, so quickly. If I stopped to think about it, the flying on my own, being miles away from home, getting all those followers, it was kind of...terrifying. Which is exactly why I couldn't think about it.

At least @realdeallogan was impressed. He'd commented with:

Flying high as usual ✈️

What it meant, I had zero idea, but I'd replied with some random globes and Christmas emojis, and he'd given it a like. Logan's comments were getting regular—and I wasn't the only one to notice. Dove had started to send screenshots of them along with ••. She'd also been tagging me in her videos from her London trip with Morgan—I got it. The bar was high. Every single thing they'd posted was like a *Vogue* video. But I had Christmas on my side, and who didn't like Christmas? Well, apart from me and my family, but no one needed to know that.

I'd had to go full charm offensive to win Mom and Dad around, but they were getting there. I'd only dropped Dove's name a hundred times. Only trouble was finding someone they were happy for me to swap with.

My little brother—well, I knew what he'd say, so I'd kept the details vague. All he knew was I might be out of his hair for a bit.

But...I had a problem.

Was there anyone I could swap with? The nearest I'd gotten was the day I posted when this came through from some girl called @HappyHol_idays.

> **Heyyyy. No jokes. That pic is frm where I live! I'm right by the duck pond! 🦆 Are you serious about coming to the UK?? How about Little Marsh?? ➡️ DM if you want any help. Have a lonely Christmas! 🎄 xxzz PS did your mum used to live here?**

I think she meant *lovely*. But who knew? People were weird—and so was British humor. I'd seen *Gavin & Stacey*—I had a grip on it.

But @HappyHol_idays had followed up.

Sorry didn't mean to sound like a creepy internet stalker.

Which it hadn't. But that one kinda did. I hadn't replied just in case.

But then hours later there had been another:

Not sure if you saw my other messages, but I am ALL ABOUT spontaneous plans. so if you want to swap then ✋ I'm 100% serious about being 100% serious #letsdothis #iamspontaneous

So I had a volunteer.

I'd spent all week investigating her, wondering if she could be an option. But despite telling my followers that I was "in all kinds of ❤ with all my amazing followers who had offered to swap," truth was, no one else had come forward. It was @HappyHol_idays or no one.

So this morning I'd clicked follow. @HappyHol_idays, my DMs were officially open.

Holly Judd. *Could you be the one to help me?* Cute profile name, although I wasn't sure it really worked year-round. She looked about sixteen, brown hair, nice bangs, geek-chic-ish vibe. I scrolled some more. It could just be full-out geek, in fact. Very into her dog. He looked like a tiny Chewbacca. No *major* warning signs she was really a sixty-year-old man, but maybe *that* was the warning sign? I clicked on her tagged photos. This supercool girl called @Ruby_Roo had posted one of Holly and her dog in bed. Maybe she was *too* into her dog actually. But she looked friendly. And Little Marsh—if she wasn't lying about that—still looked cute. That was the main thing.

I had to keep focused. Remember it wasn't really about her life, it was about how I could make living her life look. It was about bringing in new followers with the best-ever British Christmas.

And what screamed "true spirit of Christmas" more than flying thousands of miles away from my family, nailing a tight schedule of iconic UK Christmas moments on my own, all to try and beat a ton of strangers on the internet? And Clara. Ha.

I'd been making moves in case. SnapGoGo had said flights weren't a problem, as long as I tagged them throughout the trip. They'd even offered hotels. In return they wanted big numbers on my posts, so they'd lost their minds when I said I was aiming for fifteen thousand more followers. Any less, and it would be a problem. Still, I could worry about that when, no *if*, it came to it.

I could see the first post already. Plane seat back, sheet mask on, granola bar in hand, an ironic *Felt Cute Might Delete Later*. Yup, I could be that girl.

This better all be worth it.

Little Marsh was an hour's train ride from London. That

could work, and Holly's friends looked kinda fun too. One confused-looking boy really made me laugh—he had the same shirt on in every photo—with a...pastry on it?

I wondered what they'd think of someone like me?

But as I scrolled, I stopped seeing the pictures and started hearing one thing on loop. *Was I actually going to do this?*

It wasn't like I'd be missing much back home. Mom and Dad were slammed with work till the new year, Nick was being his usual noncommittal self about Christmas plans, and we could only see Grams, who normally brought all the Christmas magic, during visiting hours.

I HAD to make this work.

I headed downstairs. The fake fire was lit, Mom was sprawled over Dad on the sofa, and they each had a red wine in their hand.

Mom looked up. "Hey, peach. What's up?"

Might as well cut to the chase.

"Did your village used to have a duck pond?" Mom blinked at the conversation U-turn. Maybe a hello first would have helped. "In England? When you were a kid?"

"Ahh." A smile grew as she untangled her long legs from Dad's lap and sat upright. "Can't say I saw that coming, but yes. It did."

Okay, so at least Holly was probably telling the truth about that. Although, Google Maps wasn't exactly a top secret research tool.

"Cool." Big, confident smile. "Well, I've found someone

who's willing to swap." Mom's face didn't move this time either, but from the sharp intake of breath, I think it was more shock. "For the competition? With my account?"

Dad put down his wine and said, "I see." Which normally meant he didn't.

"So?" I needed to keep this quick. Less time for them to properly think about it. Or talk me out of it. "You said you were up for it?"

"*In principle,* is what we said." Mom was using her super-serious voice. "I think we're going to need a little more information, Elle."

"A *lot* more," said Dad.

"Well..." I had to choose the most parent-friendly info I had from the almost zero info available to me. "She's sixteen." Probably. "Named Holly." Unless she's a catfish named Roger. "Is super close with her family." *If* that was her family in those dorky matching Christmas outfits. "And loves dogs. A lot."

"I see," Dad said again.

"And..." Time for my killer blow. "She lives in Little Marsh."

Mom put down her wine—I *knew* this would throw her off. "As in...*my* Little Marsh?"

"Uh-huh." I nodded. My math might suck, but I was a master of the parental mind. "With the duck pond. So, like, we chatted." I was steamrollering the information through. "It would probably be for a week. I could go to London, see where you grew up, visit some really old stuff, y'know...all the things I've been dying to do. And the flights for both of us would be free."

Silence.

I smiled as if this was no big thing and passed Mom my phone. I hoped they couldn't see my hand shaking.

"We'd have to think about this very carefully, Elly." Mom was looking with suspicion at Holly's profile. "Do some proper research—really find out about her...and who you'd be staying with."

Dad was looking too. "We'll need to have a chat with her parents. A *real* one. It's a big decision. For them as well."

"Of course." I nodded. The more confident I sounded, the more they'd think I could handle it. "I'll send you her profile. I mean, we all need to be happy this is a good idea." I paused. "Everyone I've told's been really into it. Dove's been sending me lots of tips." See, parents—see how this is a good thing already!? "And in principle, if you like Holly, you still wouldn't mind her staying here too?" First rule of big parent questions—make them sound as casual as you can.

Dad raised his eyebrow. "Like we said, Elly, one step at a time." I couldn't help but smile at him. He always knew what I was up to. "And what does your brother say?"

I smiled. "I'm sure li'l bro will be down for it."

Nick hated when I called him that. So I did it as much as I could.

"Down for what?" Awesome. This was the second he chose to stumble downstairs. He was in his usual uniform—band T-shirt, sweatpants, dark hair that had zero style and just grew. I thought older sisters were supposed to have little brothers under their thumbs? Mine did not play by the rules. Maybe it's because I was only sixteen minutes and thirty-four seconds older.

"For sharing the holiday spirit, that's what." I hadn't told him about the challenge. What it was all for. Him never being around meant these days we stayed out of each other's lives.

Nick raised an eyebrow and grabbed an apple from the bowl. "Uh-huh?"

"I said the other day, remember? I'm getting out of your way for a bit. If Mom and Dad say I can, of course." Winning smile. "And you might have someone stay here for a few days. Y'know, bringing that Christmas spirit all the way from the UK."

He took a big bite of his apple and stared at me. "Someone like...who?"

"Like, I dunno...a cool British girl you can talk about your band with, or chat about the 1975..." Nothing. "Or..." Hmm, my music knowledge needed work. "The Beatles?"

He slowly nodded, one eyebrow raised.

"I honestly think it could be fun." And, if I was really truthful, a tiny bit of me hoped having someone new here might stop Nick from disappearing all the time. Maybe even help him find his Christmas spirit again.

"I honestly think it could be a disaster." He took another big crunchy bite. "And you wouldn't even be around to see it." But we both knew once I had an idea, there wasn't much that could stop me. "Anyway." He grabbed the car keys. "Am I all right to take these? Blake and Dean said something urgent's come up. We're meeting at the Playground in ten..."

Mom and Dad agreed, although it was clear we were all thinking the same thing. How much urgent stuff could one band have? But with Nick out the way, we spent the rest of the evening looking at Holly's profile. And about an hour in, a weird thing happened—Mom suddenly got real into the idea. *Real* into it. And all because of her old friend Jess, a decision was made.

I hit reply to Holly's message.

Video call tomorrow?

CHAPTER SEVEN

Holly

Nine Days till Christmas

This was the most ridiculous thing I'd ever done.

And I'd once dressed as a sausage roll to cheer Fred up when Eve dumped him.

Not once did Mum sound annoyed that I'd rung home three times already.

But I had to share it with *someone.*

Me! Holly Judd?! Was here. In Ameeriicccuuuhhh! Mum was almost as excited as me about the whole thing, which is maybe why she forgot to alert me that I still had my "Wake Me Up When It's Christmas" eye mask pushed up on my head. I only discovered it when I went through security and the officer asked, "Miss, is this your first time traveling alone?" in a worried voice. She then asked the purpose of my trip, and I told her all about the swap with Elle, and my snow globe, and wanting to see Central Park in the snow and a proper holiday parade like on TV. And she paused and replied, "So *pleasure* not *business*, then?"

How was I to know it was a choice of two?!

I waited for my bag to chug around the carousel—Mum's suitcase was the same size as me. Half my packing was essentials (mainly Christmas jumpers, which DO NOT like being folded), and the other half was presents for Elle's family.

Back in my room, I'd left something for Elle—tickets for the London Eye. Hopefully she'd like that. I checked her account again. Today was the day #FestiveFifteen had kicked off. Just over an hour ago, she'd posted from the plane at this very airport. How did she make a sheet mask look good?!

She must have just taken off. I waved up at the roof and mouthed, *Byeeee, Elllleeeee*. Then I realized everyone could see me.

Sleep deprivation was real, people.

I mumbled something about being British, grabbed my suitcase and dragged it toward the exit, passing TWO POLICEMEN EATING DUNKIN' DONUTS.

They looked so perfect, they could be actors. I bet if Elle saw two police officers in Heathrow eating HobNobs, it really wouldn't have the same effect. *Cops*, Holly. I wasn't in the UK anymore. I waved at them. They did not wave back.

Still, first thing ticked off on my 127-point "Perfect Christmas

Plan: Mission America" list, which took up the first few pages in my new notebook. I'd had the cover personalized to say "Holly's Book of the Best Christmas Ever," and it was probably my favorite thing I owned. I'd left a smaller list of UK stuff back home for Elle to help with her challenge. I hope she didn't think it was silly.

I'd been nervous-excited-nervous ever since we'd had that mega video call with our parents. Elle's mum and dad were just as perfect as her—her mum could be her sister. In total I'd managed to get twelve words out. Mainly because our mums wouldn't stop chatting. They couldn't be happier Elle and I were going to both have the Christmas we dreamed of. To be honest, I got the impression my mum was sort of looking forward to packing up the house in peace. So, once Elle had got the flights booked, the plan was a go. We'd been messaging loads. She'd told me her little brother was going to love a Christmas visitor but had warned me not to take it personally if he spent most of his time in his room or playing with his friends at the playground. From what she said, he sounded a lot like the twins. Which I could deal with; I just hoped they didn't expect me to babysit or anything. She also said her parents would be working most of the time, so to plan lots on my own. Which was fine—that's exactly what my Christmas list was for!

Still. It was a bit scary—for me. It was clearly a breeze for Elle. As I'd been slowly freaking out, all she'd done was post to say how excited she was. I hoped her family would like me and not feel like they'd got a dud in return for their perfect daughter.

But it had to be done. I'd been so miserable about Naomi not coming back, the house move, Mum working, and when I saw Woody and Meera snogging, Christmas at home had basically been canceled.

But out here I could have my perfect dream Christmas after all and try and finally put Woody behind me.

EURGH.

I hated that even after what happened, a bit of me was still so sad about him that just thinking his name made my chest ache like my bra was too tight.

NOPE, HOLLY. You are in America! Remember the rules on the back page of the notebook in mega-size writing and underlined ten times?

Woody and all thoughts about him MUST stay in the UK.

Closely followed by:

From this day forward, Holly Judd catches FLIGHTS, NOT FEELINGS.

Yes. Better.

With a deep breath, I walked through the big security gates and into the start of my holiday.

"*HOLLLYYYYYY.*"

Someone was shouting.

"*HOLLLLYYY, OVER HEEERRREEEEE!*"

I scanned the heads. There they were! A gorgeous woman, cheekbones of a supermodel on a good day, bright-orange lipstick, and a man who looked like an aftershave advert, waving a massive sign saying WELCOME TO THE HOLLY-DAYS!!!

I couldn't move. This was already too much!

Elle's mum ducked under the barrier, ran toward me, and gave me a huge hug.

"*Please* tell me you're Holly, or we could be in big trouble here?"

She even smelled perfect. I nodded, painfully aware my first impression was silent sweaty girl in head-to-toe loungewear.

"That sign..." Hearing my voice here made me suddenly self-conscious, like I was putting on the most fake British accent ever. "It's brilliant."

Brilliant?! I never say brilliant. That was a Fred word. Had I swallowed a Hugh Grant film on the plane and now it was escaping out of me?!

She laughed and grabbed my suitcase. "All Elle's work... You can say thanks later. I'm Jess, by the way..." She gave me another hug. "We've been SO looking forward to your arrival."

Elle's dad, Pete, joined us, the sign tucked under his arm, hot drinks in his hands. In actual red cups. "Elle said mint hot chocolate with..." he thought back, "cream and candy cane sprinkles would be the best jet lag cure." He held one out for me. "Wanna see if she's right?"

"Wow." I was holding a red cup in their spiritual home! "I mean. Thanking you, sir. You're very kind—I'm ever so grateful."

Great. Now I was becoming a Victorian street urchin.

But there was no time to stress: we were off, heading home in their massive van. And once we'd cleared the airport, New Jersey was just as I'd hoped. Cute-colored houses, big, green road signs like in the movies, huge cars with Christmas trees strapped to their roofs, streets lined with twinkling displays and trees, and best of all, the thickest, whitest snow. The kind that made a crunch-squeak when you stepped on it.

As I sipped my drink, I already knew this decision had been the best one I'd ever made—and the magic didn't stop the whole journey. Only downside was that, when I asked if they had any Christmas music, Jess put on a Michael Bublé Christmas album (confirming my worst suspicion that even really cool international mums still couldn't resist the Bublé).

I couldn't believe that my Christmas had gone from a write-off to *this*.

And an hour later, when we pulled up into Elle's street, it got even better. All the big stand-alone houses were lit up with SO MANY Christmas lights. Snowmen, sleighs pulled by reindeer, even one house that couldn't be bothered and had just written "same" in lights. There were decorations everywhere, on roofs, at the end of gardens, even poking out of chimneys.

What on earth was Elle going to think of my little house and tiny garden? I'd used words like *quaint* and *authentic* to prepare her and had made my room extra cozy, but still.

Elle's garden had the biggest decorations on the street—I couldn't wait to see inside. But when we went in, there weren't many decorations. In fact, there weren't *any*. Not even a tree. It was like the house had Christmas catfished me. And as Elle predicted, there was no sign of Nick.

But maybe that was a good thing—I was soooo tired. My body didn't know if it was night or day, and I was somehow both shivering and sweating. Jess suggested I shower, get on my pajamas, and we'd have a quick dinner followed by waffles and syrup in front of the TV and an early night. Which sounded great. Mum had said they'd make me super welcome, and I already felt at home.

I wanted to start as I meant to go on, so after my shower, I pulled on my Christmas pj's and massive turkey slippers and fished out my gifts for everyone. When I came downstairs, Pete was laying the table. Their kitchen was the size of our living room and kitchen. Hu-mong-ous.

"Wow. Sophie wasn't wrong. You seriously DO bring the Christmas spirit..." He looked down at his knitted brown cardigan over a blue shirt. "I'm feeling kind of underdressed here?"

"The slippers light up." I lifted my foot onto the chair. "Wattles AND tails. Want to see?"

"Well, who would say no to that?!" Jess laughed as she put the plates down on the table. I could tell they were impressed.

"Oh, and this is from me and Mum." I grabbed their gift. "And Naomi, I guess."

A big basket from our local market. Jams, cheese, crackers—all stuff Mum said they would like. And some chocolate that I'd chosen, because who actually thinks savory crackers are a present? It had weighed approximately one ton in my suitcase, and now the cheese looked all sweaty and out of place. You and me both, cheese.

"You really shouldn't have." Jess seemed genuinely touched.

"I've got something for Nick too." I pointed at the carrier bag. The twins had helped me choose—it was a toy-dog thing, about as big as my arm, wearing antlers and Christmas bells. When you pressed its paw, it wagged its tail, rang its bells, and warbled the chorus of "I Wish It Could Be Christmas" on repeat. It made me laugh every time.

Pete sighed. "He should be back by now. Almost six, right? It isn't funny anymore. I'm so sorry, Holly. Why don't you go and put it in his room?"

They seemed annoyed with him, or his babysitter, or whatever, so I escaped the awkward, ran upstairs, and pushed his door open.

"AHHHHHH!"

I actually screamed.

There was someone in Nick's room! In the pitch black?! A tall guy, in a hoodie, bag over his shoulder.

"WHO ARE YOU?!"

I held out the dog and pressed its paw. Yes, intruder—take that bell-ringing Christmas tune!

"Who are YOU is the question?!" the guy snapped back. "And *what* is that?"

"You okay up there?" Jess shouted, but I couldn't turn back in case the guy did something sudden.

I held the dog out farther. "Don't move, or I'll call the police."

But the intruder did something weird. He put down his bag and smiled. "The police?" He shook his head, almost laughing. "Wow, Elle really can pick them..." How did he know Elle? "You must be Holly?" How did he know *me*?!

"I'm Nick..." He flicked the light on and held out his hand.

My non-dog-holding hand stayed still. My jaw, however, dropped. Hard. Wasn't he ten years too old to be Nick? And at least seven million times too hot?

"I should have known when I saw the light-up turkeys."

The dog was still singing.

"Wattles." Silence. "Elle said she had a little brother, but..."

Nick shook his head. "By sixteen minutes. Or didn't she mention that?"

"No, she did not." And nor did anyone else.

Sorry, was living with Elle's massively hot twin brother not exactly the kind of thing that should have been put on the "urgent information" list? I had not planned for this!

Thank goodness I'd fully committed to my rules.

Catching flights not feelings.

"Now..." Nick reached out toward the dog as if it might bite.

"Are you going to turn that noise off, or are we going to have to get a vet?"

And I just stared. And blinked. And the dog went wild.

Yup, I'd been in America less than two hours, and despite all my plans, I had no idea what this trip was going to have in store.

CHAPTER EIGHT

Elle

Eight Days till Christmas

I opened the curtains. Total darkness...but still cute, from what I could make out. The whole place was so quaint. And authentic! Just like Holly said.

I rolled over in bed, Holly's sheets crinkling. Even her room felt friendly. In between her posters of Twenty One Pilots and bands I didn't recognize, her walls were packed with smiling Polaroids with her friends. I wondered what she'd think of mine? All I had was a single board of inspo pictures for my account.

I'd woken up what felt like hours ago, too tired to get out of bed, too awake to sleep. I didn't have the Wi-Fi password, so I'd lain awake worrying about the competition. So restful.

I'd gotten a voice note from Nick though. He'd told me he'd

changed his "do not disturb," so if I needed anything, to "call anytime," and then a follow-up saying he probably wouldn't sleep anyway as he was having "singing dog issues." No idea what that meant, but I appreciated it.

Holly had been supersweet and left me a gift *and* a Dairy Milk advent calendar. I was saving the gift but had eaten advent days one through fifteen in one go last night—and the rest in a five a.m. moment of "what am I actually doing?!"

British chocolate was the one! I was going to love visiting Cadbury World.

Ruby and Fred were coming over at ten—they were Holly's best friends, and apparently they wanted to take me around the village, which was really nice.

Yesterday had been the first official day of #FestiveFifteen, but my best travel posts had only pulled in 177 new followers (not that I'd burned through all my data checking). Day two needed to be better. Much better. Options might be limited in Little Marsh, so I was going with "Cute British Christmas Things I Have Zero Idea About."

But a noise stopped my brain whirring. Was something at the door? Was it...scratching?

I padded across the carpet and opened it. *Colin.* Holly's dog—and he seemed genuinely disappointed to see me. Thanks, Col. Shaded by a reject Chewbacca—great start.

He waddled straight past me, jumped on the bed, and fell

asleep on landing. This dog was a mood. But as he snored, a small, gold envelope fluttered down—and it had my name on it. I was so tired last night, I must have missed it.

I opened it up. A glittery Christmas card with a singing Statue of Liberty on it.

Hiyer Elle–if you're reading this then welcome! I guess you're here... And I'm there? Whoa. Weird huh?

Wow—Holly thought of everything.

I hope you found the advent calendar. You'll have some catching up to do, but remember, don't EVER open in advance.

Uh-oh.

Or some kind of Christmas curse will be unleashed?! (Like Iceland running out of pigs in blankets nationwide.)

Iceland? Wasn't that a whole different country?

I know we went over it, but just in case...here is Everything You Need to Know About Little Marsh. Starting with the people.

Ruby: 10/10 in every way. Will probably change her hair at least twice while you're here. Honestly—the Absolute Best.

Fred: Equal Absolute Best. He's promised to bring all the Christmas jumper fun in my absence. Be nice to him (not that you won't?!)—he's a precious treasure who needs to be protected. DO NOT BE ALARMED if he attempts to have a conversation without words. This is normal. And don't let him talk about Eve.

Obvs my mum. She's as excited about this whole swap as me. Maybe more. Don't let her adopt you permanently, please. She's getting everything ready to move into Colin-human's, so sorry if there are loads of boxes. Don't let her touch my stuff! (Muchas gracias.)

Woody. Hmm. What to say here. A friend. Who lives opposite. (And no pressure, but if you spot any girlfriend-looking people going into his house, maybe you could let me know? Although to be clear, I'm not a stalker. And don't tell the others I've put him on this list.)

Other stuff.

I have secret Colin snacks in my bedside table and the Wi-Fi network is HOLLYISINAMERICA. I changed it. I like to keep the neighbours updated.

Wonder if she meant the neighbor she absolutely wasn't stalking.

Password is HOllyIsNOtAsTallAsNaOmiButAMuchBetterPersOn.

Help yourself to anything you find in my room (especially Christmas jumpers—I left some I thought you might like). And have the best time!

Talking of which—and I'm sure you're fully planned up with #FestiveFifteen (which you will totally WIN, btw), but I thought I'd do my bit—here's my Elle's Ultimate Cross-the-Atlantic Christmas Checklist for you! (Ignore if it's cringe!!!!)

Not cringe at all. Actually really thoughtful. And it could be *exactly* what I needed—insider intel from a Christmas expert.

A London day out—don't miss the Christmas tree in Trafalgar Square, lights on Regent Street, South Bank, and the big Christmassy fountains round the back of King's Cross. Walking along the river is the best. Although it's freezing. LAYERS ARE KEY. The Tube is BOILING. The outside is FREEZING. There is no middle.

See Ruby in the pantomime. It's behind you! Oh no, it isn't! (Oh yes, it is actually—it's just right out the front door and right again.)

A pant-o-what?

Pull a Christmas Cracker.

Okay, so I'd seen these on the TV. Apparently you pull them and get a paper crown. Sounds cool. Into it.

Not a real Christmas Cracker (although that's also a must!) but Holly's "Christmas Cracker" is a thing I do every year. Basically, surprise someone with something Christmassy. No pressure, but it's normally loads of fun, so thought you might want to.

Little Marsh-mas—DON'T LAUGH—it's a big party thing. The whole village comes out (all eighty of them, hahahah) and there are stalls and stuff. Keep an eye/ear out for CAROL. Fred can help. He LIVES for this.

Eat all the foods. Have you tried mince pies? Not my absolute faves, but they're a British Christmas necessity! That Little Cafe does the best ones.

Meat and raisins? Sounds gross. But could be good for the likes.

OK, I started writing this last one and then thought, NO. You don't just want to hear from me! So—just an idea—maybe you could do a post and get other people to suggest this last one?!

Jeez—Holly was a genius! Number six could be *exactly* the big idea I'd been after. Getting my followers to post ideas for the ultimate UK Christmas challenge—tag their friends in... Maybe I could even work it into a big finale in London? My train tickets were booked for Thursday, and SnapGoGo had offered me a hotel room if I wanted, which was kind of ridiculous, but maybe I could make it all work? I could see the breakfast in bed picture already...

I closed the card, my mind whirring, but there was more on the back.

Sorry—ran out of space! This is the last bit though. As long as you're staying in my room, don't forget the three golden rules...

1. Never say no to a festive drink

2. If "All I Want for Christmas Is You" comes on, sing EVERY word. No ducking on the high notes. We must always, ALWAYS respect Queen Mariah. (Did you know they wrote it in fifteen minutes? Howwww??)

3. Have the best time.

Post everything—I can't wait to seeeeeee.

Love Holly xxxxx

PS Give Colin (DEFINITELY DOG ONLY) a cuddle from meeeeee.

I read it again, not wanting to put it down.

It was weird: it felt like I had a friend with me, despite being so far away from home, and I liked it. No one had written me a letter in *forever*. And Holly's list was packed with all the cute British stuff I really needed. Checking it off could help me win #FestiveFifteen. Although...Wi-Fi password meant contact with the outside world.

Seeing the bars of reception pop up was like taking out my hair from a too-tight ponytail. Full-on relief.

And the relief didn't stop there. My mentions had gone wild. So many likes for the photo of me on the plane. And yes, even one from Dove.

The attendants had let me sneak into first class to take it before kicking me back into economy. @_Beckywiththemediocrehair_ had tagged her friends to help me get followers, and I was now on over two hundred new ones. She was the best. Even @realdeallogan had shared my post on his stories to wish me luck AND had commented:

Wish I was there... 😉

I didn't really know him, but I knew if he shared more, if I kept him on my side, I had more chance of getting new followers. Pretending I wasn't grossing myself out, I replied with a:

I've heard London is extra ❤ this time of year...

Ick. Ick. Ick. I hardly knew the guy, but I had to remember what I was here to do—win. And right now, despite my burst of followers, it was looking hard. Seriously hard. Dove had posted the leaderboard—and I was last. Even worse, Clara was way in the lead with over a thousand new followers. In twenty-four hours?!

She'd had the genius idea of hooking up with a featured influencer every single day—guaranteed traffic. Way simpler than flying halfway around the world to eat meat and raisin pies. It was her comment on Dove's leaderboard that really got me, though.

Best of luck to all the others. SUCH a shame @OneEleOfATime had to start her account again, but I know you've got this boo! 😘 #pickyourselfup #downbutnotout #inspo

Such a shame?! It was 100 percent because of her!

And she'd deliberately spelled my name wrong so people couldn't even click me.

I hated how Clara still made me feel, but if I tried to tell anyone, gave Dove a heads-up, it would look like I was just trying to get her kicked out.

And that wasn't the only bad news. @tooblessed2bstressedxx had waded in too.

Nobody:

Not even a soul:

@OneElleOfATime: who wants more of my annoying travel posts?!

I felt that familiar sick feeling I'd had in the old days of my last account. I really thought this time would be different. Although maybe it could be—my best revenge would just have to be showing them both I could win.

Determined to get back to how I'd felt when I'd opened Holly's letter, I opened my chat with her. It was super late on her end, but she was online.

How's it going?! I feel like I slept for 2mins?! All the details, please.

You're awake! 👋

YOU'RE awake! (👋 BACK FROM THE FUTURE)

Soooo early for you 💤

Too right. These sights aren't going to see themselves...

Nahhh, truth is jet lag is ruining me rn.

🙂 same.

Thanks for the card btw.

AND THE GIFTS!

do you like them?

❤❤ LOVED ❤❤ I'm saving the wrapped one though. That OK?

Sure! I don't opeN Presents before the 25th anyway 😀

Although open it SOoooON.

If you insist!!! 😜

I LOVED your suggestions. AM TOTALLY USING all of them #Christmasexpert

Did you know it's technically illegal to eat a mince pie in the UK on Christmas Day #fact

Wow—she really was into Christmas 24–7.

From the sound of them they should be illegal every day?!

😀 In other fact news. Your house/life/ everything is AMAZING. You know it's snowing, right?

Hello!? Where you live is like a movie set!!!

Even on my drive from the airport I'd spotted all these wonky buildings, and dinky pubs, and bright red letterboxes.

HOW GOOD ARE YOUR DAD'S WAFFLES???

10/10

I paused before clicking the arrow on the next message. Should I send?

How are things with Nick?

Holly typed. And stopped typing. And typed again.

Interesting.

He's not a child?!

I had no idea what to say to that.

He said he had singing dog issues. Any ideas?!

Ermmm. Maybe.

He can be too cool for school sometimes.

Nah—everyone's been 👍

I felt my shoulders relax. I don't think I'd realized how nervous I was that she wouldn't have a good time.

What are your plans for tomorrow?

Explore Alpine Peaks. I'm checking out the lights. And baking. Biscuits. Cookies?! Whatever you call them. And lunch at Scream If You Want to Go Pasta, which is apparently...

LEGENDARY!

Legendary.

There was a knock at the door. I dropped my phone and sat up, brushing my hair down, trying to look a bit more presentable. "Hello?"

Mrs. Judd poked her head around the door, wearing the fluffiest dressing gown.

"I thought I heard you up." She pushed her glasses up her nose, everything looking slightly at the wrong angle.

I gave her a big, dorky wave. "Hope I didn't wake you." Colin raised his left eyebrow in disapproval at me making the bed move.

She shook her head. "Not at all. Tea?"

I'd been in the UK for less than twelve hours and had already learned a crucial thing. Whatever the situation, someone would offer a cup of tea. I was tired from the journey? Tea. Didn't sleep well? Tea. Stepped on a pine needle while only wearing socks? Tea.

I said thanks and headed downstairs. And maybe there was something in the tea approach, as I felt 10 percent less marshmallow-brained once I'd finished it.

Which gave me an idea. There was no way I was going to force Nick to spend time with Holly—they were chalk and cheese. Christmas cheese. He was all about spontaneous decisions, and she was like his Christmas-obsessed, plan-making nemesis. But the one thing I was going to force him to do was offer her tea.

Despite being super tired, it was nice talking with Sophie, hearing stories about when she and Mom were little. She was packing and kept apologizing for not being around more because she was getting everything ready for the move, but the truth was, it suited me just fine. I had lots to get done—it wasn't exactly a vacation, more of a mission. Which I started over breakfast.

Don't judge a sauce by its name. Apparently this is "Brown Sauce." Looks revolting. Tastes GREAT. Welcome to England 🍽️😊

I killed the next hour unpacking my stuff, sending messages for Mom and Dad to read in the morning, catching up on all my DMs and comments, and getting ready to meet Ruby and Fred. I went for big, beachy, wavy hair, a fluffy, white sweater tucked into my favorite black jeans, and some low-heel ankle boots. I wanted to wear Converse but didn't want Ruby and Fred instantly realizing how real-life me was way scruffier than the person they were expecting.

When the doorbell rang, I was a wreck with nerves. I took a deep breath, double-checked my makeup, straightened my shoulders and...opened the door to two drenched people, in matching stripy green-and-red headbands with elf ears on, a bell wobbling away. "Don't ask." The girl shook her head, making the bell jingle even more. "We thought we owed it to Hol."

The guy next to her was wearing a sweater that said, "Rolling with My Snowmies." He looked...I couldn't tell. Scared?

"Yup." The girl looked me up and down. "You actually are a supermodel. I'm Ruby, by the way. Oh." She dug her hand into her pocket. "And we got you these..." She held out a bag of potato chips...Walkers Pigs in Blankets. They looked like meat in...more meat?! Not like the ones back home at all. "Eat these, and you're basically British."

I liked her already. I said thanks and waited for Probably Fred to introduce himself. I flashed him a smile, a real big, cheesy one. But nothing. Guess it was on me.

"I'm Elle." I put my hand out. He took it, shook it, and just said one thing.

"Yes."

I guess this definitely was Fred, then. Holly *had* warned me. He then stared some more and said, "American."

"Don't mind him. He's not good with mornings." Ruby prodded him in the ribs. "Or afternoons. Want to grab your coat? I've got till..." She looked at her watch. "Two. Rehearsals are Hec-Tic."

Despite the rain, we set off on a route around the village. As we walked, Fred confirmed he was indeed Fred, which was progress, but then started reeling off all these facts ("Queen Victoria once had a sandwich here," "the plague decimated this street," "there was a massacre in that field"), all while eating a "sausage roll," which Fred had to explain through the flying crumbs. Not *exactly* the insider info I was after, but I tried to make all the right noises, as I did really appreciate them giving up their time.

Ruby got it though and helped me find all the best spots for photos and even lent me the hot spot on her phone to post them. Pics of the main street, a mailbox in front of a holly bush, a post office that had a knitted squirrel in the window wearing a Christmas hat, and a little bridge with lights all along. Fred couldn't have looked less interested in the #FestiveFifteen challenge if he tried, but it was worth it, as the likes were coming in and I hit five hundred new followers.

"So..." By the time we'd visited Mom's old house then got to the little church, I decided it had been long enough to ask the question I couldn't quite figure out. "How do you think Holly will manage? At mine?"

Ruby tilted her head back. It was a couple more paces before she spoke.

"I think she'll have an amazing time." She said it slowly, carefully, like she was choosing each word. "Honestly? She lives for Christmas."

Tell me something I don't know. I looked at Fred, who still had pastry flakes on his cheek. "What about you, Fred? And I want your honest answer..."

He looked behind him as if there could be another Fred I was talking to.

"Honestly?" I nodded. "Well, when she showed me your profile, all I knew about you was waffles and nails, and..." He did this odd openmouthed, big-eyed smile. "So, when she said you'd signed up for this competition, and that you guys were going to swap lives just so you could win? Well, I thought she was joking. Then I thought she was out of her mind. Or you both were." *O-kaaaaaay.* "And one of you would probably end up dead. Or you both would. And..." It was like he only just realized that maybe he didn't need to be *that* honest. "...Well...er...yes. I'm sure no one will die. Probably."

Great to know I wasn't going to get murdered—*probably*. A real win.

At least I knew why Fred looked so freaked out whenever he spoke to me—he thought this whole mission, my account, *me*, was a bit of a joke.

Still, I wasn't here to make friends, was I? I was here to win. If I laughed it off, then it wouldn't hurt. That's *exactly* what online Elle would do.

"Thanks for the appraisal, Fred. Ridiculous internet person who probably isn't a threat to life..." I laughed, Ruby mouthed *sorry*, but I smiled at them both. I guess it wasn't Fred's fault—he didn't really know me. "So why do you think Holly was so up for it? No offense or anything, but from what I know, it seems like she'd be the kind of person to love December at home?"

Ruby shrugged. "Well, that was her plan." I swear I caught a quick glance to Fred. "But she wanted a perfect Christmas. And she needed a change...from all the change." Ruby didn't say anything more.

What change had made Holly shake everything up so much?

But I stopped—I'd spotted something supercute. Mistletoe hanging at the end of the tiny alleyway. I got my camera out.

This time I wasn't being paranoid. There was *definitely* a look between Ruby and Fred.

Ruby stopped. "Don't suppose we could interest you in the pond instead?" She pointed in the opposite direction. "It's dead nice this time of day and..."

And clearly not a story I was getting. Never mind, I'd seen something that needed even more explanation.

A massive poster, lit up, Ruby's face splashed right across it. It was an advert for *Snow White* at the village hall, and it looked like a cross between an early episode of *Drag Race* and a Disney film—a.k.a. a must-see.

"So this is what Holly meant when she said *pantomime*?!" I hurried over as Fred shouted, "She's behind you!" even though the poster was clearly in front of me. "It looks dope! You're so famous!" I took a photo—poster Ruby looked amazing, even if real-life Ruby was staring at the ground.

"It's not a big deal..."

Fred nudged her arm but was looking at me. "Ignore her. It is. A massive one. And she's brilliant. Hol and I have seen it three times already."

"Well, I was hoping to come and see it too?" It sounded like something my American followers would really like to see. "Check out my first-ever pantomime?"

Ruby laughed. "You're going to think we've all lost it."

"That's what I'm hoping for. How do I get tickets?"

But I didn't get an answer because Fred pointed out a girl through the hall window, and immediately Ruby started striding away. I had to jog to catch up. But when we got to the green, I did a double take—there was someone I semi-recognized? *But how?*

I swear I heard Ruby say, "Seriously?" under her breath.

"Is that someone Holly knows?" I pointed over to the dude in a denim jacket.

He had brown hair, was wearing shorts despite it being freezing, and was kicking a soccer ball with his friend. He clocked he was being watched, so he started showboating—I tried not to laugh, well not too loud, as he jumped up to flick the ball up and totally missed.

"The home of soccer, huh?" I laughed. But Ruby was giving me a weird look.

"How do you know that Holly *may or may not know* who he is?"

It felt loaded, so I tried to keep it vague. I don't know why, but I had a feeling Holly needed me to. "Just a guess...?" That seemed safer than telling them that when I got Colin's snack out of the bedside table, there was most definitely a picture of that exact person tucked away.

"Guess you'll find out sooner or later..." Ruby sighed. Wow, for a village so tiny, Little Marsh was full of secrets. "It's Woody."

Ahh, the neighbor opposite. The one Holly had told me to keep an eye on. I looked over at him.

I could see why Holly had a photo of him. He was all sorts of cute. The kind of cute that my followers would love.

He stopped, cocked his head on to one side, and waved—and I waved back.

"Don't." I didn't know if Ruby was talking to me or him, but when I looked, she was staring right at him. "I know Americans love British guys, but please...anyone but him."

CHAPTER NINE

Holly

Alpine Peaks didn't do things by halves. Not even seven-eighths. Their Christmas lights were lit.

I stood in the middle of the road, snow drifting down, nodding along to a band playing jazzy versions of Christmas classics. The singer had a voice so smooth, he sounded like liquefied Father Christmas. If I weren't wearing mittens, I'd pinch myself.

First twenty-four hours were down, and it *still* didn't feel real. Six full days left already didn't feel like enough. Especially for what I had planned.

I got out my notebook and opened my Perfect Christmas Plan: Mission America list.

I'd already checked off loads of things, and Jess had just helped me get my train tickets for Thursday. It was a good way of making peace after I'd made her full-on swear when she'd come home and discovered me in her kitchen with 102 iced festive biscuits covering every surface. And they had a *lot* of surface. But the American measurements had really thrown me. How can a cup be a measurement? It's a drinking vessel of no particular size?!

Still, on the plus side, I'd discovered the train ride to New York was only one hour, eighteen minutes.

I was. SO. NEAR. To. Manhattan.

Ha. Even when I thought *Manhattan*, I thought it in a *Nuuuu Yoiiirk* voice. Me, Holly Judd, in *Maaanhatttan.* In four days. Could life get any better?!

Naomi was going to get SO many pictures. Yes, sis, I see your leopard shark, and I raise you the Empire State Building. In the snow.

My trip was already so awesome that I knew by the time I left, I really was going to be able to cross off the final thing on my list. The thing with the big stars next to it.

HAVE THE MOST PERFECT CHRISTMAS EVER!

And it sounded like things were going well back home too. I'd had a long chat with Ruby earlier, and she'd told me that when Fred met Elle, he'd lost the ability to make conversation for almost two hours and just kept repeating "American" and spouting facts about deaths and massacres. I think he even called her a waffle-loving murderer? Classic chat there, Fred. But when she'd gone, he started asking Ruby "just out of curiosity" questions which mainly seemed to be:

Did she ever post about a boyfriend?

Did she ever post about a boy who could be a boyfriend?

Conclusion: Massacres + loss of speech + interrogation = Fred was into Elle. In a major way.

I promised to do some digging to find out what Elle thought about him, but neither Ruby nor I had the heart to mention the thing we'd both noticed on her account. Elle and @realdeallogan seemed to have something going on. And he couldn't be more different from Fred. I mean, sure, he might have just announced a trip to Finland to shoot for some underwear brand, but personality-wise, his chat seemed to be... Well, let's just say if you are a fan of American football, cars, or going to watch American football in cars, then maybe it could be true love. And Elle seemed way better than that.

Ruby had a point though; maybe Fred finally liking someone was enough. At least it meant he was finally moving on from Eve. Of course, I'd had to immediately ring Fred—who denied everything, but did say Elle was "chill," they'd had a "dope" afternoon, conversation "totally flowed," and when I'd asked if she was as hot as I'd imagined he said he "hadn't noticed." Hahahaha. Worst liar ever. He also said she looked surprised when he got a sausage roll out of his pocket—maybe I should have warned her.

I just hoped he didn't get too attached. Just in case she wasn't into him. I mean, she should be—he was the best human in the world—but I knew how it felt to like someone who didn't seem into you. Someone like...

NO, WOODY THOUGHT, GO AWAY—YOU ARE NOT MEANT TO HAVE GOTTEN THROUGH PASSPORT CONTROL.

I see you, unwanted Woody thought, and I raise you the biggest light-up festive pineapple I've ever seen. He was *not* going to ruin my evening. I tugged down my woolly hat and marched over to it, and as I sent photos of it to Mum, Elle's name popped up.

Btw, thought you'd want to know, I'm already on it with your list ❤

My chest went all warm—and it wasn't the Christmas churros I'd just eaten. Elle really *did* like my list—she hadn't just been saying it! Regardless of the fact we'd life-swapped, truth was, I was still a total fangirl of hers.

Awesome. Alsooooo, not related to anything, but where I live, it's not considered weird to keep pastry snacks on you for emergencies.

Yes. Subtle.

Now I know you ❤ lists, I made one for you... My way of saying thanks for loaning out your dope friends. You up for it? #ChristmasChallengeRightBackAtYa

Great news that she loved Ruby and Fred, but less-great news was an extra to-do list. Especially if she was challenging me to complete it? Sure, I wanted to be all "yes, of course, I'm up for anything!" just like her, but truth was, I already had a packed daily (some would say hourly) plan.

Could I dodge it?

They thought you were dope too.

That word had literally never come out of my mouth before—and never should again. It was like when Colin-human once said Mum's date-night dress "slayed." Actual shudder.

Did you get panto tickets? Think Fred has a spare one for Wednesday??

A little white matchmaking lie never hurt anyone. Ruby and I had come up with the plan—she'd get a pair, and I'd do the setup.

Thanks but I'm already on it

Ouch. Was that a brush-off? Maybe facts about massacres weren't her thing.

You didn't answer though. Say yes and I'll do an extra Christmas Cracker. I've got the best idea for a surprise for our moms

That sounded awesome, but handing over my holiday—me, a girl who packed turkey slippers—to someone who talked her way into first class on the plane sounded like nothing but a disaster.

And what if I don't?

The holidays will be ruined hahahahhaha.

Sorry—slightly dramatic. How about if either of us don't do them...

She was typing. And untyping. The suspense was too much.

Yes!!

But when I looked at my message flying out of my phone to Elle's I yelped. I'd meant to say "Yes??" not "Yes!!"

What kind of twisted keyboard inventor would put *!* and *?* next to each other? She was going to think that was me agreeing to it.

But my message explaining didn't send. And it didn't send again. And it didn't send even when I went back to where we'd started the conversation, waving my phone around as much as I could without causing a security alert. Wi-Fi, why have you dropped at this crucial time?! Why, Wi-Fi, whyyy?

I huffed so hard, I created a face full of steam.

Guess there was nothing I could do except wait for reception. And enjoy the lights. And fret. And buy emergency hot chocolate.

Which I finished in record time. I took aim with my empty cup at a bin that was a penguin with a giant hole for a mouth and threw.

I shot. I scored. I celebratory danced.

"Well, hello there." A deep British voice popped up beside me. I stopped dancing, spun around, and saw someone I didn't expect. Nick.

"What are *you* doing here?" He'd given me a fright. Mainly due to the fact he wasn't wearing a coat. In the snow.

"Just testing out my British accent on strangers." His voice was back to normal, and he almost, almost smiled. Maybe it was the cold affecting his face. "Or maybe I thought I'd come see if you'd found everything okay..."

Well, that was nice of him, especially as Jess said he had basketball practice. "I thought you were with your mates?"

This time he definitely smiled. "Mayyyyytes."

"Needs work. See Daniel Radcliffe for details."

But then I didn't know what to say. And neither did he by the way we were both just standing and looking at each other. Normally I wouldn't be able to function around someone who looked like him, but luckily my brain was otherwise engaged trying to stop thinking about thinking about Woody.

"Elle told me to tell you the hot chocolate here should not be missed."

Oh, I see. She'd sent him. Designated babysitter. That made sense. Still, it would be rude to say no after he'd made the effort to come.

"You know it's a Christmas rule of mine to never turn down a festive hot drink?"

Nick grinned. "I did not know that, no."

I fished out my notebook. "Yup, alongside never leave Mariah hanging. It's all in here." I couldn't tell if he looked alarmed or impressed as I flicked through.

"Holly's Book of the Best Christmas Ever?" He raised one eyebrow. "No pressure, huh?"

Oh—I hadn't meant him to take it that way. "No. Honestly no." I opened the front page. "I've already planned it all out."

I handed it to him, so he could see. It meant he could back me up when I told Elle I wasn't sure I had time for any more plans. He scanned the list. "You sure have. All hundred things..."

"A hundred and twenty-seven."

He whistled as he read down. "'Go into a 7-Eleven (they might have Twinkies?). Watch a Christmas film and get popcorn, soda and best-named snack... Ask for the check, please, and keep a straight face.' You haven't left anything out, have you?"

"Nope." I shook my head. "You can't leave something like this to chance, right...?"

But judging by his face as he read points sixty to seventy-three, I wasn't 100 percent sure he agreed.

"And what's this?" Oh no. No, no no?! I grabbed my book back. He'd seen the back page—the page that only I was ever meant to see. "'Flights, not feelings?'"

So this is what dying inside felt like. I did NOT want him or his perfect sister to know what a dweeb I was.

"Don't ask." Why had I been such an idiot?! "So, are we getting these drinks or what?"

We headed back to the stall I'd just come from, and I tried not to make eye contact with the person serving, whom I'd only ordered from six minutes ago. When they said, "Back again, huh?" I pretended I'd dropped my mitten in the snow and disappeared to look for it. I only dared to sip it when we were around the corner.

"I *cannot* get enough of this..." It was soooo good.

"I owe you a thanks, by the way." Nick took a sip. "For those cookies. Tasted delicious—looked..."

"You don't need to finish that." Neither of us wanted him to say it out loud—the red and white icing had run, so they looked like flesh-colored, slightly bent, er, rods.

"I didn't think you were into Christmas stuff?"

"Being attacked by a singing dog, I can take or leave, but cookies, I can handle"

"Anything else?"

Nick looked around. "I mean, all this isn't really my thing..." He shrugged, almost apologetically. "Guess my only plan would be to not have a plan."

Okay, this guy was clearly weird, so changing the topic quickly, we walked around the stalls. I wouldn't have said I was that overexcited about things (a really good snow mound! A dog wearing a brussels sprout costume!), but compared to Nick, I was a total Christmas freak. We even looked opposite. He was wearing a checked shirt open over a white T-shirt, and sort of retro, faded-blue jeans, with a black jacket pulled over it. I, however, looked like a sweaty, walking ball of wool. Just like Elle, he was painfully good looking—like in science when you can't look directly at burning magnesium, or it would burn your eyeballs...but with cheekbones, and dimples, and these amazing long eyelashes.

Still, we'd been thrown together by his sister, so we talked and tried to find common ground. When we walked back past the stage, and the band was covering "Last Christmas," we found it—music. I was as obsessed with American bands as he was British ones, and we agreed to swap playlists.

"So, are you missing Elle?" I'd stopped to take another photo.

Nick raised an eyebrow. "It's been less than two days."

"My friends love her, by the way."

This time he did one of his semi smiles. "Everyone loves my sister." But it quickly faded, like he'd remembered something. He realized I had noticed and quickly turned the attention back to me. "So are you missing your 'maaates'?"

"'Course. Like massively. They're the actual best. But

Christmas at home sort of got canceled, and this was my plan to salvage it. So here I am." I pointed at a giant, lit-up, red-and-green plastic dinosaur. "A T. rex in a Santa hat." I closed my eyes and breathed out. "I. Am. Blessed."

"Really glad that even after pointing out the last three hundred displays, you're still not bored." I couldn't tell if he was joking or not.

"And I never will be. So buckle up. Same with people genuinely saying 'happy holidays.' And them playing 'White Christmas.'" I looked at the band.

Nick shook his head. "It's the third time they've done it since I got here."

"Look, you've already told me you can 'take or leave' Christmas dinner, so frankly your opinions are not to be trusted." But I had learned *something* from what had happened with Woody, even if someone thought I wasn't fun or exciting enough: I should still just be me. Which is why I didn't mind Nick looking at me with confusion while I two-stepped to Bing Crosby.

"Yeeeesh." Nick checked his phone. "Sorry to do this, but I need to go see Blake." I nodded. Elle had told me he'd be like this. "Want to fit in a super-quick meeting with grumpy Dominic? He's only a five-minute drive."

I was intrigued, so we headed off.

"Holly, meet Dominic. Dom," Nick held his hand out. "Meet Holly."

I didn't know what to say. I was surprised by two main things.

One, Dominic wasn't grumpy. And two, he wasn't a man.

"He's a reindonkey." Nick nodded. "A rare breed found only in somewhere as deranged as, well...here." Maybe I should have guessed when we drove out of the town and parked up at Alpine Parks Community Farm.

There Dominic was. The other side of a fence. Eating some hay. Being a donkey. Dressed with a head collar that had antlers on it and a ball of white fluff on top of his tail. He ambled over, and I stroked his nose.

"Erm, so he's amazing." Wow, anti-Christmas Nick had come through with some surprise festive gold.

"You should see him with the full nose on."

Dominic made a sort of fluttering hello through his nostrils as I rubbed his neck.

"But I don't understand. He's not grumpy at all?"

"It's because he's grumpy the *rest* of the year. When they don't have him all dressed up as a reindonkey. Seriously, Holly, I'm not a donkey psychiatrist." I saw him check the time on his phone. "I mean, is anyone? But when he gets those antlers on... He's a whole new man. Donkey."

And something about Nick saying *donkey* again, and Dominic loving the attention, made me burst into an impromptu rendition of "Little Donkey" but with the words changed to "Little Reindonkey."

It was only when Nick laughed (I think with humor, not with fear?) that I realized what I was doing.

"Blame the jet lag. And the hot chocolate." I left off the *s*.

But time was tight, so we said bye, and I promised Dominic to try to see him every day. See, Nick, I can be spontaneous too!

As Nick dropped me back, I tried to find out more about him and Elle, starting with his band, the Au Revoir Hairs—apparently his grandma used to try and go in the mosh pit before she got ill. She sounded unreal.

"So, did you not fancy going with your sister?"

Nick shrugged. "Nah, that whole scene is more her thing."

"Scene?" As in what? A free holiday? The UK?

"You know..." Nick checked his mirror, avoiding eye contact. "I've just got stuff here." He paused. "Dean. Blake. The band. That's all."

I had no idea who Blake was, but he kept mentioning her, so I figured girlfriend was the obvious choice. In my head she was drop-dead gorgeous too, like Blake Lively. "Sooo..." I rummaged for another question. "Do you like Alpine Peaks, or would you have rather stayed in Nashton?"

"Nah." Nick shook his head. "I'm glad we left. In fact"—he cricked his neck, like I was making him tense—"I just wish we'd left sooner."

Well, I'd definitely managed to kill the vibe. Which was extra impressive as we were now driving slowly around a herd of small children dressed as elves.

Maybe I needed safer conversation ground?

"Elle's trip is off to a great start, though!" I couldn't sound more enthusiastic. "Those follows are pouring in." But this time Nick just stared ahead. It took him a good ten seconds to answer.

"Look, I just try and stay out of her business. And vice versa." He said it like he was almost saying it to himself. But then he shrugged. "I just want her to be okay, that's all."

So did that mean he hadn't seen all the amazing stuff she was doing? As he pulled up on their drive, I felt it was my life-swap-buddy duty to talk her up. "But she's killing it. Her followers love her!"

He switched the engine off and turned to look at me, his big, brown eyes full of concern. "But it's not them I'm worried about."

And I had no idea what he meant—but there was one thing I did understand. There was something going on here that I didn't know about—and I couldn't help but wonder if Elle was in the dark too.

CHAPTER TEN

Elle

Seven Days till Christmas

I stared at my laptop—I had a lot I needed to get done. Edit videos, book Cadbury World tickets, sort out the trip to the German Christmas market in the next town (which about a billion people had recommended), and get set for the Little Marsh lights switch-on tonight. Luckily I was feeling motivated—I'd gotten 1,230 new followers. Well, semi-motivated. I was still only in fourth place, and @CallMeClaraT was on 2,300 already, way in the lead.

It was time to step it up. Holly's idea was GO. I'd just posted to say:

Watch this space >>> It's about to get big.

Announcement coming in 3 hours.

On Thursday, I wasn't just going to London—I was going to have #OneElleOfAChristmasDayInLondon. My big push. I was going to complete FIFTY things, all suggested by my followers. The ultimate #FestiveFifteen challenge! And hopefully my ticket to beating Clara and getting into @thingsthepeakgirlsdo.

And I'd already gotten my first reply... Oh.

tooblessed2bstressedxx: Can't wait. Have set my watch. Highlight of the year 😘 xoxo

I shut my screen. I know I shouldn't let it bother me... But it did.

Still, at least Holly had been up for the challenges I'd sent her, which meant she had no clue what I was up to. I'd gotten the idea after talking to Ruby. She didn't say it exactly, but I could tell what she was thinking—Holly needed a hand getting over Woody. So I'd emailed them over this morning like an official contract. Risky. But hopefully worth it.

What Ruby said definitely made Holly's sudden enthusiasm to swap lives with a total stranger make sense. Guess we both had big things riding on this trip. Ruby had even asked if there was anyone in Alpine Peaks who could bring some Christmas romance to Hol's stay. I'd been trying to come up with someone worthy, but the best I had so far was asking Nick to set her up with one of his bandmates. Although then he'd have to believe in the concept of love. I'd never known him to even say he liked anyone, let alone have a girlfriend. Blake? Hmmm, he only had eyes for his boyfriend, Lance, but Dean... Yeah, Dean wasn't a bad option.

Ding.

I opened the door expecting to see Ruby, but instead there was Fred, giving me the kind of smile that meant he was either pained to see me or had eaten something bad.

"Hey." I stepped back. "I wasn't expecting you..." Well, that came out badly. "I mean, great to see you. I just thought you'd be—"

"Ruby. She's meeting us later." Pause. Silence. "She's running late at the matinee, so she said to come call for you." So he was here under duress. I'd made a good call yesterday then—Holly had suggested I go with him to the pantomime, but I knew he'd hate being stuck with me for a whole evening, so I'd made it seem like I had other plans.

"Wow—you've gone big." Under his open coat, Fred was wearing a blue sweater, a tiny, headless dancing elf knitted up to the neck, like his real head was on the elf's body. "Holly..." He pointed at his chest with both hands. "I promised. The back says 'Elf and Safety Monitor'..." He stopped. "Ironic considering most accidental deaths happen at Christmas." He trailed off and started doing his coat up, even though seconds ago, he'd been taking it off.

Confusing to know how to respond to that. I went for a low-key "awesome..."

I hoped he knew I meant the sweater, not the fatality fact.

I grabbed Colin, and we headed to That Little Café. Their speakers were blaring out Christmas tunes, and as I waited in line, I Shazamed the one where a man yelled, "It's Christmaaaaaas"... *Slade*. I made a note to tell Nick, in case it was a new British band I could impress him with. The café was full of vintage stuff, and they had all these posters that said things like "Keep Calm and Christmas On."

I got three hot chocolates, one each, and managed to try the mince pie from Holly's list. Turns out they weren't gross and mince-y. They were gross and raisiny.

Fred filmed it, and when I put it to a "Tradition or Terrible" vote, it was fifty-fifty.

"Wow, people are really loving your pie chat." He looked at the numbers going up.

"Uh-huh. And look..." I showed him my photos of the drinks already had 230 likes. "Et voilà, the café is famous." I cringed. Why did I say that like I was some sort of celebrity?! He already thought I was weird enough.

"So many comments..." Fred leaned in. "*Save one for me...?*" He read the one that had just popped up at the top from Logan. He was starting to creep me out—I was *not* into the hearts he'd added. I took my phone back.

"By the way, you've got glitter on your nose." It was red gold from the drink. "Very festive."

As Fred opened his mouth to speak, Ruby pulled up a chair. "Sorry I'm late." She looked at Fred, who still had his mouth open but with no words coming out. And he still had his coat fully zipped despite the café being so hot, all the windows had steamed. "Are you not boiling, Rudolph?"

"You know raising your basal temperature indoors helps you keep warmer outside."

Ruby nodded slowly, giving him a funny look. "Which explains everything."

The four of us huddled under Fred's umbrella (he called it a brolly!) (and Colin seemed genuinely fearful of the rain) and headed out to the tiny stage in front of the gigantic Christmas tree. It was so windy, my cheeks got a temporary face-lift as we walked.

"Now, look." Fred leaned over to whisper, "Yes, the tree is brilliant. In fact, so good, Holly named it Tree-yoncé. BUT trust me when I say you need to be standing as near to the lady in the beige bobble hat as you socially acceptably can."

I spotted her in the crowd, standing just by Colin-human and the twins, who all waved us over.

Fred led us a bit closer. And as soon as the carol singers started, I knew why.

I was experiencing Carol. *Carol singing*. The thing on Holly's list for me. And it was a blast. In the worst-best way possible.

I didn't know it was possible to get the words to "Away in a Manger" so wrong. So loudly. And the *tune*? At one point I did wonder if she was doing a different song altogether. Most of the crowd was watching her just as much as the pros.

But that was only the start. As they were singing the final note of a song about staying another day (depressing, and not really anything to do with Christmas so far as I could tell, but actually quite a tune), a big finale of fake snow was released from the roof of the post office. But the wind was so strong, it just whipped, in one big white blanket, straight on the stage and attached itself to the announcer who was walking out. He was wearing the biggest gold chain I'd ever seen. But with a suit.

"He's the mayor." Ruby took a deep breath, trying to regain herself from the carol singing-laughing. "It's a thing."

"HELLO, MIDDLE MARSH!" he yelled.

Carol looked close to exploding as she shouted back, "LITTLE!"

"Sorry, yes. LITTLE MARSH! It's time for us to all say a big..." The mayor walked forward with his hand in the air but slipped on the fake snow and cursed loudly into the microphone. "Erm, sorry. I meant 'happy Christmas.' Let's start again, shall we? Are you ready for the big switch-on?"

The crowd cheered.

"Let's kick things off by welcoming the big man himself..."

Santa Claus walked out from the side of the stage. Even across the crowd, I heard the twins squeal with excitement.

Fred leaned over. "He was once on the quiz show *The Chase*." He stopped. "As in the guy in the suit, not actual Father Christmas." I had no idea what he was talking about, but I appreciated the detail.

Mom would love this. I flicked on my data to send a picture. But I instantly wished I hadn't, as out of habit, I found myself checking my DMs. One from Dove.

What's up? You're still on for this right? The drinks looked ❤ but have you seen your follow count?

Ow. What she meant was had I noticed I was very nearly back in fifth place. I fired off a quick reply before I could overthink it.

I'm on it! Watch this space 👀 Got something much more than hot chocolate planned!

That wasn't a lie—I had #OneElleOfAChristmasDayInLondon. But I knew I needed to do better in the interim, not leave it all to the end of my trip—and I wasn't sure this dinky lights switch-on was what Dove and the rest of my followers would be after. Fred saw me looking stressed and mouthed, *Are you okay?* I nodded. But my phone buzzed once more.

Please tell me it includes something else hot... Cute British guys. I'll be waiting for the post...Grid not stories 😘

As if I didn't have enough on my hands—now I had to find 14,000 new followers AND someone cute I could post about. I switched off my data and looked back at the stage.

And it was perfect timing. Santa's hat immediately blew off. Followed by his beard, and one eyebrow. And effectively we were left with a stressed-looking man wearing a bad red suit on stage. He was clutching his tummy so it didn't blow around to one side.

"Happy Christmas, kids," Santa yelled, waving, before looking to the edge of the stage for a kid who had been picked to come and meet him. But two walked forward—Zai and Kai holding hands, their jumpers flashing "Ho Ho Ho." Colin was side of the stage filming and cheering them on.

"*Whoop, yes, guys!*"

"Now, young men..." The last of Santa's stick-on eyebrows had shifted by an inch and the end was flying free in the wind. He bent down. "Have you been good this year?"

They nodded sweetly—I hadn't seen this shy side: they normally never shut up.

"So what would you like from Father Christmas this year... ZaiandKai?" Clever—Santa said it as one name.

They grabbed the microphone, turned to the crowd, and with the cutest smiles, shouted in unison, "CHICKEN NUGGETS!"

Colin looked like he might faint with embarrassment—he probably wanted them to say "classic reading material," but everyone else was cracking up. Santa said something about checking the freezer compartment on the sleigh and bundled them off to the claps and laughs of the crowd.

This was WAY better than back home.

The mayor cleared his throat. "Well, that was lovely." He then muttered "five minutes to fill" before telling a joke about angry mice sending "cross mouse" cards and then in desperation moved on to talking about road construction that was starting in the new year.

This was the best entertainment I'd had in years. When the countdown finally started, I began to film.

The huge tree, lights strung up around every lamppost, a big "HAPPY CHRISTMAS" sign swaying over the bridge all ready for their big moment. It was going to look awesome. This was just what I needed.

"Five...Four..."

I joined in with everyone shouting. The mayor held up the big, red button.

"Three... Two..." Pause. "ONE!"

He slammed his hand down on the big, red button. We all *ooohed.*

And literally one light on the tree lit up. One. Then went out.

And then all the normal lights around the crowd went off too.

Pitch blackness, except the mayor's flashing necklace.

It was more of a lights-off ceremony. Everyone was silent.

Until Ruby, Fred, and I got the same idea and cheered

wildly—everyone joining in with us. The band started up, and phone flashlights came out across the crowd as an impromptu street party kicked off.

Fred leaned into me. "Told you it would be memorable. Now, fancy some mulled apple juice?"

"Ew, no!" That sounded god-awful. "Why would anyone drink moldy apple juice?"

Fred laughed. "No, not *moldy*. Forget it—you'll see what I mean."

So we weaved our way out through all the dancing and, as we reached the edge, the lights finally flicked on.

I couldn't help but stop. The village looked gorgeous, so Christmassy. Even better than in Mom's photos. I took so many photos for her and even a video to show Grams when I was back. The band was playing "White Christmas," her favorite song.

Ruby had to head home, so Fred and Colin got in line while I went to have a look around. I swung my legs over the railings next to the green and headed toward the fairy lights on the middle of the merry-go-round. I sat on a swing and swished back and forward, scrolling through the photos I'd taken. What could I post next? Bald Santa and Chicken Nugget moment were gold, but not exactly Dove levels of perfection. And when she said *cute guy*, as much as someone like Fred was my definition, all scruffy hair and big, brown eyes and a smile that took up his whole face, I had a feeling that was not what she was after. Someone like Logan was much, *much* more her type.

"So, have you been naughty or nice this year?" A guy's voice made me jump. I put my feet on the floor and stopped swinging.

Woody.

Face-to-face with a moral dilemma. A really cute moral dilemma.

"Kind of creepy." I sat more upright. After what I heard yesterday, what he did to Holly, I felt like I was going into battle even though I wasn't 100 percent sure what the war was. His smooth smile disappeared. Had I caught him off guard?

"Sorry... I, erm..." He waved at a friend in the distance, which gave him the second he needed to get his Woody-ness back. In his other hand was a cone of fries, the paper wrapper covered in snowmen. "You're Elle, aren't you?"

I raised my hand as if guilty as charged. "What gave it away, y'all?" As if I'd ever say that back home. Still, he didn't know me—so I might as well live up to the version he might have seen. "Although, hot tip. Next time try and find out *before* following someone to an empty play area."

"Fair." He chewed his fry slowly, not hurrying to finish whatever he was saying. "I didn't mean to alarm you."

"No worries. I'm like the twins earlier. As long as there are chicken nuggets...or fries." I swiped one. "I'm all good."

He smiled. A very good-looking, superconfident smile, and pulled himself on to the swing next to me.

I hated having this thought, but deep down, I knew he was

exactly the kind of snack Dove would like. I mean, to be fair, that anyone with eyes would normally like too... Nope. I swallowed. I had to forget the accent, the smile, the confidence, and the, yup, bright-green eyes, and remember that Holly was more important than the challenge.

"You're the dude from the house opposite, right?"

He nodded. "Sure am. Why? Have you noticed me?"

Wow, he didn't come to play. "Nah. Just heard he was the kind of guy who would come creep on strangers."

But Woody laughed. "Just like I heard the American internet girl filming around here liked to put guys like that through their paces." He took his beanie off, flicked it out, and pulled it back on. Cute move—and he knew it. "So may I ask? Who *exactly* have you been hearing these terrible lies from?"

"Well, that would be telling..." I paused. I didn't want it to sound like Holly and I, or even Ruby, had been talking about him. "It's not Holly, though, if that's what you're asking."

He dunked his fry in the ketchup. It was the size of a full potato.

"Why would I be asking that?"

He knew exactly why. But what did he think I knew? I had to be careful. "And it wasn't your girlfriend either."

I gave him a sweet smile—I wanted him to know I was on to him. He couldn't play those games with me. And I *definitely* wasn't finding out if he was single...was I?

"Don't know what you mean." He slowly chewed, not reacting at all. Maybe he and Meera weren't a thing after all? "There's nothing wrong with keeping options open. Until something *great* comes along." I didn't know how I felt about him smiling at me when he said *great*. "How is Hols getting on?"

He held out his fries. I took one even though it somehow felt like a truce. A confusing truce. But I had only heard one side from Ruby. Was Woody actually that bad?

"She's doing great. Hardly heard from her, she's been so busy." Still, whatever was going on, I could still score some points for her. "And Nick. Blake...Dean. Allll those guys who knew she was coming. Honestly, 'dying to arrive' doesn't even cover it. That accent? Kryptonite." He didn't need to know I'd mentioned my dead-inside brother and the rest of his band.

But Woody just held my eye contact.

"You mean the accent like mine?" Well, I'd messed that up.

"Maybe." We both knew he had me there.

"I've got to admit, when Hol told me she was going, I didn't know if she was for real. She was kind of...freaking out at the time."

"Well, it's very real." I stretched out an arm. "I mean. Here I am. Just waiting for some moldy apple juice or whatever."

And that's when Colin found us, dragging along Fred, who was trying to balance two steaming drinks in front of him as he tripped his way toward us.

"One semi-delicious, semi-gross festive hot drink coming up! Ah..." Fred stopped dead when he saw Woody. He passed me my drink without even looking at me. "Woody."

"Fred," Woody replied. "Nice to see you." Fred did just a short, sharp nod back. "And Elle, if you need anything, anything at all, you know where to find me." He threw the greasy paper in the trash can, getting it in first time. Of course he would. "And you can look out for my follow later." I swear he winked as he said it—just a small one so Fred couldn't see. And as he walked off, I tried to figure out—who was the real Woody? Ruby's version, or the one I'd just met?

But I didn't have long to think, as my phone lit up my pocket with a text. Must be serious for someone to have gone off Wi-Fi. I pulled it out.

WHAT HAVE YOU DONE?!!!!

If there's one thing to make you not-relax about a decision, it's an all-caps reply.

CHAPTER ELEVEN

Holly

I slumped on Elle's floor and dropped my head back on to her bed. Which was way springier than mine, so it bounced straight back and almost gave me whiplash. I turned up my Christmas music and looked back at what she'd written. Why hadn't I checked my email earlier?! It was Elle's list of challenges for me.

One to four were fine. Fun, almost.

1. Take on New York. If I don't see a pic of you skating in Central Park, it didn't happen.
2. The lights at City Hall in Peakstown. And while you're there. Hauuuul. You need to hit the shops. Hard. What does Holly look like not in a Christmas sweater?! (Sound of my mind blowing.)

3. Party America style—a costume party, so festive-themed outfits are required (my family can/will help).
4. Holiday menu at Cheeze Pleaze Louise. You won't regret it.

Yup. Fine. They sort of matched what I had lined up anyway. I'd already planned a trip later today to Peakstown, which was the big town nearby, and put the word *Christmas* in front of any food, and I was there. And a party could be fun. But number five?!

5. Snag a hot Christmas kiss under the mistletoe.

Kiss under mistletoe?! What? With whom? Elle had even written the whole thing up like a contract. Did she have no clue my heart was still in a bin outside Woody's house? That I was dead to love? Still, at least it meant Nick hadn't told her he'd seen the whole Flights Not Feelings cringeathon.

But what would happen if I didn't? The Christmas surprise for our mums that Elle was sorting would be off. And I did love a Christmas surprise. And mums.

I should have let her know I wasn't up for it when I got back home, like I'd meant to. But after my unplanned meet of Grumpy Dominic, I made a spontaneous decision to try and be more spontaneous.

Which I was now deeply regretting.

New plan for notebook—never be spontaneous again.

I looked down. What was Elle going to say back?

Typing. Stop. *Typing*.

Keep calm and Christmas on?!

KEEP CALM???

I took a second to compose myself. I needed to try and be a fraction cooler about this. A very small fraction, maybe 1/17882732879797.

Look. Earlier today I found out Nick has NEVER SEEN ELF. And now this?!

He'd told me when he'd turned up for breakfast and I'd asked if he fancied watching it with me later in the week. But he'd said it seemed ridiculous. So I'd told him HE seemed ridiculous and had woken up knowing (a.) my annual tradition was officially off, and (b.) I was spending pre-Christmas living with a maniac. Guess me and my traditions were too boring for Nick—and it increased my suspicion that he was only doing Christmassy stuff with me on Elle's request.

Is that a no then?

YES!

As in "it's a no"

Can you think of something else?!

Elle must be trying to think of something, as the back-and-forth paused. I refreshed her profile as I waited. Dove had announced that Elle had held on to fourth place, with just over 2,000 new followers, but @CallMeClaraT was firmly in the lead with 4,000. Elle looked fine about it though and had posted a celebratory shimmy—my ramshackle room had never looked so glam. Even the semi-dead poinsettia couldn't dull her shine. She didn't seem bothered that she'd started to get some really mean comments on her posts either. It all seemed to be from one person though, so if it got worse, maybe I could report them.

I brushed my hair, which felt like a rope after getting blown about at the Christmas Makers market this morning. I should never tackle my knots when I'm this stressed. I yanked out at least five clumps—enough to make a small hair hedgehog on the floor.

I'll confer with Ruby later 😜😉😜

Breathe, Holly, breathe.

It was only a list, and I could just not do it. But...then as well as not getting something cool for our mums, I'd disappoint the law of lists. I loved lists. Not completing a list was sacrilege. I mean, I think it was? I'd never not done one before.

I had to speak to Elle. Nip this in the bud. It was now or never.

RING.

RING.

Make that, *now or in a bit.*

Elle messaged to say she was on her way home and would ring when the Wi-Fi didn't keep dropping, so I rang Mum instead.

"Hello?!" She always answered the phone in a panic, like I was ringing to report my kidnap.

"Mummmmmm." It was lovely hearing her voice. But there was silence.

"It's me. Your youngest daughter...Holly?"

She laughed. "Sorry, yes. Was just..." Another pause. "... sealing up a box. We're doing a run to Col's. The tidying is ENDLESS... One sec." I heard a thud. "Now, packing isn't what you rang for, is it? Tell me your news! I want to hear EVERYTHING."

Well, she said it, and who was I to deprive her? So I took her through a minute-by-minute account of the amazing time I was having. But she still had questions. So many questions. Everything from what I'd eaten to if I needed her to ask Jess for long johns.

"And what about things your end?" Weirdly I'd had enough of thermal underwear chat. "Is it Christmas a-go-go?"

"Just work. Packing. Same old. Elly has been a delight, though!" Oh good. "Funny having an American accent in the house. But the biscuits are definitely going down slower than when you and Nay are home."

Mum hadn't mentioned any of the things we'd normally be doing—by this time the three of us would usually be spending evenings watching Christmas TV, wrapping presents, and eating meals that were entirely party food from the freezer. I hoped Mum was enjoying pre-Christmas fun too.

"Well, I'll be back to eat those biscuits in full force. In what..." I counted on my fingers. "Five days." I couldn't believe my flight on the twenty-third was coming around so quickly. "Then, it's Chriiiiiistmas!" It just popped out. Mum laughed. I liked hearing her happy.

"Are you still up for doing the full works on Boxing Day? When your sister's back?"

"You KNOW two Christmases is my dream. Well, three hundred and sixty-five is, but y'know, this is a step. Lemme know if you need anything from here, or if there's anything I can do to help, seeing as you're a chief elf down?"

"You just keeping being you, darling, and having a good time. That's all I need."

I promised I would and told her I loved her, but she had to go as Colin had an incident with a vase. I didn't tell her how much I was missing her, in case that made her worry. But it was perfect timing as Elle was ringing. As soon as I saw her face, I felt a bit better.

"Hello, Engerlanddddd," I yelled as if we were doing a live TV broadcast.

Elle waved back as she pushed her AirPods in. She looked all flushed from being outside. "And hello, Alpine Peaks?!"

"How was the switch-on?!" Her pictures had made it look so much more glam than I remembered.

"A blast. And you were right about Carol..."

I nodded. "Genuinely gutted to have missed her."

Elle grinned. "Which is why I took some serious surreptitious video for you."

I mouthed *thank you*, while putting my hands together in gratitude.

"Sorry, but I'm still not over you being in my room, and us having NEVER MET."

"Yup. We messed that one up." Elle swiveled around in my chair "Why didn't we think to overlap somewhere?"

"Because we didn't really think?" We both laughed.

"Sooooo," I started.

"Soooooo...." she finished, grinning as she could tell what I was trying to get at.

"The, er...list you sent me."

She nodded, totally straight-faced. "Uh-huh? All good? I know you love 'em."

"Well..." I gave up trying to be cool. "We both know number five is never going to happen, right?!"

Truth was I'd started to have a sneaking suspicion why she'd said it. Had she heard what happened with Woody and me? Was this her way of helping me move on? 'Cause I wasn't moving anywhere. I was stationary. For life.

"Never say never..."

"But that's what I am saying. Literally that. It will *never* happen."

Elle's smile softened as she picked up I was freaking out for real, not just pretending.

"Well, look. It's your call. But if I can take on the fifty challenges in London, maybe you should see what happens over the next few days on your end?" *See what happens?* Did she not know how I operate?!

"And maybe *you* could tell me what the thing was you were thinking of doing for our mums?"

"My lips are sealed." She put her finger to her mouth. "Unless you pull it off, of course."

I laughed. She was impossible.

"Fine. FINE. But what about you?" It was the perfect time to do some digging of my own. Some Logan-and-Fred-shaped digging. "Met anyone who, er...takes your fancy?"

Why was I so strange with words?! "No." She almost snapped at me.

"Oh, okay..." I didn't mean to annoy her. But Elle looked almost embarrassed.

"I just meant, you know, keeping my options open."

Okay, something was definitely up here, but I did really want to know if Fred was in with a chance. "And by *options*, do you mean international male model and professional pants-wearer Logan?"

"Maybe..." Elle fiddled with the ends of her hair—the first and only time I'd ever seen her look truly awkward.

"C'mon, spill. As an impartial observer, I can honestly say he makes Harry Styles look like a seven out of ten." I didn't mean it, Harry would always be a straight ten, but I needed to use whatever I could to get info for Fred.

"Look, I'm sorry." She rubbed her face. "I'll give you the full story later, I promise."

"Full hot details of your secret boyfriend?" Desperate times.

"If that's how you want to describe it!" Finally, she laughed. Guess that was as close to a yes as I was going to get, especially as she launched right back into her normal chatty mode. "Anyways, it's like, what...almost three at your end? You look like you're heading out?"

"Yup—going to Peakstown. Checking out the City Hall lights like you said." Elle gave a big "wooo" and raised her hand up. "Your dad's dropping me off. Honestly, your parents are legends."

Elle properly smiled. "Give them a hug from me. And my li'l bro, if he's going with you?"

I didn't say anything, but Elle knew what the silence meant. He'd disappeared again.

She sighed. "Have you even seen him at all?"

"He took me to meet Grumpy Dominic, so how much better can anything get?" I was relieved Elle smiled. "But he's had band stuff, and last night I think he stayed over at Blake's?"

"Surprise, surprise." Elle laughed, but like she didn't find it funny. "When doesn't he?"

Could I lighten the mood? "Helping you escape a house takeover from an international visitor, isn't that what friends are for?"

"If only they were just friends." She rolled her eyes. I'd been right then—Nick was coupled up, but his parents had no idea. Elle and Nick were as bad as each other! "Those two are just so much more. I sometimes think if he didn't talk to me about Blake, he wouldn't talk to me at all." She laughed, but there was a sadness to it. I wondered if it had something to do with what Nick said yesterday?

And something even weirder. Did confirming that Nick definitely had a girlfriend make me have a...sadness too?! What was happening? That feeling could GET IN THE BIN. Sorry. GET IN THE TRASH. Either way, I needed to focus on the way more important thing. "Are things...okay with you two?"

"Sure." So neither a yes or a no? Time to find out if I could figure out what he'd meant in his car.

"Has he said much about @OneElleOfATime? Fourth place, huh?!" I raised my hands in celebration.

"Better than fifth, right?" But Elle didn't look pleased. In fact she looked uncomfortable and had gone back to fiddling with her hair. "I mean, if you want me to be honest?" I gave an "uh-huh." "Back in Nashton, when I had @NoWayNoelle, Nick used to be my biggest supporter. But then, I dunno. Something changed. And now he doesn't even really know about #FestiveFifteen. Or anything about my life. Not that I know much about him either..." Did I hear her voice crack? "So New York, then..."

And with that she shut the subject down. After a catch-up about our London and New York plans, and me asking if there was any Ruby and Temi news, we said bye.

Probably best—I was trying to avoid giving away I had two pages of hour-by-hour notes for my New York schedule already, and I needed to head out anyway. I'd already had a busy morning and now was going to the City Hall to see the Christmas lights, Christmas shopping, finding some Christmas nibbles, and maybe even seeing a Christmas film at their cute vintage-y cinema. Yup, definitely a theme there. Normally I'd do stuff like this with Naomi, but there was nothing normal about this year. I did miss her, though—so I messaged her to tell her. She replied straight back with a picture.

A big, white, cute-revolting flat sea creature, with sort of holes for a face.

Erm thanks. Today, and not being weird, but this stingray genuinely reminded me of you.

How heartwarming.

Maybe I should tell her Dominic has the same ear hair as her or something. But there was another message.

> Hey Hols. How is Amuricah? Your new roommate is jokes. Pretty hot too 😊

Wait.

Woody was messaging me?

And messaging me about liking Elle?! This was NOT OKAY.

My heart tripled in speed.

How dare he just send me a message?

He hadn't been in contact for almost a month. Not since that night.

And he'd met Elle? Why hadn't she mentioned it?!

What did he want me to do, set them up? What about Meera?!

I felt sick. Like eating-a-whole-selection-box sick.

Maybe two. Just from thirteen words.

I screenshot and sent to Ruby and—after multiple messages that were mainly very inventive insults—she said to ignore. She'd left Fred and Elle at the switch-on, so she had no idea what had happened with Woody.

But the worst thought was creeping in—was this why Elle was being weird when I asked if she'd met anyone she liked?

I'd thought she'd meant Logan. She couldn't mean... No. This was too bad.

Woody would love nothing more than a model influencer girlfriend. A really exciting, spontaneous one.

Ruby and I did the only thing we could think of—went in deep on every comment between Logan and Elle. Which calmed me down. It was all there for everyone to see—they were all over each other.

Although it sucked for Fred—he was going to be gutted. Ruby said she'd let him know on the d-low to save him getting even more hurt later on.

Eurgh. Why couldn't liking people not be completely rubbish?

We decided there was only one way I could handle Woody—by ignoring him entirely.

But after ignoring him for at least twelve minutes, we figured he might not know he was being ignored, so I decided I should send something that showed how over him I was (now wasn't the time to mention to Ruby the technicality that I wasn't).

This is what we went for.

Yup. She's great. I'm having the best time out here. Think Elle might be into someone else though. Soz. Have a good Christmas and New Year.

Ruby wanted me to put "and life" at the end. But after I put the phone down to her, I felt at least half as brave, so I went with:

Yup. She's great. Think she's into someone else though... Soz. And I'm having the best time out here.

My finger shook as I sent it. I immediately headed downstairs to try to stop thinking about it. Pete was on the phone, I think to Elle, and Jess was on her laptop in the kitchen.

When she saw me, she stopped and snapped her fingers. "I KNEW there was something I had to tell you." She slid a thick, cream-colored card over across the table. It had posh gold writing on it. "Nick told us you were a fan of Twenty One Pilots?"

"Who isn't?" I blurted before I could think of something better.

"Well, we got this..." She nodded me to open it. Out popped a 3D version of the band, and loads of other musicians all in Santa hats, gold writing underneath.

"Oh wow." I realized what I was holding. *THE SNOW BALL. December 24. Madison Square Garden.* The one Nay and I watched every year on YouTube, and this year Twenty One Pilots was playing! And so were SO many amazing people?! Lizzo, Billie Eilish, Harry Styles. Everyone! "Killer lineup!"

"Turn it over..." Jess stepped beside me. I flipped to read the scrawly black handwriting.

Scrawly black handwriting inviting Jess, Pete, and family to a VIP box and after-party.

Whyyyyy did this have to be the day after I left?!

Jess rested her hand on my arm. "It's a thanks for all the work getting the decorations for the dressing rooms."

"Elle is going to DIE." I said it so forcefully, Jess looked a little alarmed. "But in a good way."

"It says family, Hol—and while you're here, we hope you very much feel like that."

"Oh yeah, you guys have been amaze."

"Now I know Elle said the flights are flexible...so if you wanted to stay a little longer, go home on the twenty-sixth..." She rested her hand on my arm. "We'd be delighted to have you. Only if your mum was happy, of course..."

"I..." How was this happening?! I could be at the Snow Ball? In New York? Seeing my favorite bands? At Christmas? With my own eyes? Going backstage?!

This was the icing on the Perfect Christmas Cake! Totally off plan, BUT I still liked it. A lot. THE MOST.

I stared at Jess, millions of thoughts battling for first place.

Was I going to cry? Or hug her? Or just squeak? This was beyond anything I could have imagined! Although...reality check. Then I'd have to be in America for Christmas—there was no way I could make it home any quicker.

Although, *although*. I *could* leave Boxing Day? Mum was working Christmas morning anyway. And she kept saying her best present would be me having the best Christmas. Maybe she would even prefer one with just Colin-human?

Although, should I be home if Naomi wasn't going to be?

Although, although, if I stayed I could properly meet Elle?!

Too. Many. Thoughts.

Jess coughed. I was still gawping at the invite. "Sorry. This is my completely overwhelmed face. Thank you. THANK YOU. This..." I waved it. "You guys...everything is amazing. Although, can I have a think about it? Talk to Mum?"

I didn't want to not be home if she wanted me there.

But...the Snow Ball?

This required an *extensive* pros/cons list.

"Whatever you need, honey." This would be the ultimate thing to cross off my Christmas list. I'd even take on Elle's mistletoe kiss challenge if it was Harry Styles, hahahaha.

"C'mon then, Hol." Nick burst through the front door and straight into our conversation. "I'm switching in for Dad."

"Here." Jess grabbed the keys that were by the sink and tossed them over. Guess he was giving me a lift then? "Oh, and Nick—we're planning to drop in to see Grams later. Any messages for her?"

Nick just shrugged—he didn't even bother properly replying. Weird considering he'd been telling me this morning how much he missed her living with them. Sometimes I just didn't get him. We headed out to the car.

"So, if you're up for it." He put the keys in the ignition. "You can consider me today's Christmas crew." So he was coming with me? Had Elle said something to him?

"Consider yourself considered." I plugged my phone in and

looked out at the heavy snow. I'd never not love it. "Do you, er... like Christmas shopping then?"

"Isn't that why the internet was invented?" Nick was checking out his rearview mirror. "But it's all on that list from Elle, right?"

"You know about the list?" Elle must have told him—including point number five. Cringe.

"I know everything, Holly."

"Did you know in Japan millions of people have KFC for Christmas dinner?"

"I did not." He pulled the car out on to the road. "So I take it all back. Now, what's in the notebook for today's schedule?"

I told him the key things and then put on "Christmas Time (Don't Let the Bells End)" by The Darkness. He gave it a few seconds.

"Is this a Christmas song?" he said, like he was asking if milk was in date, after he'd drunk it.

I smiled. "Uh-huh. And it's a certified bop, so don't even try and tell me otherwise." He opened his mouth to protest, so I had to shush him. If he wasn't into Christmas, fine—but he wasn't going to kill my vibe.

And what a result. By the time we got to the second chorus, he was singing along under his breath, which turned into a full-on headbang. Which turned into a really fun day. Despite Nick saying he wasn't that into Christmas, he knew all the cutest bits of Peakstown to show me around. But all the Christmassing made me hung-er-reeee. Nick said he knew the perfect spot, and when we got there, it was the one Elle had suggested—Cheeze Pleaze Louise, a burger joint, with little booths and the staff wearing cute 1950s uniforms with snowman-shaped aprons. Actual heaven.

Nick pointed at the menu up behind the counter. "Time to get feasting. The holiday menu is..." He closed his eyes and nodded like he loved it in all sorts of inappropriate ways. "A Christmas thing I can get into." He looked toward a corner table. "Oh, and if you don't order a shake, you WILL go down in my estimation."

The nice guy serving asked if Nick wanted his regular. He was called Rohan, and after introducing himself, he asked after Elle and said he was missing her face. I didn't think the guy in That Little Café would notice me if I put two chips up my nose and pretended to be a walrus, let alone just "miss my face." I ended up telling him about our swap. He had no idea about Elle's account and followed her there and then. Yesss—get me helping with #FestiveFifteen. I ordered a Santa's Stuffed Sack, which was a veggie burger topped with roast potatoes and cranberry, and a Merry M&M's milkshake. Nick and I didn't speak for a full five minutes, but only because the food was too good to delay chewing for talking. And I was feeling a bit better about things at home too—Ruby messaged to say she'd popped to Fred's and had given him the heads-up about Elle not being single (without him realizing that's what she was getting at) and instead of being sad, it was almost like with the pressure off, he felt he could be more normal around her. I loved that everyone was getting on so well.

Including Nick and me. I was beginning to realize that, despite his dubious approach to Christmas traditions, whenever he was around, things were even more fun—the only problem was I never knew when he'd be around or how long for.

"So, Nick." I did a drumroll on the table. The light was fading, and the displays were coming on. It was time to shoot my shot. "The big one. I'm giving you another chance. A chance to have the best evening of your life." He stopped chewing. "Probably." I took a deep breath. "At half six, the Regal Cinema is playing one of the best Christmas films ever made. Give or take *Home Alone*. And *The Muppet Christmas Carol* and..." I could see from Nick's rising cheekbones I was losing the room. "*Die Hard*?" I'd never seen it, but desperate times... And it was showing tonight as well. "Watching it with me would mean bringing my favorite UK tradition here. To you. So..." I did a drumroll again, even though the moment had passed. "How about today being the day you finally see *Elf*?"

But Nick was looking at his phone. And he looked concerned.

"Sorry, Holly." He looked up, realizing he'd missed whatever I'd said. "I need to head out. Blake needs a hand with something." He grabbed his stuff. "Band stuff. I'll make sure Dad can pick you up. Or, here"—he pushed some dollars across the table—"just in case you need a cab." He apologized again, but seconds later he'd disappeared.

And I was alone. Sipping on a novelty milkshake that was almost as tall as my upper body. Which suddenly felt a whole lot less fun.

But as Nick dashed out, someone I recognized walked in. Dove. Wow. She was even more perfect in real life. She stared at Nick as he raced off—if anything, she looked shocked a guy hadn't stopped for her. I felt normally most things would—guys, traffic, birds, gravity.

But she was on the phone, and it sounded heated. Wow—I wouldn't want to be on the wrong side of her. She was waving her arm around, she was so mad. Or was she stressed? She shouted something about that too. I think it was Morgan on the other end, and she was yelling at her for something not being more. More *what* I had no idea, but I definitely heard the word *payback*. I tried to watch without her noticing me but sucked on my straw so hard, it made a gurgle.

Great.

Dove glared at me, and I don't know why, but I waved. She ended the call and walked over.

"Sorry, do I know you?" She tossed her hair over her shoulder. How did it bounce when it landed?

"Erm, no." I smiled. "I'm Elle's friend." Nothing. "You know, @OneElleOfATime?"

I was expecting a smile, something about my accent at least, but all I got was a "right."

Weird. Elle had been telling me how friendly she was in real life. "Did you just hear that?" She nodded to where she'd been on a call.

I shook my head. "Nope..."

"Good." She did a smile that lasted 0.000001 seconds. "Top secret challenge planning with Morgan."

"Well, your secret's safe with me." I wish I'd heard more now, maybe I could have tipped Elle off. "I'm actually the one who swapped with Elle."

Dove looked at me and the pile of knitted accessories next to me. "Makes sense."

Did it? The way she was looking at me made me feel uncomfortable—like when you're swimming in the sea but the water goes all cold and you can't feel the bottom and you wish you'd never left the beach.

"Elle's doing so well, isn't she?" Nothing. "She's got some amazing stuff lined up!"

Dove's mouth quavered. Ever so slightly, but I saw it. "Like a...'pantomime'?" Too late, she laughed. "Yeah...sounds rocking."

Wow—she was...mean.

And confusing. She'd been throwing all the love hearts on Elle's grid. Maybe she just didn't get it. I tried to explain, how funny it was, how great Ruby was in it, and how it would be like nothing they had over here, but when I got to the end, all she said was, "Watch those followers flood in, right?"

Well, this was *not* what I thought she'd be like. "Did you see her announcement about #OneElleOfAChristmasDayInLondon?"

"Uh-huh." Dove reached over and took a sip of my milkshake. A really long one. "Gotta hope she's not leaving it too late. Thanks for the shake, by the way."

In a normal situation, I'd make an excuse and leave, but as I was sitting in a cubicle, I was a bit stuck.

"Ermmm...no problem?" I was being as upbeat as I could. "Anyway, I won't stop you, but thought I'd say hi." I waved up at her. "And fingers crossed Elle wins, right?"

I'd gone for killing her with kindness.

"Sure." Dove pushed her lips together. "Time will tell, huh?" And that was that, off she went to the counter.

I couldn't stop thinking about it as I sat on my own in the cinema. All this time I'd been hoping Elle won #FestiveFifteen—I mean, I'd literally swapped lives to make it happen—but now that I'd met Dove, unless there was something I was seriously missing, I wasn't sure I wanted her to.

CHAPTER TWELVE

Elle

Five Days till Christmas

"Tell me they're your panto pants?" I pointed at Fred's jeans. He immediately doubled over and started patting himself like he was on fire.

"Oh God..." He was actually panting as he stood back up. "Pants? I thought you meant I'd forgotten my trousers... Again." He was too funny. "Anyway." He thrust his hands out. "I brought these." Twiglets? Did he expect me to eat tree bits? "Ten out of ten brilliant. And a can of this."

Vimto? I said thanks but looked at it suspiciously.

Still, what doesn't kill me makes me stronger, right?

After Hol had messaged the night before last to say she was watching *Die Hard* on her own, I'd bitten the bullet and asked

Fred if he wanted to come with me after all. When he said yes, it made me happier than I realized it was going to. And now we were outside, the hall all lit up in the dark night. It felt all Christmassy and twinkly and magical.

"Great minds think alike. For you..." I handed over the massive bag of Mis Shape chocolate I'd gotten him from Cadbury World. "Ten out of ten sweater, by the way." I'd only just made it back in time—but I'd had the best day. And even better, I'd jumped up to 8,329 new followers. Not just second place, but less than three hundred behind Clara. The announcement about #OneElleOfAChristmasDayInLondon, and all the suggestions coming in, had turned things around, and if London went well tomorrow, I really could be in with a chance of overtaking Clara. Not just keeping my account. But actually winning.

But there was something I had to do first. And when Fred went to pick up the tickets, I knew there was no time like the present. After Holly asking me all those questions, and his comments over the last day and a half, I needed to sort out the Logan situation before anyone else got the wrong idea. Most of all Logan. Sure, I was all up for doing what it took to win the challenge, but I didn't want to mess with people's feelings. Especially not someone who was so very, very interested in cars. Ha.

I'd hated dodging Holly's question, but I didn't want her to think badly of me. The truth was, I'd gotten so caught up in the competition that I'd let it go too far—so now it was on me to clear it up and say sorry if I needed to.

Earlier he'd posted on his stories telling his followers to "give the hottest US ambassador to Britain a follow." I wasn't 100 percent sure it was me until he followed up with one of my posts of my silly smiling face. It had given me a follower boost, but I knew it had to stop.

So here it came. The awkward slide into Logan's DMs.

Thanks so much for the support. This ambassador can report that this trip is brilliant.

Such a Fred word. But getting to the point was hard.

Could I actually do this?

Looks it. How about we meet in person when you're back so you can tell me all about it?

I almost spat my Vimto out. I looked at Fred in the line to see if he'd noticed, but he just gave me a goofy wave—and something about it made me feel as brave as I normally pretended to be. It was now or never.

It would be great to put a proper face to the...internet face! And it would be nice to say thanks for all the support. Just friends though, right? ☺

So brutal.

But I'd done it. Dropped the friend bomb.

Logan was typing back. I didn't mean to, but I stopped breathing as I waited.

Whatever you want. I'm still gonna back ya—a local girl's gotta win right? #AlpinePeaksPatriots

Jeez. That went *way* better than I thought. Maybe I should have given him a bit more credit from the start? I was so relieved, I did an accidental fist pump.

"Two tickets to probably one of the most confusing nights of your life." Fred held them out. "And can I say you look surprisingly happy about it?"

"What can I say? The Vimto was a pleasant surprise." I smiled at Fred, who just gave me a happy shrug and asked if it was okay if he went to say hi to his neighbors.

After months of having a crappy time, finally things felt like they were going my way. I felt so good, I even posted on my account to nudge everyone to get ready to help me get my followers up tomorrow. @_Beckywiththemediocrehair_ immediately replied to tell me I was going to smash it. Then Dove commented too.

Big day tomorrow. Fifty things is epic! 🤞 Did you see my suggestion? A photo at Platform 9¾ at King's Cross. Can't be a proper London challenge without it 🤞

Ermmm, okay. It wasn't on the plan, but I guessed I could make it work. But before I could reply, someone else did. @tooblessed2bstressedxx was back in full force.

@DoveAllLove @CallMeClaraT any spare good ideas? Think someone could give them a good home when London doesn't work out @OneElleOfATime xoxo

Great. Just like that, everything good I'd been feeling vanished.

Not helped by Dove replying to it with a 😂. Was she trying to make me feel like trash?

I shoved my phone out of sight, mad at it. I hated this feeling—the exact same out-of-control feeling I'd had back in Nashton when I'd started to get bitchy comments on my old account.

But Fred was heading back, and I didn't want him to know what was going on. What had changed so quickly.

"Now tell me"—I gave him the biggest smile I could find—"how do we go say good luck to Ruby?"

A girl dressed as a court jester looked around. She was on a call but put her hand over the speaker. "Are you looking for Ruby?" We nodded. *One sec*, she mouthed at us, gesturing that the call was wrapping up and laughing to herself as the person on the other end didn't get her hints.

"She's nice..." I whispered to Fred—I felt like I'd seen her before.

"She's Temi," Fred whispered back. "And don't tell Ruby I told you, but..." I nodded to stop him. I already knew from what Holly had said, and I was officially on alert.

"Follow me, then. Got to be quick." Temi was off the phone and beckoning us through a side gate. "Talent entrance." She cackled. "As if!"

She pushed open a heavy, wooden door into the building, and a burst of light, noise and hairspray shot out. Fred peered in. "Ruby..." he sort of cooed, literally no one noticing him. "Rubbbesss." He turned back, looking flushed. "I've never been backstage before."

"Fred." Temi shook her head, but she was smiling. "It's the village hall, not the BRIT Awards." She grabbed his arm. "Come on!"

As we searched for Ruby, Temi filled us in on how the show was going and asked all about my trip. She seemed really impressed. When we finally found Ruby, she was alone in a small room, sitting in front of a big mirror—and she looked absolutely fire. Like a sexy disco ball.

But she was busy looking at Temi. And Temi was looking at Ruby.

And they were both trying to hold in what looked like face-wide smiles.

Ermmmmm. I looked at Fred, but his eyes were shooting from Ruby to Temi to Ruby like he was watching an intense game of Ping-Pong.

Should we slow-walk backward out of here and close the door so they could be alone?

Temi and Ruby had *serious* energy.

"These guys were looking for you. Hope it's okay..." Temi grinned.

"'Course. Yes." Ruby was nodding and smiling and nodding. "Thanks. That's great. Excellent. Thanks."

Temi turned to us. "Have either of you seen it before?" Fred put his hand up like he was in class. "Well, then, Elle, be prepared. Ruby is killer."

"No, *you* are!" Ruby almost interrupted her, she said it so quickly.

"No, it's all about you," Temi shot back.

When they finally stopped "no, you-ing," Temi said she'd leave us to it, gave me a hug bye, and shut the door behind her. Ruby was still beaming. It would be gross, if I weren't totally into it.

"So, you want to fill me in?" I pulled up a chair for me and Fred.

"I don't know what you're talking about." Ruby pretended to be indignant. Holly was right—her acting skills *were* good.

"Well, *I'm* talking"—Fred waved his finger—"about the fact Ruby's finally sorted out a date. With Temi. In two days' time. Yes, after three months, it's actually happening."

"It's not a date." Ruby didn't sound like she was even convincing herself. "Just two people. Hanging out."

"On a date." I couldn't not join in, but before Ruby could protest, I carried on. "I'm stoked for you. She's awesome."

Ruby grinned. "She is, isn't she?"

"Yup." I gave her my last packet of Swedish Fish as a good-luck offering. "And so are you. Invite me to the wedding, please."

By the time Fred and I were in the frow (as only Fred kept saying), I was feeling actual nerves. The lights dimmed, and they did an announcement about turning off phones, but I was already on it. After tooblessed's comment earlier, I'd decided that this evening, I was switching off. Not just my phone. Everything. Worrying about #FestiveFifteen. Worrying about the comments. Worrying about if I'd beat Clara.

So tonight's pictures had just been for me. Me and Fred laughing as we messed around in the props cupboard (side point—that boy could rock a bald head), him giving me two thumbs-up as he got a kiss from the dame, and the video of me trying my first festive sausage roll. I already knew Dove wouldn't approve. In fact, her exact reply to my earlier picture of Ruby's awesome poster was, "Isn't that kinda dorky? Not being a downer, just want you to be having the best time and getting those followers in! Kisses."

BOOM.

A drum banged. The panto was starting.

Fred leaped so hard out of his seat that our popcorn flew up into the air and onto the stage. The curtain paused dramatically in midair, kernels stuck to it. There was no option but to stand up and brush it all off as a hundred people tutted behind us, and we tried not to crack up. And as soon as the main cast took to the stage, with the worst innuendos and age-old jokes (that, ngl, made me howl) I was loving it. Sure, it was weird as hell. Including how Ruby made a reflective surface so funny, so swaggy and badass, but she did. My hands actually hurt from clapping. And by the time it ended, all the kids in the audience getting up and dancing in the aisles, I was on a high.

We managed to grab Ruby after to tell her she was amazing, but she had stuff to do backstage, so Fred and I stopped in a cozy pizza place where I ordered the Christmas pizza with sprouts and pigs in blankets on. It was delicious. I was very much getting on board with Holly's idea to eat all Christmas everything.

Just the two of us, Fred and I chatted more than we ever had before. About Ruby, about life, about the suggestions that were coming in for my London trip. We talked about how Fred's brother kept waking him up at three a.m. to ask if it was Christmas, how I'd managed to change Holly's flights, so she wasn't going to be back till the twenty-sixth (which he called Boxing Day?!), and somehow, without knowing why, I told him the thing that I hadn't told anyone else.

The reason I was so bothered about #FestiveFifteen. It wasn't just that making my way into @thingsthepeakgirlsdo meant I'd finally have something in Alpine Peaks. It was how I was done making friends that let me down. That I was done with goodbyes. How online, I could finally be the one in control. And this challenge was finally my chance to prove to everyone that I could be okay on my own. Especially to Clara.

I still had no idea how she'd found out the things she posted in Nashton. Why she'd turned like she did. But when she started posting about Nick, that's when I knew I had to put an end to it.

I hated we were now in a head-to-head to win this thing with Dove—and if I didn't manage to overtake Clara, and quickly, I'd have to delete my account, and she'd win all over again. It was like whenever something good happened to me, there she was.

Which is why I had another suspicion.

Was it Clara who was trolling me? Again? I didn't want it to be true, but once I'd thought it, I couldn't shake it.

And I told Fred how nice it was to finally tell someone. How Nick used to be my person, but the move, and Grams getting ill, had just made all the distance and disappearing even worse, and now I felt like neither of us had a clue about each other's lives.

Fred seemed genuinely shocked—shocked about what happened and maybe a little shocked I'd told him. But he listened, and he didn't judge, and he didn't tell me I was wrong, or brave, or should have told someone sooner, he just listened and told me that whatever I wanted, he really believed I could make happen. He even offered to come with me and Ruby tomorrow to help with #OneElleOfAChristmasDayInLondon.

And I listened too, when he told me about Eve—how hard it was to get over someone you liked, even if none of your friends got it. And how he wished Holly would realize how great she was and that she wouldn't worry so much about life not going to plan. And how sometimes when he finished a pizza, he wondered if it would be okay to order a second.

So we did. To share.

CHAPTER THIRTEEN

Holly

Go to a festive costume party, they said.

Americans are incredible at it, they said.

It'll be fun, they said.

Well, *they* meant Elle. And Elle was a liar.

"Take me through *this*." I pointed at what Nick had laid out on her bed. "One. More. Time."

"Well..." He walked across the room. "Elle said you'd be up for Dean's party?" Dean wasn't just the lead singer of Au Revoir Hairs, he was Elle's science partner. "And...well, I didn't want to disappoint on the costume front."

Disappoint? The theme was Christmas?! But we only had an hour to get to the party. So instead of arguing or trying and failing to look as glam as Elle would, I decided to suck it up. Do things Nick's way. Maybe it was because I was still on a high about the Alpine Peaks Christmas Tree and Furry Friends decorating competition I'd been asked to guest judge earlier (the tiny stuffed Father Christmas riding a patient-looking Labrador was a thing of beauty). Or maybe it was because everything was sorted to go to the Snow Ball on Christmas Eve. With Elle. Mum had been really sweet and told me that us two meeting would just be an extra present for her. She was the best.

But as we walked into the party, I knew, crossing off Elle's challenges to me or not, that I'd made a huge mistake. A huge, meat-shaped mistake.

In a room full of sexy Santas, cute reindeer, and snowsuit-wearing Mariah lookalikes, I was a giant piece of bacon. Crispy, American bacon. An equally giant bacon strip waddling alongside me. We were only a couple of pieces of bread away from a sandwich.

The only good thing was that no one here knew me to tag me into any of the photos. Maybe I'd use a fake name to be on the safe side. Christine Petra Bacon. Chris P. Bacon.

"One cream soda." Nick passed me a plastic red cup. He'd been gone ages getting it. "I know that trying one was in your notebook. And..." He wobbled the plate.

"Mac-and-cheese-flavored Christmas trees. Don't say we don't know how to do nutrition."

A bit of his furry rind clipped my ear as he passed them over. "So, is this what you expected?"

I looked around Dean's packed house. I wasn't sure how to reply. I mean, it *was* amazing. Everyone seemed really friendly, and the house and music and decorations and everything were exactly as I'd hoped. Maybe a tiny bit of me felt that standing on the edge of a party of people I didn't know felt kind of the same whatever country you were in.

But that bit of me was an ungrateful Christmas parsnip, so it could shut up.

"It's BETTER." I looked up. "I mean, did Dean hire in those lights?!" There was a rig spinning around, projecting actual snowflake lights. Ruby and Fred would LOVE it.

Nick laughed. "You wait until you see the hot tub. Might be one to add to the list—Dean's legendary for them."

Well, this rasher was going to be legendary for avoiding that at all costs. I hadn't even done an emergency leg shave. Change of subject needed. "So..." I balanced my drink on the arm of one of their huge sofas and picked up the mac and cheese thing. "Excited about Christmas yet?" I threw it in my mouth. It tasted of feet. Mac and feet. Must. Not. Gag.

"It's not that I'm not excited, Hol..." Nick moved to stand beside me, both of us now leaning against the wall, like porky party observers.

"It's just that you don't want to hear any Christmas songs, or put any decorations up, and you come to a Christmas party dressed as meat?"

He tried not to laugh. "When you put it like that..." I still felt there was something he wasn't telling me—like there was something they *all* weren't telling me. Like there was a ghost of Christmas past knocking about that house and we all had to pretend we couldn't see it.

"I got the impression you used to love it when you were younger?"

"'Course. But y'know." He hesitated. "Things change." And as much as I wanted to make a joke, tell him why he was wrong, all I could do was nod. I was the one out here who'd had to swap countries on my mission to make Christmas great, because the one I loved so much back home was changing beyond recognition.

So instead all I said was, "I get it."

Nick seemed surprised, but before he could ask what I meant, "Don't Let the Bells End" came on. The song I'd played the other day in the car. I looked at Nick, and he shrugged. I looked around to see if anyone else knew it, but as I did, Dean gave Nick a thumbs-up over the room. Had Nick requested it? For me?

I looked at Nick. "Was this you?"

"What can I say? My friends have great taste. Now..." He took the plate of mac and feet out of my hand. "Want to dance?"

I don't think the party, maybe even America, was prepared for two pieces of bacon jumping around, arms fully out, yelling along to every word. I definitely wasn't. I hadn't seen this side to

Nick before, and I liked it. All his friends joined in—even Blake. The very male, very much in love with his boyfriend, Blake. Well, I couldn't have got *that* more wrong.

And it meant Nick was most definitely single after all.

Not that it mattered to me. At all. FLIGHTS, NOT FEELINGS.

When the song finished, Nick leaned over. "Sorry I missed the meal last night..." Wow. That came out of nowhere. I'd made Mum's infamous Christmas Treefle (chocolate trifle with a Christmas tree design on top of the cream, all covered in caramels), which Pete had at least eight helpings of. "It sounded great. I just...had to be...somewhere."

There was definitely something going on with Nick and his family, and I felt like, as a mix of both in- and outsider, maybe I could be the one to help? But before I could ask any more, a random girl dressed entirely in stick brown bounced into us.

"LOVE THE OUTFITS!" She put her hand to her mouth and shouted, "Guys—we have the party winners, you might as well go home." She giggled and looked down at her body, brown cushions attached, a sort of lid attached to her head. "This was the best I could think of. A mother-freakin' Christmas pot roast."

"Pot roast?" I asked, confused.

"Tell me you're not British?!" Pot Roast's jaw actually fell open. "Sorry. Little Bacon. You are TOO MUCH." She stepped back, fanning her face, then looked at Nick. "And Big Bacon. Aren't you the guy who just did the store run?" She held up her can of Mountain Dew. "I owe you big-time. This pot roast was getting hangry."

"Sorry?!" I cut across her more rudely than I meant. "You ran to the shop?" THAT'S why Nick had been so long?

Nick didn't make eye contact. Pot Roast punched him gently in the arm.

"When a guy's on a mission for cream soda, and your party host has none, what's he gonna do, huh? I'm telling you, this little streak of pork can run."

Wait. Nick had gone for me? And hadn't even told me?

"You shouldn't have..." I began to say, but Nick had already turned to leave, saying something about catching up with Blake.

Wow—he was a master of avoidance.

I stayed and chatted to Pot Roast—she was Fred levels of funny and knew Elle too. Apparently they'd worked on a science presentation together, and she was as in love with Elle as I was. I showed her @OneElleOfATime—she didn't have a clue about it, so she hit follow. It was weird: from Elle, I got the impression that people only knew her from her account, but everyone I'd met hadn't even known about it.

But all of a sudden, a stressed Nick came over, keys in hand.

"Elle, I'm so sorry, but something urgent's come up." Again? If he was about to say band stuff, it wouldn't fly, as we both knew they were all here. "I can drop you off, unless you want to stay?"

Pot Roast made an awkward excuse about heading to the hot tub to become a "pot boil" and left. Probably best. I was fuming.

Nick had asked me to this party, and now he was ditching me. And I knew why it stung extra hard—sure, I'd only known him for a few days, but sometimes the way he acted made me feel like Woody had. That I wasn't enough—that there was always somewhere better to be.

And this time, I'd had enough.

"Take me with you." I crossed my arms. "If it's so urgent? I'll come."

We'd been driving for ten minutes, but Nick hadn't said a word.

I stared out at this amazing town that just over a month ago I didn't know existed and now felt a tiny bit like home.

But where were we going? We'd gone past their house five minutes ago and were heading to the edge of town.

Nick's knuckles were tight around the wheel. Maybe I shouldn't have pushed him into this. "Look, if you want, you can just drop me off."

"As long as you swear this is just between you and me, Hol?"

"I promise." And I meant it. What could be so bad?

"No Elle, no anyone?"

"Sure. No rash-er decisions." I mean, I didn't know what he

meant, but one of us had to acknowledge we were still dressed as bacon.

When he hit the indicator, I swiveled in my seat—finally, I was going to discover where he'd been running off to. But when I saw the big, white building and the huge sign by the big gates, I thought I must have gotten something wrong.

ALPINE PEAKS SENIOR LIVING. About half of the bulbs in the sign had given up life long ago.

"I'm confused..." Nick was definitely pulling into a space. "*This* is your guilty secret?"

"Not guilty, no." He turned off the engine and unclipped his seat belt. "But not something the others know, if that's what you mean. Come on." He opened his door and gestured for me to do the same. "I've got someone for you to meet."

I pointed at what I was wearing, but he just raised an eyebrow. "You said you wanted to come..."

So I shut up, put up, and followed him in.

"Well, look at you!" The receptionist waved her pen up and down at Nick. "You should have told me you were making a special effort!"

She was *definitely* a fan of Nick's.

"We like to try, Charl." She beeped us through, and we walked down some quiet corridors into a big room, sort of like a giant living room, comfy seats facing all directions, and a TV blaring. Nick headed toward the corner, where there was one armchair facing away, with an old lady sitting quietly, staring out of the window, even though all there was to see was headlights going back and forth along the main road.

"All okay?" He crouched down.

"All good—you shouldn't worry yourself," she replied gently, putting her hand on his. As she turned round, as I saw her face, there was no doubt who she was. It was like looking at Elle, just in sixty years' time. The same brightest green eyes, the same dimples, the same confident way she held herself.

"Holly, meet Grams. Well, Dottie..." Nick pulled another chair over. "Grams, meet Holly."

Dottie looked up at me and smiled, a big, whole face smile.

She held her hand out. "This is *the* Holly, I take it?"

"Well, I'm *a* Holly?" I shook her hand as I sat down. "And a Holly that's very pleased to meet you."

She laughed. "And is it you I should be thanking for those delicious cookies?"

"Grams, please!" Nick was laughing. "I acquired those by very surreptitious means..." He must have taken a box from home.

"Now," his voice dropped, "Grams, when I called to check in, they said that you'd had another fall?"

"Oh, it was nothing—I'm here and fine." Dottie clearly didn't want to talk about it. "That's the important thing." She twisted slowly to plump up her cushion. I stretched over to help, but she didn't want any. "Charl promised they weren't going to make a mountain out of a molehill. Although you promised you weren't going to always panic and, look, minutes later, here you are..."

And as they bickered about how protective he was, I tried to figure out why on earth Nick seeing his grandma was something he wouldn't just admit to his family.

"I don't suppose you have any more photos you could show me?" Dottie waited till Nick had gone to get tea before she asked. She reached for her glasses case. "Of Elle's big adventure? Between you and me, Nick can be a little lacking in that department."

But I had more than enough, so I showed her everything—the ones Elle had posted and everything from Ruby and Mum. Whenever I tried to flick through, Dottie would quietly put her hand on mine to stop me so she could study each one carefully.

"What a lucky girl. What a brave girl. She'd been so nervous as well." Dottie clearly didn't know Elle was immune to nerves. "I bet she's having the most wonderful Christmas, isn't she?"

I nodded—I didn't want to correct her that Elle was more into winning the challenge than festivities.

"I am too. I've been having the best time here... I'm a biiiig Christmas fan." I looked around the room and tried to ignore that there was just one piece of tinsel up and a faded, folded-out poster that said "Happy Holidays," which looked like it had been in use since 1952. "I heard you might be too..."

"Oh boy, am I *ever*!" And it was like I'd opened the floodgates.

Sparkly, happy festive floodgates. Dottie's eyes came alive as she told me about the traditions she'd had—that the whole family had, how Elle and Nick used to love it, about all the things they used to do together. I loved hearing about it but was sad it had changed so much for them.

"So come on then, Dottie. What would your perfect Christmas be?"

"Well, that's a toughie!" She closed her eyes and breathed in, a smile on her face—almost like she was doing a séance with Santa Claus. "There has to be carols. And..." She started gently singing "White Christmas." I joined in too. "Lots of gingerbread. I could survive on that stuff! Oh, and the best bit was a proper dance with Jack." That was Elle's granddad—Dottie looked at her wedding ring. "But I guess those days are long gone."

"Sorry to interrupt." Nick slid a tray down in front of us, unaware that his gran and I were about two minutes away from best-friend status. "This should be everything. Two teas and..." But Dottie had already started munching on a biscuit.

I had no idea why this would be something Nick didn't want his family to know about.

And I was still wondering when we left and Dottie took both of my hands in hers and said, "Look after him." And I was still wondering on the way home, when Nick promised he'd tell me tomorrow.

But figuring out Elle's family would have to wait. When I got back to her room, I put on "One More Sleep," shook up my snow globe, and instead of dreaming of a white Christmas, I dreamed of my biggest Christmas wish coming true.

Tomorrow, I was finally going to be in Manhattan.

CHAPTER FOURTEEN

Elle

Four Days till Christmas

I folded my coat onto the rack above my seat, as Ruby mouthed *sorry* for the fifteenth time from the other side of the train window.

She'd been messaging us a live commentary of her being stuck behind a tractor, which had turned into a live commentary of her missing this train by seconds.

"Guess it's just you and me then." I gave Ruby a big wave, sat down, and cheers-ed Fred's cardboard cup with my Diet Coke bottle.

My phone rattled on the table.

@RUBY UK: Good luck Elle!! If anyone can make a

Beefeater smile, my money's on you xx

Yup—that was challenge number twenty-eight. I gave her a thumbs-up back, even though she was so far away, I wasn't sure she could see.

Not the best start, though, and I was already tired—my alarm had gone off at six so I could make sure everything was perfect. I'd even put on my favorite red Lady Danger MAC lipstick, so I looked braver than I felt.

Everything depended on today. Thanks to lots of amazing people tagging on my account, I was now up to 9,201 new followers—but Clara had just hit ten thousand. The others were way behind, so one of us two was definitely going to win. The race was really on to be first.

Dove hadn't made my day any easier by adding Platform 9¾ into the challenge, and I'd woken up to her tagging me into a video asking if I could pick her up a souvenir. And some really hard-to-find candy. I didn't have time, but I also didn't have a choice, so I'd said yes.

I'd posted the full list of fifty this morning, so everyone could check them off as I went. The idea was, for each one I did, people would tag in a new friend, and the person who suggested that exact one would tag in ten. I was asking a lot, but I really hoped they'd do it.

I looked back at the list. The long list.

Photo with a Beefeater (or any novelty Londoner)... Ride a double-decker bus... Take the Tube... Zara... A ride at Winter Wonderland... Carnaby Street lights...

Even though I'd never met her, this whole day was making me think of Holly. I couldn't believe we were going to the Snow Ball AND spending Christmas Day together. I swear I heard Nick humming a Christmas tune when I spoke to Mom last night—and he'd asked me if it would be a good idea if he went to Manhattan with Holly as "we haven't actually seen the Central Park ice-skating rink in years." I thought he would hardly hang out with her, but he'd done something with her every day. *Interesting*. Something Christmassy too. *Even more interesting*...I dropped Hol a message.

> Checking off London >> So so vibed for the London Eye. THANK YOU!! And send me everything about New York!!!

All I had left from her to-do list for me was the Christmas Cracker. And Holly had done almost all of hers too—even if she didn't get a mistletoe kiss, I was still going to do the extra surprise for our moms. Not that Holly needed to know that—she still had Woody to get over. An extra incentive never hurt.

Fred leaned over the table. "Soooo, tell me. What cunning plan do we have to achieve this ridiculous day?"

He raised an eyebrow and tried to look cunning. But he didn't look cunning.

The truth was... *The truth was.*

Nope, I wasn't going to go there. Today was hectic enough, without having a mind melt.

Lack of sleep must be getting to me. Holiday romances were not my style. Not even romances, really. Even with cute British boys who wore bad knitted stuff because they'd promised their friend.

Get a grip, Elle. I didn't get feelings for people. Especially when, in less than three days, I'd never see them again.

I downed my Coke and focused on the plan.

When we pulled into King's Cross, we headed straight for Platform 9¾, but the line was a hundred people long. Not a great start. The helper wizards recommended coming back in the evening, so with no choice, we had to move on. Maybe I could talk Dove out of that one?

We raced to Buckingham Palace then headed to the park and did the bumper cars at Winter Wonderland that looked like sleighs (good, but it was so early that there was only one scared-looking kid to crash into). Everything in London was so cute—even the lampposts and trash cans looked museum-worthy. The Tower of London put Hogwarts to shame, even though it was right in the middle of normal London. Like, Tube stop, busy road, INSANE MASSIVE CASTLE THING THAT THE ROYAL FAMILY USED TO LIVE IN. Fred really hit his stride telling me all about the murders there. They had an ice-skating rink outside—I was nowhere near as good at skating as Nick, but I still had some skills, so I pulled out some spins and backward skating. Fred was meant to be filming but ended up falling backward over a kid clinging to a giant penguin. Then we went top deck on a double-decker bus past St. Paul's Cathedral and over the Thames. The view was incredible. On the left was Tower Bridge, and on the right was the rest of London, its jagged skyline piled up around the river, like a theme park of really old stuff. By the time we got to the South Bank Christmas market, despite not stopping at all, we were running late, so we decided to have a quick lunch.

"Okay, so the option seems to be..." Fred looked around the wooden stalls along the river. "German sausage or...German sausage." He turned to the long line of restaurants behind me. "I mean, there's a zillion other places, but the people serving in them aren't dressed as elves, so I'm guessing I already know how you feel about that."

I nudged him with a giant gingerbread heart I'd picked up for Mom.

"Hey. You're making me sound like Holly!"

"Excuse me?!" He flared his nostrils. "In all Holly's years of jumper calendars, film screenings, and commitment to all things Crimbo, I have NEVER done so many Christmas things in one day."

"But this isn't Christmas, Fred, this is a competition." I said it as a joke, but Fred didn't laugh. I sure had a weird way of saying thanks for his help.

"Well, let's go get that sausage then. I'll be back in a sec." Fred gestured for me to wait, so I used the spare minute to check my phone for the millionth time today.

Thirty-two things left to do, and only six and a half hours before our train. It was going to be tight, but there was no way I could not do it. Especially as Clara was posting as much as me. I'd managed to get 150 new followers today, but despite it being super early for her, she'd gotten 450 already—her day of livestreams was doing well. Too well. And she'd just replied to my latest post.

Nice work @OneElleOfATime 18 done!
#OneElleOfAChristmasDayInLondon

I could tell she was throwing shade at me.

I sent back a thumbs-up, hoping she could tell how seething I was.

And even worse, the other name I really didn't want had made an appearance on my timeline. @tooblessed2bstressedxx

@DoveAllLove is the rule that if all fifty don't get done
@OneElleOfATime is out the comp?! 😱😘 xoxo

I was relieved when I got a notification that Dove had replied—maybe now would be the time to tell her in private I didn't think I could get the Platform 9¾ photo.

@tooblessed2bstressedxx ooooh now that IS an idea. Love me some Xmas drama!

What? Was Dove agreeing?!

As if today weren't stressful enough.

I looked over at Fred, who was now chatting to a stranger about the perfect mustard to ketchup ratio. I didn't want him to know I was freaking out. I guess, if worst came to absolute worst, I had been offered a hotel room by SnapGoGo. But there was no way I wanted to leave him to head back on his own.

Pretending I had everything under control, we headed up to Camden and chowed down a snowman-shaped ice cream made with liquid nitrogen. I don't know if it was the ice cream on the coldest day of the year, or talking to Fred and not checking my phone, but it made me feel a little bit less stressed. We then burned through lots of things in a few minutes when we got to Oxford Street. Fred snapped a quick shot of me marching down the escalators in Zara, then I posed outside Liberty's windows and ended up on Carnaby Street. The evening was settling in, and if I'd been loving London earlier, now I wanted to marry it and have all its babies.

"You all right, Elle?" Fred asked, as I looked for the perfect spot to take a photo of the lights, which were Christmassy but themed around protecting our oceans.

"It's just..." I knew this was going to sound silly, but it was

Christmas, so who cared. “It’s just ridiculous, isn’t it? Better than I ever thought.” I lined up the photo. “Holly might be on to something, you know!”

Fred laughed softly—I only really knew because his breath showed up in the cold. “Would this be a good time to tell you that you’ve officially overtaken Clara?”

Wowsers. I stopped taking the photo to check. He was right! @_Beckywiththemediocrehair_ had messaged to tell me too. I’d not only just tipped 10,000 new followers with only 4,213 to go, but I was 50 in front of Clara.

And as everyone bustled around us, and the sound of “Last Christmas” spilled out of the coffee shop as its door opened and shut, and Fred stood beside me, singing the “very next Dave you gave it away” and pointing out his favorite whale light, for the first time in forever, I felt something. A little spark of magical excitement I hadn’t had in years.

About all the things that seemed to happen on the cold winter evenings in December that couldn’t make sense at any other time.

About the way Christmas made anything feel possible.

Like this.

Me realizing this weird feeling, the one that had been fizzing up for days, wasn’t just Christmas magic.

It was because of the boy standing next to me.

CHAPTER FIFTEEN

Holly

"Still not over it." I flicked a crumb off the train table at Nick. It bounced off his jacket with a satisfying *ping*. To help me get up so early for the train, he'd blared Sia's "Candy Cane Lane" at full, and I mean *full* volume through the bedroom wall.

He looked out the window. "I thought you liked Christmas songs?"

I huffed, but it was more of an air laugh. I was no good at pretending to be in a mood when I was this happy. Today was the day I'd been dreaming of. For years.

And last night, out of the blue, Nick had asked if I would like company. Which I really did. I didn't think this was his thing, but Elle must have twisted his arm.

And now I didn't just have a New York buddy, I had a whole day to get to the bottom of what happened yesterday.

"Never forgiving you aside—thanks. For coming." I found sincerity mega awks. "This is literally my lifelong dream come true."

Nick grinned. "A lot of people say that about spending the day with me."

"Ha very ha." I waited for my phone to hook up to the train Wi-Fi. "I more meant my ultimate Christmas Day in New York." I waved my notebook at him. From the second we got into Twenty-Third Street Station, I had a minute-by-minute must-do of all the best Christmas things. "All three beautifully planned pages of it." Nick looked like he might be working out how safe it was to jump off a moving train.

But I didn't need to explain—he knew me by now. Anyway, I needed to ring Mum. Nick knew she'd been on my mind. I'd spoken to Nay last night, and she'd said Mum had sounded weird. Tbf, Naomi didn't exactly sound super happy either. She'd run out of money, and all her friends had flown back, so she was being a "beach loner" until she caught her flight on the twenty-fifth. I pointed out it was quite hard to muster up any sympathy when the only beach I'd seen this year was in Wales, but she'd asked me what time my train was to Manhattan. Touché, schwester.

"Hello?" Mum answered like whoever was calling was a total mystery, not like there was a photo of me, with my actual name on it.

"Mother dearest!" I liked to mix up my greetings. "Guess where I am?"

"Well, if I've got the right day..." I loved seeing her happy face. "Hopefully on the train to Newwww Yoooiiirrkkkk."

And that's why I should have put my headphones in first. Mum on speaker + quiet train carriage + bad American accent = many, many dirty looks.

I clicked them in. "That's better—and yup. Look!" I flipped the camera so she could see the snow. "Actual snow. I'M LIVING MY SNOW GLOBE DREAM."

Mum grinned back at me—she knew what this meant. "Your plans sound incredible." I'd read her the highlights on a quick call yesterday morning. "I can't wait to hear ALL about it."

I waved my book in front of the screen. "Trust me. I'm ready. I'm prepared. It's going to be the best day EVEEEER!"

"Of course you are. Then it's the parade, then the Snow Ball, right? What a week!" I beamed—I knew how lucky I was. "Oh, by the way." She leaned back—revealing my penguin jumper with the snowball pom-poms.

"YESS, MOTHER!" Definitely too loud.

"Thought you'd like it. I gave Fred a lift this morning, and he was wearing his too."

I closed my eyes, balled up my hand, and kissed my fist.

"No words." My friends were ICONS.

"Sure we'll get Elle in one too by the time she leaves." I tried not to be disappointed that she hadn't already. "Did you hear Ruby missed the train?"

"I did not!" Weird. That was not like Ruby at all. "Maybe she's got something on her mind." Mum had no idea I meant Ruby's hot, hot, hot date with Temi tomorrow. I smiled smugly to myself—yes, I was making in-jokes, with...myself. "Only five sleeps till I'm back. CAN'T WAIT. And you've got your first proper Christmas with Colin and the twins. Imagine—not having to rely on me and Nay to help with dinner!"

But the big, smiley reply I was expecting didn't come. "Well, I will sorely miss your excellent carrot-peeling skills. And the twins are off to their mum's, so Col and I were thinking of treating ourselves to takeaway." Takeaway? She wasn't doing turkey for the first time ever?! "Less danger from Colin-dog. Maybe a nice glass of wine and something good on TV." No mention of stockings? Or even a game? What positive could I take from this?

"Well, takeaway beats what people used to have...pig's head and mustard."

Did Nick just snort?

"Not sad to have missed that one." Mum laughed. "Thought I might even put the old Christmas onesie on!"

"I *will* require a video call with you BOTH in them." I did well not to ruin the surprise. Once I'd realized I was going to miss the big day, Naomi, Elle, and I had managed to organize stockings for all of them.

"Of course! I'm excited already." I smiled at her, but I didn't really want to talk about it—although we'd chatted every day,

I'd been really careful she didn't realize I was freaking out a bit about spending my first Christmas away. So instead I asked her the question I'd already asked a million times.

"And you're still sure you don't mind me being here?"

"Of course not. You're meant to be having the best Christmas ever, remember? And if you are—I am."

I realized in that moment, I could never be a parent.

They were too good.

But I had to go. Nick was jabbing me in the arm. I pulled out my headphones.

"The train's stopping, something on the line. We could be stuck here for a couple of hours—but if we run, we can jump on the express to Penn."

Stopping? Penn Station? This wasn't the plan?

But neither was being behind schedule! Help!

I said bye to Mum and stuffed everything in my bag as Nick scrambled around under the seats to unplug our chargers. Clinging on to armfuls of things (mainly woolen and mine), we made the train by seconds.

I sank back into my chair until I could manage words.

"Right." Breathe. "Phew." Oxygen. "Soooo." I got my phone out. "Can you show me where Penn is? I might have to jiggle some stuff around."

Nick moved the map around as I got my notebook out to fix the schedule.

"Nick?" I patted my jeans. And stuck my hands in my coat pocket. "Have you, er..." I rummaged in my bag. Then rummaged harder. "Have you seen my notebook?"

Nick looked blank. "Sorry—not since you showed your mom."

An icy thud hit me harder than a perfectly thrown snowball.

I had picked it up off the last train. Hadn't I?

But after emptying every pocket, even checking in my bobble hat, it was nowhere.

All my research! All the timings! All the perfect Christmas things!

THIS WAS A DISASTER.

"Don't worry." Nick was checking my coat again after I'd flung it at him in a mild breakdown. "We can figure this out."

"But I can't remember everything! I can't remember *anything*!" I started typing the bits I could into my phone, but the more I freaked out, the more I forgot.

How had I messed this up? I'd been planning it for EVER!

"Hol." Nick sounded genuinely concerned. "Look..." He paused. "A swede is a cross between which two vegetables?"

What?!

"Good." Nick was looking me straight in the eye. "You're back in the room...train, whatever. It was cabbage and turnip by the way. The closest to a Christmas fact I could get. Now, I've got a suggestion..." A voice boomed over the speakers:

"PENN STATION."

"As I see it, there are two options." He was talking quickly. "We try and remember what was on your list. Or..." He shrugged, a little grin on his face. "Or we do Christmas in a new way. We figure it out."

Figure it out?

Figure. It. Out?! This was meant to be my perfect Christmas day!

But as the train stopped and the doors cranked open, I didn't feel like I had much choice.

Without him seeing, I reached in my bag and clutched my snow globe, hoping the Christmas magic that got me here could work its charm today.

And off we went.

We stepped out on to Seventh Avenue, yellow taxis and "Don't Walk" signs flashing. And it was better than anything I'd ever dreamt of. I was finally here. In Manhattan. And I loved it.

Nick leaned over. "Welcome to New York."

"It's been waiting for us," I replied, but his face told me he didn't necessarily get the Taylor Swift reference.

"Shall we walk around the block first?" I nodded, too busy taking it all into speak. "We can grab a drink. Central Park is pricey."

Frankly even if he said, "Let's jump in front of the traffic, waving our pants above our heads," I'd probably agree. Anything felt like a good idea right now. WE WERE IN NEW YORK!

As I tried to remember how to form words, Nick got our drinks and hailed us a taxi. As we drove up Sixth Avenue, you could already see where the buildings stopped, dropping away as the enormous Central Park started.

I was living my dream. I finished my entire drink without even noticing one sip. Almost as bad as accidentally finishing toast. But there was no time to mourn, we had to hurry to make our ice-skating booking at ten. Luckily, my phone had the details of that one.

I didn't want to hold Nick back, so I told him to do his own thing on the ice—I'd seen how good Elle was in her stories this morning. But Nick said he hadn't skated in ages and edged his way around with me. I was so busy concentrating on not falling over that I forgot to look up until he reminded me. The skyline above us looked amazing, like a film set of skyscrapers, letters mounted on their roofs.

I couldn't believe after years of dreaming, I was finally here.

I also couldn't believe I fell over and took out a very small brother and sister, but as Nick said, "If you can't handle the heat, then don't go really slowly in front of an out-of-control British tourist whose scarf has blown over her eyes."

Once we'd survived, we walked up through the park to this perfectly still lake that reflected New York back off it, and as we stood and stared, a man riding a street cleaner went past and shouted "happy Holidays" at me.

It was like he'd appeared there just to make my day. I actually whimpered, I was so happy. When we got to the nearest subway, Nick said I shouldn't stress about remembering what should be next, I should just choose a stop I thought sounded fun. So I chose Grand Central, and after gawping at the terminal hall, which I recognized from every New York film ever, we walked a few blocks up to Rockefeller Plaza and their huge tree. That *was* something on my plan, but weirdly I was enjoying all the walking in between just as much. I wasn't scared of heights, but when the lift started going up the seventy floors to the Top of the Rock, I did feel a bit odd.

"Okay, I admit it." Nick was leaning against the glass at the edge of the roof. Nick was an idiot. We'd been walking around the top for about five minutes. "This was a great idea." He peered down. "I've always avoided it, but it's like looking down at the Sims. But real."

We could see everything from up here. The Hudson and East Rivers, the huge bridges over them, the Empire State Building...

"Whoa, is that the Statue of Liberty?" The good stuff just kept on coming.

"You want a photo with it?" Nick asked. He took one picture for every three hundred that I did. I shuffled in front of the view and held out my fingers, like I was pinching the air.

"Does it look like I'm tweaking the top of it?" He moved the camera a bit higher, told me to move a bit left, and then said, "Uh-huh." Nailed it the first time. We then did photos with me leaning on the Empire State and pretending to stir the river. Comedy gold.

It wasn't till we were down that I realized he'd been teasing me, and I was miles off in each photo, grinning like a clueless sausage, while doing poses that made no sense.

"Sorry..." Nick looked apprehensive. "But you did say you wanted something unique?"

And they certainly were—in fact, they were hilarious. I loved them and sent some to Ruby and Fred, who I knew would enjoy laughing at me from afar.

Back at ground level, it was so freezing that we ditched my original idea of walking over the Brooklyn Bridge and instead started strolling down to the market at Union Square. It was far, but there were shops and coffee shops to dive into along the way. I spotted a cool one with homemade Christmas decorations and saw the perfect thing for Colin and Mum. It took a while to get done, so Nick waited outside for me. When we met back up, he asked if we could take a little detour. But no plan meant it wasn't a detour, just a tour, so we walked around the corner to stand outside what looked like a derelict building, "Houston & Beats" painted above the big window in white paint.

"And this is...?" About to be demolished? The scariest place we'd seen so far? The set for a film about the end of the world?

"Where Au Revoir Hairs just got asked to play!" Nick looked dead chuffed.

"What? It's open?!" Was the exact response I didn't manage to stop coming out. He looked a bit hurt. "I mean..." Could I dig my way out of this? "This very second? For us to go in?" Big finish. "I would LOVE to see you play here!"

"They've asked for Christmas Eve." Nick was peering in, grinning at the empty stage. "Last minute. But don't worry. I'm not expecting you to choose the Hairs over Harry Styles!"

He laughed, but he had no idea what I was really thinking.

That actually it *was* a tough choice—because these last few days, I'd seen less of the grumpy Nick I'd heard about and more the one that Elle kept describing from Nashton.

"Holly...?" Uh-oh. He'd caught me giving him a funny look.

"Sorry—you got the full glare of my 'thinking about seeing Twenty One Pilots' face there." I laughed slightly too manically. "Now, how about I take some photos of you for a change? I want full posing in front of the venue, like a proper band douchebag, please."

And surprisingly he obliged.

We made Macy's our next stop. I'd planned to do some serious shopping—but it was so crowded, I switched for a quick in and out. Nick was down for that—but was less down with how I got on the escalator. Full-on lunge. I was trying to get photos for Ruby and Fred of me re-creating the scene from *Elf* they shot there, of Buddy doing accidental splits on it. But the escalator went faster than I thought, and what with me also trying to take a selfie, I ended up in a real-life-medical-emergency splits. Nick had to physically scoop me up as I wailed, "Help meeeee," whilst at least two hundred confused tourists stared at me.

And then I remembered Nick hadn't seen the film anyway.

After that, things went more smoothly. Give or take my limp from pulling twenty-three muscles I didn't even know I had. By the time we hit the cute stalls at Union Square market, I wondered if it was time for me to bring up what happened yesterday.

"So Dottie said you used to come here with your family for Christmas, right? What did you used to get up to?"

"Oh, you don't want to know..." Nick was looking with suspicion at a stall of terrible Christmas trees painted on old records. "Stupid stuff."

"Stupid stuff is my favorite." A person dressed as a candy cane offered me a piece of cinnamon-toasted white chocolate. I paused my investigation to take it. Never say no to free festive food. "So?"

"Guess it was just the usual..." Argh. Sometimes he was a Christmas nut that I just couldn't crack.

"There is no *usual*. C'mon, Nick. You're talking to someone who is losing their mind over those steamy magic jets things." I pointed to the street where the steam was billowing up from the floor.

"Pipe condensation outlets?"

"The *magic*?! Soooo? What was it? Stockings? Carols? Matching family onesies?! What?"

He laughed at the merest suggestion of onesies. Which made me doubt whether I should unleash the personalized ones I'd packed for them in my suitcase. The Millers were probably way too cool for matching.

We sat down on a bench under a speaker playing "Driving Home for Christmas." My mum's favorite. Wow, I wished she could be here right now.

"Fine, fine..." Nick sat next to me. "And this song is a stone-cold classic, Christmas or not." He rubbed his hands together. "Yes, we had stockings when we were little. Mom and Dad too. We even hid one for Grams every year. We'd pretended Santa had gotten soot in his eye and gotten lost, so she had to hunt it down."

"Might have to steal that one for myself!" I was not ashamed to borrow a great idea.

He nudged his knee into mine. "In fact, you'll like this. Mom and Dad were both really big on cooking, so they'd each cook a special dish—sort of US vs. UK style—and we'd declare a Christmas winner. Although—and don't tell them"—he laughed at the memory—"Elle and I would always choose opposite, as they took it way too seriously and we couldn't risk ruining Christmas." So he did have some Christmas joy in there after all? In fact, quite a lot by the big smile on his face. He dropped his head in his hands, shaking it as he laughed. "And oh wow—the singing... How could I have forgotten that? Grams used to get on the piano. There was no stopping her! I know you've only seen her the once, and y'know..." He tailed off, not wanting, not needing to say the obvious—that she wasn't well. "But she used to be the life and soul."

"So..." Time to ask the awkward. But it had to be done—maybe it could be the first step I needed into understanding whatever else they had going on. "How come things aren't like that anymore?" How could he have gone from loving it, from having all these traditions like me, to not caring one way or the other?

"Like I said, things change."

"But Dottie's only around the corner?"

He shrugged. "I don't know. It's normal visiting hours only on Christmas Day. And you know we do our thing in January now. Have done for years." He looked at me. "Bet your mom is going to love having you and your sister home."

"Erm..." Back to Nick's life please. "Yes. But I'm here for Christmas Day. So you, me, and Elle can do something big, right?" I mean, it was a nonnegotiable for me.

But Nick was chewing on his lip. Miles away.

Thinking.

"Nick—why don't you tell everyone where you're going? When you see Dottie?" There it was. I'd asked it.

He sighed. "Thought that was coming." He rolled his neck back. "You really want to know?"

I nodded, letting the music fill the silence.

"Okay, well..." He looked up at me. "Promise you won't tell anyone? Not Elle, not anyone?"

"Uh-huh."

"It's...it's Mom and Dad." He stopped. "They've been worried about me and Elle." I wasn't expecting that. "About us settling in. My hunch is they're thinking of moving again. That's their reaction—something's wrong, we move, we fix it. And that's the last thing Elle wants. I just know it." He paused. "So, when they started to worry about me after Grams had the fall, I knew I had to do something to make them stop. Show them we were doing okay here. Take the pressure off Elle too—she had way too much to deal with after everything that happened back in Nashton." *What happened in Nashton?* "And spending all my time with someone who was eighty wasn't exactly their definition of 'settling in.' So, thinking it's the band, Dean, Blake, basketball, whatever just means zero questions..."

Whoa. This was so much bigger than I thought. And I couldn't help but think I was the first person he'd told.

I knew Elle hated all the moves, that she wanted to stay in Alpine Peaks. I guessed that might have something to do with wanting to win this challenge with Dove. But I couldn't help but think Nick not being honest, all the disappearing, wasn't taking any pressure off—it was giving Elle more to live up to and maybe more to worry about.

"WANT A PHOTO WITH A PRINCESS?" A blue giant with the voice of a man who smoked fifty a day crashed between us. "ONLY TWO DOLLARS!"

"ELSA?!" The burn holes in its face were extra creepy. I grabbed Nick in terror, and we both ran. By the time it had chased us down the path, yelling, "PHOTO? YOU WANT A PHOTO?" Nick and I were too busy laughing to try and get back on to serious stuff. So we headed to the subway to take us over the water to Brooklyn.

But as I watched Manhattan stretch out behind us, I couldn't shake a feeling. Everything I'd done here had been amazing—but was it finally time to move something else to the top of all my Christmas plans?

Helping Nick and Elle get everything out in the open.

CHAPTER SIXTEEN

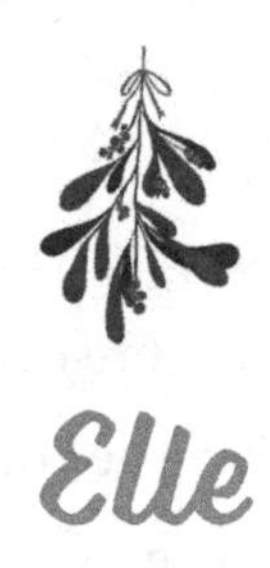

Elle

"C'mon, then." I had to shake this weird Fred thing off. Whatever it was, it was going nowhere. I was flying home in just over two days. Back to real life.

Real life, where I needed to have won this challenge. What *was* this trip doing to me? Other than mess with my sanity, totally proved by the fact I was now wearing some antlers Fred had found on the ground.

I leaned against the brick wall, using the coffee shop's Wi-Fi as Fred used my rapidly running-out pounds to get us some gingerbread-spiced lattes in Covent Garden. I didn't even like coffee, but I needed energy. Big-time.

Sixteen things left to do today—and my phone was on overdrive with comments about whether I was really going to do it.

HappyHol_idays: How many iconic photos in one day?!

tooblessed2bstressedxx: Tick-tock 😊 Hope you don't have to delete this account like your last one 🤞 xoxo

I didn't like it one bit, but when that reply had come just after I'd overtaken Clara, I was convinced that tooblessed could be her. As scary as it was, one more comment, and I was going to have to find out. I couldn't have her ruin everything—again.

I'd turned my rage into energy for a jog down to Leicester Square, panic-darting into any store, desperate to find a souvenir for Dove—and the candy too. Luckily I found a London Bus gross-cute decoration that I hoped would do the trick and the chocolate, which cost a fortune.

But my success was short-lived, as just as I was about to tell her, she DMed me.

Hey Elle. Change of plan. Don't get me a souvenir, I wanna see a hot British boy instead. I mean, I did say before... I'm SURE you can get me a selfie with one before anyone hits 15,000... 😘

All that effort for nothing. And even worse, she was backing me into a corner I really didn't want to be in.

Fred would hate it, and I didn't want tooblessed, or Dove for that matter, to weigh in with their hot take on him. Which left me with only one option. Ignoring the knotted sick feeling in my stomach, I messaged my new follower whose ego was so big, they'd be happy to help. I'd have to explain to the others later.

And that included Fred—I didn't want him to know what was going on yet. So with a breezy smile, I led him through the crowds to Trafalgar Square. When we spotted the huge Christmas tree, the singers underneath were packing up—so, pretending we both weren't embarrassed as hell, we completed another challenge by launching into carol singing for two, with our own rendition of "Deck The Halls." When we got to the "Gl-o-ooo-oo-ooo-ooo-rrii-aaaa" bit, Fred went full Carol from Little Marsh. It should have made people run a mile, but instead it made them laugh, and soon a crowd of twenty people had joined in. We ended up doing the full song and then "We Wish You A Merry Christmas" too. Hilarious...but a massive time suck. We had to sprint across the bridge to get to the London Eye on time.

We were totally out of breath by the time we got there, but as the pod went up, I found the perfect view to de-stress with. Holly and her mom had picked the perfect time, the very start of the evening. The city was twinkling below us, and the traffic on the bridges and boats underneath looked like tiny little toys. I was worried about Fred though. He was unusually quiet, like when we first met, but whenever I asked if he was okay, all he said was "we're on the London Eye" and then started telling me about the Great Fire of London. Or the plague.

We touched down an hour before our train was due to leave, with six things still left to do. Despite being totally exhausted, we rushed straight back toward the Tube.

"Twenty-three thousand, one hundred and thirty-four steps. We should have gotten sponsored for today." Fred flopped back on the Tube seat.

"Oh yeah? And who would we raise money for?"

"Overworked elves," he replied immediately. "I couldn't even hack a day."

"Only one thing left though." We'd gotten creative on the sprint to the station. "And we're done. Like done, done, AND done." There was no way I was getting thrown out of the competition—not after all this. "How long have we got?"

Fred looked at his watch. "Fifty minutes. And it takes ten to get there. We should be fine..."

"Yup." I liked this. Say it to bring it into existence and all that. "Hopefully there'll be hardly any line for that dumb photo now." I jumped on the Underground Wi-Fi and posted an update to my followers to let them know I *was* going to do this. "So what was your favorite part?"

"The London Eye, probs... I'm not a huge fan of heights." So *that's* why he kept reading death facts from his phone. "Everyone's got to do it once, right? And now my once is done."

"I'm sorry..." I felt like a bit of a jerk for not realizing sooner. "Was it worth it?"

Fred turned to me but took a long time before he answered. "Absolutely."

And we both grinned. For so long that it gave me enough time to think, *We're really both smiling at each other, aren't we?* And then, *Is this weird?* And then, *No*, and then smile some more.

But my smile vanished as an announcement came on. *THIS TRAIN IS BEING HELD DUE TO THE PASSENGER ALARM BEING PULLED ON THE TRAIN AHEAD.*

What?

The old lady next to me leaned over, seeing my panic.

"Nothing to worry about, it just means we'll be stuck here a while."

But that's *exactly* what I was worried about. "Thanks, but I need to get to Platform 9¾!" I blurted, like she could somehow sort this out. Or I really did have to get to Hogwarts. By the time the train finally got moving, my heart was racing, and when we got aboveground, we only had ten minutes spare.

I put all my track training into practice. But it was too late.

The line was huge. There was no way I could get the photo and catch the train.

Totally drained, I dropped into a squat right there in the middle of the concourse.

The nightmare had happened. I had to make a choice.

Stay here and finish my #OneElleOfAChristmasDayInLondon to keep me in the competition. Or head home and admit defeat.

I had to put someone—or something first. But would it be the challenge and Dove? Or Fred?

CHAPTER SEVENTEEN

Holly

Not going to lie, I was surprised by the group messages between Ruby and Fred. But my Wi-Fi was dodgy, and I didn't want to put Nick in an awkward position by asking if he'd heard anything.

We were having the best time in Brooklyn and, with only a few hours left, I wanted to keep it that way.

"Okay, so even though this wasn't on the list, I'm giving it a straight ten." We'd found a place that only did desserts, and I'd gotten the birthday cake shake—it was so good, I didn't even mind that it wasn't Christmassy.

Nick grabbed the table as if he might fall over in shock. "Wow—are you, Holly Judd, really saying that maybe list life isn't the only way to happiness?!"

"Never!" I did a slurp so loud, the whole place looked around. "Just maybe, maybe you lucked out just this once."

"But we've done most of what you had planned, right?" I nodded, and in truth the list was pretty much the last thing on my mind right now. "And hang on—haven't you finished the ones Elle sent too? What was it... Cheeze Pleaze Louise..." Nick picked up his empty cup and shook it at me. "Done. New York. Check. Party. Yup, Ms. Bacon... Which leaves what?"

I waited for it to dawn on him. But it didn't.

"Justthemistletoekissthing," I said as quickly as I could, like it was no big deal. Too quickly though, as Nick had to say "excuse me?" two more times.

"JUST THE KISS. UNDER THE MISTLETOE," I eventually yelled, so loud, everyone stopped talking.

"Oh yeah," is what he said. I wasn't sure why, but when we first chatted about it, it felt fine, funny even, but now, it felt... weird.

"It means little dung twig." Pause. "Mistletoe. Because it's spread by bird poo."

"I see." Nick took another slow slip. "Well, guess there's nothing I can do to help with that one."

Did he think that I was hinting?

"I know," I snapped. "I wasn't asking you to." Why was this making me so stressed?

"I also know," he said just as quickly.

"I know you know." I sounded like I was having an argument with Naomi. Time to move things on. "Have you seen Elle's smashing her London challenge?" I got my phone out and showed him her story with a punk in Camden (extra likes for the baubles on their spiky hair). "She's up to over eleven thousand new followers. I really think she's going to win." Although it wasn't all good news. I'd seen tooblessed's latest work. "But sheesh, some of those comments... How rude are some people?"

Nick's eyebrows dropped. "What comments?"

"Oh, who knows? Just a random who doesn't want her to win, I guess."

But Nick was already on his phone, scrolling though Elle's grid. The more he saw, the quieter he got. "And what exactly will she win?"

Weird that Elle hadn't told him—but there must be a reason, so I kept details light. "Nothing except getting into Dove's @thingsthepeakgirlsdo crew. It's a new thing they're doing. Oh"—I finished my drink—"and whoever loses has to delete their account."

"This isn't good," is all he said as he looked through.

"I know. Full-on, right? Dove is an evil genius!" But he didn't answer. "What do you, errr, think of her? Of Dove?" I really wanted his opinion. Elle was clearly a fan, but I really hadn't gotten the best impression.

"Honestly?" Nick put his phone down and rubbed his face with his hands, like he was trying to wash something off. "It's a weird one... My ex used to be obsessed with her, and then we move, and boom, we're decorating her house, and now she's somehow gotten my sister to fly to the other side of the world." He sighed. "And, if it's okay me saying this, I really can't see the appeal. She's always seemed a little..." But he didn't finish. And I didn't fill in with *mean*, which is where I thought he might be heading. "So you really think Elle's doing okay?"

"Uh-huh. I reckon she'll win." I'd just checked, and Dove had posted an update telling the others it was now or never to catch her. "Unless @CallMeClaraT does something preeee-tty spectacular."

Nick almost broke the table, he slammed his drink down so hard. "Sorry, what?" He opened his phone back up. "This cannot be happening," is all he said but definitely to himself, not to me, as he clicked on the FestiveFifteen hashtag. "When is Elle back at your place?"

"Soonish, I think? It's just a day trip."

"Okay... Sorry. Give me a sec." He opened his messages and began typing super quick. I had no idea what was going on, but I did know I'd never seen him this on edge. Those guys needed to talk—and soon.

But seeing as Elle was so busy today, maybe it was my turn to help him out for a change? I waited until he'd pressed send and looked a little less stressed.

"Look, how about you choose what we do next?" Yes, I was effectively handing over my ultimate Christmas day to the Grinch. "Got to make it Christmassy though..."

So, with the dark hitting, we headed out. Outside was so cold, I couldn't speak without my voice wobbling, and the freezing wind blowing off the river brought serious danger of snotsicles. I buried my face in my scarf and tried to suck air in and out of it to provide my own central heating. But we both liked being outside and, as we chatted and strolled, we managed to put whatever weirdness just happened behind us.

Nick's first stop was a museum dedicated to noodles in cups. So basically a Pot Noodle museum. And I was here for it. He smugly found a Christmas-dinner-flavored one, which meant he achieved being festive after all. Then we walked up Bedford Avenue, which had the coolest shops I'd seen in my life, all vintage sunglasses and candles that cost fifty dollars. But it wasn't that Christmassy, so I told Nick he needed to step it up. And less than two minutes later, he stopped by two big guys in suits, standing outside a warehouse door. As someone pushed the door open, a burst of "All I Want for Christmas Is You" popped out. Well, a weird guitar-hipster version of it, but I'd take it.

"Shall we?" Nick asked.

"What—sing or stop?" He knew my rule about never leaving Mariah hanging.

"Stop..." Nick looked at the guys on the door. "We okay to go in?"

Neither of them moved. Not even their eyes. The one on the right said, "Guest list only, sir."

But Nick just smiled. "Oh, I know. We're with Au Revoir Hairs?" He looked down at the iPad the guy was holding. "Nick Miller... And Holly Wattle." I knew he'd only discovered that word when I was showing him which bit of my turkey slippers lit up. Nick lowered his voice as if asking me a private question. "Hol, what time did you say your flight was tonight? The lounge for London is WELL worth getting there in time for."

I tried not to show fear. Or anything that resembled not a British celebrity. "Not till nine." I used the poshest voice I could.

"Are you sure you want to stop?" Nick put his hand on my arm. "The restaurant's only another block?"

I couldn't believe they were buying it, but somehow the threat of a fake celebrity leaving did its job. The guy stepped to one side and pushed the door open. "Have a great evening, sir. Ma'am."

I did a loud extra posh "brilliant, thank you" and tried to look not at all excited, as I think that's how famous people handle everything. Beyoncé on a trapeze? Fine. Finding out Father Christmas is alive and living in Birmingham? Happens every day.

But what was inside was not fine. It was EPIC. Nick had struck gold. And green. And red.

"What. Isssss. This. Place?" In the middle of the ginormous room was a life-size gingerbread house, wooden lodges scattered around, fake snow covering real-life trees. There was an adult ball pit with fake snowballs and a sign that said "Happy Holidays" made out of marshmallows that you could skewer off. There was even a hot chocolate machine where you could choose all the options and toppings—and it got delivered to you in mugs on tiny skis on a conveyor belt thing. "I think I've died and gone to Lapland."

And, oh my Christmas turkey—they were even printing pictures on the hot chocolate foam.

My actual heaven. Nick's idea of hell.

But when I turned around, he was smiling at the back wall. "I haven't seen that movie in forever."

I looked over. They were projecting up a subtitled *Gremlins*. So we jumped in and out of the ball pit, drank some hot chocolate, pulled on some bobble hats they were giving out, grabbed blankets, and sat down on the snowball cushions. Who cared that I had a cleaning brand on my hat—or that we'd crashed a party designed to show "the only mark Christmas should make is the memories." Free knitwear was free knitwear. I grabbed one each for Ruby and Fred too.

As Nick and I watched the film, it was the perfect time to check in on Fred.

Home yet?

Also hypothetically, would you want a bobble hat that's promoting disinfectant?

How did you know what's NUMBER ONE on my wish list?

Prepare to be very excited then. Good day???

Yup. And yup.

I was hoping what Ruby had said earlier hadn't really happened. That Elle hadn't ditched Fred and made him travel back alone, just so she could get a picture for the challenge.

Is Elle with you?

Nope? Thought I'd said? She had to stay.

Hmm. She didn't *have* to do anything. I hadn't said anything to Nick, but his sister had chosen to ditch my friend, and I wasn't best pleased about it.

IMO, that's nooooooot cool.

But IYO, a disinfectant yellow hat is, soooo

He always wanted to keep everyone happy.

Don't stress about it Hol, it's all good. I had the best time.

Wow. He sent me a picture of him on the London Eye—this from someone who sometimes got vertigo when looking out of his bedroom window.

I guess, despite knowing she wasn't available, he was still totally into her.

OH AND YOU'LL NEVER GUESS WHO I RAN INTO ON THE TRAIN BACK?

I asked him who, but he'd gone. And that's why phones should be charged more than once every three days, Fred.

But as chill as Fred was, I couldn't make myself not be mad about what happened. My friends had done so much with Elle—and she'd just ditched Fred? Fueled by the adrenaline of friend loyalty, I messaged Elle and asked if she was around tomorrow for a chat. But she sent back a short reply saying she was busy. Weird. As far as I knew, the only thing she had planned was the Christmas market.

"So we're literally in a place that looks like a snowman barfed—and your face looks like...that?" Nick looked concerned.

"Numb bum." I didn't want to go into it. "Jury's out on if snowballs make the best cushions."

"Come on, then." Nick stood up and reached for my hand. "We can watch *Gremlins* for real when we get home. But for now..." He looked toward the large stand behind a huge, hanging red curtain. "How about I get a picture of you in that?"

How had I missed it?! Behind the curtain was a huge,

twenty-foot-high snow globe with real trees and a real NYC cab inside. In the background was a mini Statue of Liberty, the ice rink at Central Park, and an Empire State Building.

"Nick! It's..." I couldn't believe what I was seeing. "It's my snow globe." Uh-oh, my voice was shaking like it wanted to cry. "In r-real life?!" I gulped. Not only was this a little emosh, and a bit weird, but it was also categorical proof Ruby was an actual wizard. "Is this Christmas magic or what?!"

"Well...I mean. They are kind of famous landmarks..." He saw my face. "But sure, yes. Christmas magic. You want to go in?"

"Together or not at all."

He stepped back. "It's not really my thing."

'Course not. Way too Christmassy and cheesy. But I had guilt on my side. "Pleeeeease?" I'd gone low, but I could go lower. "It is meant to be my perfect Christmas trip..."

So in we went—the fake-snow fans firing up as a lady shouted poses at us. "Throw snowballs! Sexy spin! FROLIC!" Watching Nick not wanting to do it, but also not wanting to look rude, was a Christmas present in itself.

They emailed us the GIF straightaway—hilarious but I loved the strip of photos even more.

I kept them safe as we headed back out for our final hour. We'd decided to not use a map, but my feet somehow found the huge Brooklyn Bridge, and we walked along the river. I felt like I was walking through my dream New York scene, and it made me sort of teary. Again. Luckily it was so cold, I was kind of eye-leaking anyway, so Nick didn't realize I was having another solo deep and meaningful moment.

We walked in happy silence, both of us staring over the water, the lights glistening away. To think that none of this had been on my list! Was I sort of glad I'd lost it? As we turned off to catch the subway back, Nick spotted a hotel he recognized and asked if I'd follow him into the coffee bit.

But when we got to the lift—elevator!—Nick didn't press the button for the café—he pressed the one for the top floor.

"This is great in the summer," he said as we went up. "But in the winter..."

With a ping, the doors opened. Nick put his finger on his lips, and I snuck out after him. He walked past the "No Entry" sign and pushed open a huge glass door that led out onto a massive roof terrace full of piled-up chairs and tables. Putting his hand out for mine, he led the way, and we weaved through them, around the corner, him helping steady me so I didn't slip on the fresh snow.

And when I looked up, there it was.

We were right above the edge of the river, Manhattan twinkling away in front of us. The two of us in our own secret spot as the snow fell.

I'd spent ages planning the perfect Christmas day in New York. But doing it Nick's way had made it even better.

CHAPTER EIGHTEEN

Elle

I *should* be looking around the amazing hotel room I'd been #gifted, or more importantly, taking photos while it still looked perfect, but I couldn't be bothered to even pick up my phone. I felt awful about leaving Fred—he'd been so sweet about it too, which made it even worse. Damn him and his all-around awesomeness.

After standing in line for an hour, I'd gotten the photo at Platform 9¾ but ended up running in time to miss the last train, just as Fred messaged to say he wasn't alone on the way back home—he'd run into his ex, Eve.

Great. Job. Me.

Oh well, if they got back together, at least he'd remember me for helping out.

Sophie had totally freaked out—she'd been seconds away

from jumping in the car to come and get me. In the end, I'd had to get Mom to call and tell her it was all fine. But then Mom was pissed at me for stressing her out and even more mad at me being on my own in London. Oh, and Holly had asked to "chat tomorrow." No kisses, no nothing. She was mad about me leaving Fred, I could tell. I told her I couldn't make the call, but I didn't tell her why. She'd find out soon enough. Until then, here I was. Alone, in London, with all the people I liked in two countries mad at me.

Still, I'd done it—completed my #OneElleOfAChristmasDayInLondon. And if I got 553 more followers, I'd be first to hit fifteen thousand and win the challenge—unless @CallMeClaraT managed something major. And it was unlikely, because I still had more posts to upload that I knew people would love.

And I felt...nothing.

I'd spent the past few hours trying to figure out why.

Turns out, I hadn't just used my account to put on a face to the world—I hadn't been honest with myself either. I'd done all of this to win the challenge—to prove to myself I could make it work, all on my own. And I guess so I could finally feel like I belonged somewhere. In Alpine Peaks. As part of Dove's crew. Prove it to Mom and Dad too.

But now what I really wanted was... Well, it was hard to admit.

Because if I were honest—really honest—what I think I really wanted was...Fred.

Whoa.

I'd thought it.

I like Fred.

And the more I thought it, the more I knew it for certain.

"I like Fred."

I said it out loud to the empty room.

And instead of letting him know how much I'd loved today—in fact, had loved every day we'd spent together—I'd ditched him at the station. All for this stupid challenge.

I knew when he'd told me about Eve. It was selfish, I know, but I didn't feel happy—I felt jealous, and sad, and like I was the biggest dork in the world for paying more attention to this challenge than to how I really felt.

Nothing like realizing how much you like someone because you find out they like someone else.

Everyone always says to do what makes you happy, but if you don't ever stop to figure out what that is, you sure can make some bad decisions.

I flicked TV channels trying to give my brain a break. 2:53 am. Great. My train back was at 7:51, so less than five hours to fall asleep, wake up, and get there.

I spread out on my bed, a message coming through from my brother. A selfie? Nick must have been on the hot chocolates.

I'd been worried earlier when he'd asked if I could give him a call—it had sounded urgent. But when I'd called back a few hours later, he hadn't picked up, and now if I wasn't very much mistaken, it looked like he'd gate-crashed his way into that Christmas party he'd found. He'd sent it to me yesterday to see if Holly might like it, but we both figured she'd want to stick to her plan, so I thought he'd decided not to mention it?

I messaged back.

👏❄️⛷️👏☃️

What I'd give to talk with him right now—like we used to. When he had my back.

Wanting to feel closer to him, I went to Holly's profile. Wow. So many photos on the grid—and no wonder. Their day looked awesome—Nick looked like his old happy self, like back in Nashton. Out of habit, I checked Dove's too—her last post had been announcing that I was in the lead, but as I reread it, I couldn't help feel that, despite her smiling photo, something sounded like she wasn't pleased.

Was I being tired and paranoid?

@OneElleOfATime has taken the lead—but has @CallMeClaraT got time to post her way to victory? It would take hundreds of you to >>> her way and click that follow button 😉

Was she telling them or asking them?

And @tooblessed2bstressedxx had been at it again on my arty post of the Carnaby Street lights. It had started with @_Beckywiththemediocrehair_'s super-nice comment:

That shot! Chef's kiss! Is there anything you can't do?! 📷🔥

But @tooblessed had replied immediately.

@tooblessed2bstressedxx: why yes. How about an original photo?! 😘 xoxo

But this time someone I didn't recognize had replied.

@betterplayliststhanyou: @tooblessed2bstressedxx... when you can't even manage an original comment? The door's that way ➡️👋

Yeah—they'd gone there. I bet they were going to get the same treatment too. I clicked on their profile, but it was locked down on private. And I don't know if it was their support, or the tiredness, or the mess I'd made of the day, but I decided to finally do it. Message Clara.

Hey. Nice work with the challenge. Hope you're not feeling too blessed to be stressed??? And don't pretend you don't know what I mean.

I pressed send before I could wimp out. I didn't know what she was playing at, but I didn't like it. Not one bit. Still, I knew sleep would make everything a bit better—so I did what I always did when I was desperate to fall asleep.

I went on a deep dive.

Real deep. On Clara's profile. On Dove's. Even on @thingsthepeakgirlsdo and @tooblessed2bstressedxx.

And the more I looked, the more something just...didn't... feel...right...

"Would you like us to ring back?"

Words.

Need. Words.

What time was it?

"You did say you wanted a seven a.m. alarm call, miss?"

"Arrgheuthankayou," was all I managed before dropping the handset down—must apologize later. If it was seven—my train left in less than an hour!

I plugged my phone in that had died overnight and jumped in the shower—not sure why when I could only get dressed in yesterday's clothes that I'd slept in. The only evidence that I gotten any sleep was the massive pillow crease in my face, but I'd woken up knowing exactly what I had to do.

Today I could finally win the challenge.

Or I could try and do something even harder.

CHAPTER NINETEEN

Holly

Three Days till Christmas

I was worried. Very worried.

That's why I'd ditched getting ready for the parade later and taken a ride with Pete to pick up some groceries from the farm store, where I could get away from my worries for a bit and check in on Dominic the reindonkey instead.

Ruby's date with Temi should be about to start—but I hadn't heard from her all day. I mean, she could just be a capable human who didn't need to message every minute to help her deal with this... Buuuuuuut, I had no idea what that felt like.

I'd sent her loads of good-luck messages anyway and reminded her to use the mirror I'd gotten her (and magic pebbles now that the universe had confirmed what power she held).

There was no way I was going to make her worry by telling her what had happened on my end. That I'd woken up to the worst message yet from Woody.

And Fred was being weird. Very weird. It was December the twenty-second, and he'd sent me a voice message saying he needed urgent help with our Macbeth English assignment. That wasn't due in for fifteen days.

Apparently he had to make a start on it now as his sleep was being affected as he—and I'd listened at least ten times to check I'd gotten it right—"kept dreaming he was a modern Lady Macbeth." Worrying on so many levels. We'd agreed he'd ring me at one to go through it. And I was still mad at Elle, in fact, peak mad now that she was ghosting me. She'd been online as well—her true colors must be finally coming out.

I'd never tell the others, but when she'd refused to speak, I'd left her a message to tell her I didn't think ditching Fred had been cool. And since then, things had only gotten worse. A lot worse.

I took my millionth look at what Woody had sent. I'd screenshot it and couldn't stop myself going back to it, despite how much it hurt.

> Hey Hol. Hope you're having THE BEST CHRISTMAS EVER. Thought you'd like to know Elle isn't into someone else—she's into me. Got a date today. 😊😊

At first I didn't believe him, but he'd followed up with a screenshot of her message she'd sent him yesterday, so I knew he was telling the truth.

You free tomorrow? I can come to you. E.

So that was why Elle couldn't talk to me. She was busy with Woody. And was that why she'd challenged me to "snag a hot Christmas kiss under the mistletoe," so she could move in on Woody guilt-free? I really thought I'd been getting to know her the last few weeks, that in real life, she was even better than online. But clearly she'd just been taking me, and all my friends, my family, for a ride to win this stupid challenge.

I'd messaged her again telling her we needed to talk, urgently, but like the whole world, she was ignoring me. I really thought Elle wouldn't have gone there—not after Ruby filling her in. I'd made Ruby admit she'd told her the other day. And wasn't Elle with Logan anyway?

Guess she was as bad as Woody.

Fred must never find out—he'd be heartbroken. EURGH.

It was such a massive mess. One thing was for sure though—Elle clearly never meant me to find out. If I'd thought we were becoming friends, at least now I knew I'd been very much mistaken.

It wasn't just her brother that was good at secrets after all.

I thought after our chat yesterday about what he'd really been up to, things might have changed between Nick and me—but this morning, even though we were meant to be having Christmas pancakes together, he'd disappeared, again. Maybe he was just like Woody after all? Maybe I was only good enough until something better came along. And even more bizarre, in the living room, a Christmas tree had appeared (which I'd already named Spruce Willis due to its stocky action-heroesque branches). Jess and Pete had brought a spare one home and said they didn't want my decorations to look lonely.

It was like the world was all upside down.

But what problem to sort out first? I let them all whirr around my head as I watched Dominic have his mane washed. Never had one reindonkey looked so happy. But I had to dash back to make my call with Fred.

When we got home, Nick had reappeared and was watching *Gremlins* in the living room. He was impossible, even if he did look all sorts of cute under his Christmas blanket.

"Don't suppose you're making tea?" he shouted through. Luckily he couldn't see my suspicious look. First Christmas songs, now hot drinks?

"Well, I wasn't..." Their kettle was so annoying—you had to heat it up on a cooker like it was 1825.

"No worries...I was just in the mood for a Christmas tea." I'd brought some with me. That's how cool I was. "And no one makes it like you..."

How would he know? He'd never had one. But with the day I was having, I wasn't exactly in a hurry to chat to Fred about Shakespearean bloodbaths, so I agreed. Plus, I could ask Nick outright why he'd ditched me this morning. I had my suspicions—was I right that he only spent time with me when Elle told him to? And as if I needed another sign I was on to something, when I carried his tea through, he'd gone again.

He wasn't in his room either. Way to make me feel great.

Surely he'd have told me if there had been a Dottie situation?

Dominic was genuinely the only normal one today.

I left Nick's tea in his room, settled down on Elle's bed with my laptop, and waited for Fred to dial. Which he did. On the dot.

I was determined to be as happy as I could—Fred worrying about homework was not normal, and I had a hunch maybe he was sadder about what happened with Elle than he was letting on.

"Punctual?!" I laughed as I hit answer. Fred's timings were normally just a rough guide.

"I'm a changed man." It was so good seeing his face again—he always cheered me right up. Although...

"Erm, why are you in my room?" I recognized my wardrobe, all my photos pinned around it—and the now fully dead poinsettia. RIP, Stemi.

"Ah." Fred rubbed his nose, buying time. "Did I not say?"

I shook my head.

"Sorry. My bad. I just thought if you needed any notes or anything..." He lifted a pile of books. My books.

"Er, okay." I spotted what he was wearing. My favorite "Son of Nutcracker" top. "I'll guess I'll let you off as Mum said you've been repping the jumpers."

He opened his eyes wide and wiggled his fingers just like Will Ferrell did in the film. We both cried, "Santaaaaaaa!" and creased up.

"Maaaan, I've missed you guys." I wiped my mascara from where I'd just smudged it laughing too hard. "I mean, I'm having the best time here." Don't mention Woody. Don't mention Woody. "But if I ask Nick one more time to watch *Elf* with me, I swear he'll poke a Christmas tree in my eye."

Fred shook his head. "Ohhh, I'm sure he wouldn't." Trust Fred—so nice, he'd stick up for someone he hadn't even met. "Anyways, your pictures from New York looked brilliant." He'd been on my account? That wasn't like him. "Elle showed me." Elle. Ah. Just hearing her name made me feel fidgety. I really didn't want to talk about her if I could possibly avoid it. "I heard you lost your list? Did you...survive?" He was grinning.

I put my hand on my chest.

"Well, it was touch and go, as you can imagine. But then Elle's brother, y'know Nick, the man who hates Christmas, pulled it out of the bag. I'm still in shock now!"

Fred laughed, but not as much as I hoped. "I'm sure he doesn't hate Christmas..."

To be honest, I wasn't sure about anything to do with Nick anymore. But I was annoyed at him for going back to his usual disappearing ways and wanted to make Fred laugh, so I decided not to hold back.

"Fine. Not hate...just the word anti-Christmas springs to mind." I thought about Nick's Christmas tea going cold. His poor, lonely tea. "He's probably allergic to tinsel. And all things festive and fun. Seriously, he makes Colin-human look like Father Christmas. A really jolly Father Christmas."

But nothing. Not even a reaction.

"Some people are just different, Hol," was all Fred said. Well, he was fun today. Lady Macbeth must really be getting to him. "I thought you said you liked him?"

"Hell-o. I catch flights, not feelings, remember?" I laughed. But I wasn't sure if I was laughing because it was funny, or because there were moments in the last week where that had really felt possible. Not that I would tell anyone that. Not even Fred.

"Er...I didn't mean like liked, but...yeah, of course." Fred coughed awkwardly. "So, erm, did you see Elle finished the full fifty things? It was hec-tic!" I fixed a smile on my face. The less said about her the better—now I knew what she was like, there was no way I was going to let her hurt Fred too. "I really think she's going to win—isn't that amazing?"

"Well, London looked amazing. Or at least, an amazing opportunity for picking up followers, if not hanging with you." I rolled my eyes.

"Come on, Hol—are you just jealous that"—he tried to wiggle his eyebrows even though we both knew he couldn't and only his hair moved—"your Queen of Christmas crown might have been taken?"

He was joking, but when it came to Elle, I was not in the mood.

"It's not that, Fred..." How could I not say the thing I was trying to not say. "Just people like her work in different ways to us. Challenge or not, her life will bounce back to being perfect."

Bounce back to forgetting about all of us.

"Okaaaay, not sure I know what you mean. But...moving on..." He picked up a book and put it down. "How are the challenges you set for each other? Wasn't there a surprise for your mums riding on it?"

"It's a no from me." Unless that kiss with Harry Styles did happen. Fred looked surprisingly disappointed—he really did love my mum. "I know. It sucks—I'd love something nice for Mum." Although if Fred was insisting we talk about Elle, it did mean I could try and find out about something else. Nick's reaction to the challenge.

Did that have anything to do with her ditching Fred? "Don't suppose Elle said anything yesterday about Nick, did she?"

Fred just shook his head. "Nope. No. No. I don't think so. So anyway, what about the list YOU SENT ELLE?"

Why was he so obsessed with that list? Especially when I actually needed to speak to him about something important.

I lowered my voice in case Nick came back.

"One sec, Fred. This is important." Even though I was done with Elle, and Nick was heading that way too, now me and my friends had been dragged into it, I wanted to get to the bottom of what was going on.

"Issss itttt?" he asked like he didn't believe me. "Did I mention I actually don't have that long?" He looked at his wrist even though he didn't wear a watch. "Maybe ten minutes?"

I better get to the point then. We hadn't even started on his work.

"I'll be quick, I promise..." Here went nothing. "You know Elle made out something's been going on with Nick?"

"Uh...Holly, I don't think..." Fred looked horrified—I knew he hated getting involved in other people's stuff, but I had to carry on.

"Yes, remember? And the thing is, she's right. He told me. Well, bits of it." I'd promised Nick I wouldn't share what he told me, so I wouldn't, but I was hoping that even being vague might make Fred jump in with some ideas. But nothing. "I have no real idea what's going on between them, but what I do know is those two really need to talk. When I showed Nick the #FestiveFifteen challenge posts, he fr-eaked out."

Fred didn't even let me finish. "All right, Hol! You don't need to tell me. Probably just talk to Nick about it?"

He was properly flustered. Why wouldn't he hear me out?

"Talk to him? But that's the problem! No one in their family talks about anything! That's why they're all mad about him disappearing. He hasn't even told Elle that—"

"SO THE LIST." Fred yelled it so loud, I actually jumped, despite being on the other side of a laptop. Why did he keep looking behind him like there might be a ghost of Christmas past lurking?

Christmas past...

"That was it!" I actually snapped my fingers as the thing I knew I wanted to talk about popped back into my head. "How was this not my first question? What happened with Eve?! You never gave me the full story, and I tried to get the details from Ruby, but she's gone AWOL."

"Erm." Fred looked peak awkward. Like he really wanted to end this chat and get on to the lighter topic of Shakespearean murders. "Maybe she just didn't see her phone?"

"For three hours?"

He shrugged.

"Naaaah, it's weird. She better not be avoiding me. I need full details on her HAWWWT DATE. If you get news before me, message me. Immediately. You know what Rubes is like. She probably wouldn't even admit she liked someone after being married for ten years."

"I'm sure you'd be first to know." Tough crowd today.

"Well, I'm last to know what happened with Eve...sooooo, tell all?!"

And finally, finally, I got Fred to smile again. A happy, relaxed smile. "She sat by me the whole way back..."

"And?" If something had happened with Eve, that would mean he was over Elle—and I'd be into it!

"And...it was really good to speak to her again."

"And..." I left it blank for him to fill in. But he didn't.

And still didn't.

And he was still smiling.

"Fine, Fred, I'm not saying anything here. Nothing about that massive grin on your face. And I'm definitely not saying anything about karma being pretty cool if getting dropped by Elle—in what was a total sly move, if you ask me"—uh-oh, it was coming out—"after spending all day doing her stupid challenge led you back to the love of your life."

"Bit harsh, Hol..." But he didn't know what I did. About Logan, and Woody. And I couldn't pretend anymore.

"C'mon, Fred. Putting followers over someone who has been an actual friend? Who literally gave up a whole week for her?! Not cool."

"There are always two sides, Hol..."

"Sure. But for what it's worth, I reckon as soon as she wins the challenge, she won't even think of us ever again. And you want the other news flash." It was all coming out now. "Y'know Dove? I honestly think she might be mean, Fred. Like mean mean." He dropped his head in his hands. I sipped my Christmas tea. "If Elle ever asked what I thought of her, not that she'd care what someone like me would think, I'd say she was a total wet wipe." My ultimate insult. "Genuinely—don't you reckon she sounds like she doesn't even want Elle to win anymore? It's all so messed up. I'm mean, I've loved being here, but I can't wait to get back home to some normal people." But Fred had slumped forward.

"Fred?" Nothing. "I meant that in a good way. Normal is good?!"

And then it dawned on me.

Woody. Maybe that's why he was being weird?! And why Ruby was buying time to talk to me—they already knew about what had happened with Elle.

"Oh, Fred. It's okay..."

"Is it?" he mumbled up from having his head in his hands.

"Yeah. I know about Elle liking Woody. And frankly"—I smiled to let him know that sure, it had hurt like hell, but I was going to be okay—"they're perfect for each other. Honestly, for all Elle's online nice-nice, in real life, she's just as two-faced as him."

I thought Fred might look relieved.

But he didn't answer. And as the silence grew, I noticed something.

Where he'd leaned forward, something about my room wasn't as I'd remembered.

It had been covered in even more decorations. And had three little hats hanging up.

"What did Elle have left to do, Hol?" Fred's muffled voice came up even though his head was still buried in his folded arms. "From your list?"

Weird timing, but he clearly needed an answer.

There was only one thing I could remember. "I think only the, err, Christmas Cracker?"

There was a moment's silence before Fred said, "Bingo."

And the two wardrobe doors behind him opened slowly.

Standing there, in matching elf onesies, two unpopped party poppers in their hands, were Ruby and Elle.

And a fed-up looking Colin. "Surprise."

They couldn't have sounded more miserable. Oh. My. Actual. God.

They'd heard *everything*.

"This was meant to be it. My Christmas Cracker." Elle pulled her party popper.

They looked like they might be about to cry. Or shout. Or both.

Everyone had heard *everything*.

Well, except Nick, which would have completed my worst luck ever.

"I guess this is the moment I make my excuses and leave." Or not. Nick crawled out from under the blanket over Elle's desk. "Ruby, Fred, great to meet you." He waved up at the screen as he walked toward the door. He couldn't get out of here quick enough. And I didn't blame him. "Thanks for the invite. Shame..." But he didn't need to say it.

Shame I had ruined EVERYTHING.

CHAPTER TWENTY

Elle

Never let them see you cry. That's what Mom always says.

But then Mom had never been crouched in a closet hearing what I'd heard.

"Well, that went well." Fred broke the silence.

After all this, *that's* what Holly thought about me? I knew from her message she was pissed about me leaving Fred, but did she really think I would stab her in the back like that with Woody? That I cared more about likes from strangers than I did about her friends? About her?

Just because I posted all the good stuff, did she really not think I had feelings in real life?

Ruby took the laptop from Fred and turned it around so Holly could see what we'd spent the day doing—decorating her whole room with stuff I'd picked up on my way home this morning.

I'd walked back with it, and it had weighed a ton. I'd made the decision to cancel the Christmas market, put my challenge on hold, and try and make it up to everyone here instead. Holly's message last night had only made me more determined. I'd only not replied so this could be a real surprise. A Christmas Cracker like she loved.

And what was all that stuff about Nick and me needing to talk?!

Did it have anything to do with the reply Clara had sent earlier?

Ruby put the laptop back down. Holly was just saying something that sounded like "errmmmeeeggaaddd" on repeat.

"Just putting myself out there with this, but I sort of feel like the moment might have gone?" Ruby put an arm around me and gave me a squeeze. She already knew exactly what had happened with Woody. After going to Fred's this morning to take him an apology sausage roll, I'd given Ruby the Snow White mirror decoration I'd picked up for her and explained everything.

"We *were* going to watch *Elf* with you." I was glad Ruby was talking, as I didn't know if I'd shout or cry. "Go transatlantic with the tradition. Elle's idea."

Holly was gawping like she'd seen a ghost. "Is that..." Her face was now so close, it was taking up almost all the screen. "It that why I couldn't get hold of you?"

Ruby nodded. "Uh-huh."

"But aren't you meant to be on a date?" Her face was scrunched-up trying to process it all. "Like...now?"

"Postponed." Ruby put her hands in her front jean pockets. "I thought seeing as we weren't seeing you till after Christmas, this came first."

"Oh, Rubes?!" Holly sat back on my bed. Well, more of a collapse really. "I'm so sorry. SO sorry. You should be there! And you know I didn't mean what I said?! And, ahhh." She dropped her head in her free hand. "And Fred. I mean...it all makes sense now. I couldn't understand why you were going on about that list..." Fred was looking at the floor, even more awkward than normal. "You sounded worse than me!" But no one laughed.

At least I knew now Fred was with Eve, so I didn't have to humiliate myself by thinking me and him could be anything more.

How had I been so stupid as to let myself like him? This was exactly the reason I didn't let people in anymore.

"But, Elle?" Holly finally made eye contact with me. "I don't understand. Why would you do all this for me if you were getting together with Woody?"

I totally got why she was so angry—I would be too. But she had me so wrong.

"I can explain... It's not exactly how he said."

"Well, it looks very much like it." She held up her phone. "According to this..."

I leaned in to take a look—he was such a slimeball for sending her that.

"But that's because he's a total creep..." I got mine out to show her the whole thing. "I didn't send him one message, I sent him two."

I held up the second one I sent, straight after, when I'd realized how someone like him might take the first one. I knew he might say no, but I'd rather that than him not realize I was 100 percent team Holly.

Holly read it out.

"Sorry—full disclosure, all I need is a selfie with you, for a challenge. My US friend is into British boys, and while I personally much prefer personality, and, y'know, boys who don't cheat on their girlfriends, I thought someone like you wouldn't say no to more attention."

At least I had the proof to clear that up—I didn't want Fred thinking it either. But when I looked around, he'd gone. I didn't even hear him slip out.

"We were going to tell you." Ruby looked sullen. "Before the film...so you knew what was going on." She laughed through her nose. "I even thought you might find it funny. Woody's got a track record with trying to ruin movies, after all..."

Holly shook her head. "But he got in there first. He is just..."

"THE WORST," we all said together. Finally—something we agreed on.

"Elle—I am so, SO sorry." Holly looked mortified. "I should have absolutely chatted to you before I'd jumped to all sorts of conclusions. Especially before trusting Woody over you." She looked on the verge of tears. "Just the thought of Fred being on his own, and the whole mistletoe kiss thing for me, and then this message came through, and then...well. Sorry. That's what I'm saying."

I could tell she really meant it, so I was going to accept it—I hadn't exactly made some great decisions myself. "Don't worry, Hol—I guess a lot of it was my fault. Like the whole Logan thing all over again."

Holly looked even more stumped. "Logan? As in boyfriend Logan?"

She shot Ruby a look, but Ruby looked as confused as her.

I had to laugh. "Logan as in a guy I've never met and probably never will after I told him to back off."

But Holly and Ruby weren't laughing—they looked kind of horrified. And did they just mouth *Fred* at each other? "Wait, you guys thought I was cheating on Logan...with Woody?"

Wow, they really had a high opinion of me. But as they both apologized and tried to explain, something else was gnawing at me. Something about the screenshot Holly had showed me of Woody's message. "Hol, can you show me that picture again?"

I squinted at the screen.

What was it that wasn't sitting right?

Screenshot of the message. Eleven per cent battery.

Camera roll underneath it.

A couple of photos back was one of Dominic.

And then...

"You've met Grams?!"

"Erm..." Holly's whipped her phone out of view. "Well..."

Mom hadn't mentioned anything?! But then it suddenly all clicked.

And it clicked HARD.

"Nick took you, didn't he? That's where he keeps going, isn't it?! I *knew* it wasn't band stuff, but wow..."

And although Holly didn't say anything, we both knew I was right.

And so was she—Nick and I had some *serious* talking to do.

CHAPTER TWENTY-ONE

Holly

I was such a mug. A massive Christmas mug, full of idiot tea.

Thank goodness Elle and Ruby had let me explain—and apologize.

Nick though, he'd fled the scene and was nowhere to be found. No wonder, after all the stuff I said about his sister—and him. So great that I'd said none of them were normal. Well done, me.

And now it was only a matter of time before he found out Elle knew about Dottie. He'd trusted me—and this is how I'd repaid him.

I had to find him—and fast. Which is why, for the past hour, I'd been risking full-Bambi sliding over as I power marched through the snow. But I'd had company—I'd only just gotten off the phone to Ruby. Ruby, whom I needed to make this up to big-time. She was looking for Fred—turns out he didn't want to get back with Eve at all—he'd been smiling because he'd admitted to Ruby that seeing her made him realize he was finally, finally over her.

Could I have gotten things more wrong?!

There could have been a chance with him and Elle? And I'd ruined it by assuming she was with Logan, never actually getting her to confirm it. And now Elle only had a day left in Little Marsh, and even if she did like Fred, she thought he was with Eve.

Well. Done. Me.

I'd messaged Fred a billion sorrys then a million thanks, but none had been delivered.

And as I finally got to my destination, I just had to hope that being numb from the knees down, and even my bra being soggy with snow, was all worth it. When I saw the car park, I started to panic jog.

But phew.

My gamble had paid off. There was Nick's car—in front of the broken sign and falling-down Christmas tree. But his engine was running.

"Nick!" I yelled, not caring that I looked like some sort of snow creature emerging from the wilderness. "Nick!"

I tried to run faster, but I couldn't bend my knees, so I looked like a knitted triangle waddling. But I had to hurry—he was moving toward the exit.

"WAIT!" I lunged at the back window, giving it such a massive thump that a heap of snow fell off. But it did the job; his brake lights flicked red.

"Holly." He looked surprised. "What are you doing here?" I couldn't exactly say he looked happy to see me.

I tried to stop my teeth from chattering long enough to get words out. "Just thought it was a nice day for a stroll." Was I shaking from nerves or hypothermia? I looked around the empty slush-filled car park. "Take in the sights."

"You want to get in?" He popped open the door, and I climbed in.

So this was it. My big moment. I'd spent the whole walk, when I wasn't on the phone, planning exactly what I needed to say—and I'd come up with the perfect thing, which I'd now completely and utterly forgotten.

"So, erm." I pulled off my mittens with my teeth, bits of snow-frost flying across the car. "I just wanted to say sorry. And thanks. Sorrythanks." Nick was staring out of his window, so I had no idea what his face was doing. "For the surprise." I rubbed my hands together, trying to bring them back to life. "I can't believe you were going to watch *Elf*. I mean, it's the *right* decision, but still...the whole thing, I really appreciated it."

Ruby had explained the reason he'd disappeared this morning is because he'd been out getting festive American snacks he and Ruby remembered from my list. Nick turned to me. "We don't need to do this, Hol."

"Well, I think we do. Because I'm sorry. For what I said. I don't think you're allergic to tinsel." Dying inside at having to say that. "Or the anti-Christmas." And that. "I've actually been having the best time. I don't know why I was being such a..."

"Wet wipe?" He raised his eyebrows.

"I think I was raging you'd left your tea..."

I gave him my biggest smile, but I didn't get one back.

He flicked his key ring. "Look, we don't need to go over it. It's all good."

But it felt very far away from good. It felt like it never had before. Awkward and weird.

And I was about to make it even worse.

"There's something else, Nick." This was going to be awful, but I had to be honest. "I promise I didn't mean it to happen, but...Elle knows about you seeing Dottie."

I tried not to notice his shoulders slump. "I see."

"Are you mad?" I twiddled with my mitten, not really wanting to hear the answer.

"What would the point of that be? We'll never see each other again in a few days." Yup, he hated me. Nick stuck the keys in the ignition and flicked the engine on. "Although, I did think you'd promised you'd keep it between us?"

I fully turned in my seat to look at him, but he wasn't making any eye contact.

"I did. And I'm sorry. It really was a stupid accident. With my stupid phone." The stereo sprang into life—"Blue Christmas" by Elvis was playing. Literally one of the saddest Christmas songs ever—even the radio hated me.

"Well, this Christmas-hating Grinch is heading home." He put the car into gear. "Want a ride?"

I needed to clear things up. I didn't think he was a Grinch—he just didn't love Christmas like I did.

"We're just different, that's all." I was trying to sound positive. "I like Christmas one way...and you just... Well, not everyone has to be into it, right?"

Nick looked at me, holding my eye contact like he was hoping I'd understand without him needing to spell it out. But I didn't know what it was that I was missing here.

"If that's how you see it." He ran his hands around the wheel. "Elle will be back tomorrow, so I'm sure she'll be a lot more fun. A lot more festive."

Yup—he really, really hated me. Just as I'd finally figured out I really, really liked him. And it was all my fault.

"Well, at least she won't do a double take at this." I pulled at today's Christmas jumper. "And songs like that..." I was cross with me but taking it out on him. "The little bits—they all add up, y'know? They make people happy. And if you ask me"—he wasn't, in fact he was hardly saying anything—"they make Christmas Christmas."

Nick tilted his head as if I was the one not understanding.

"And you don't think there's something more than that?"

"Nope. Actually I don't."

"Cool, then..." He nodded.

"Cool," I said back.

"Oh." He reached into the back seat and grabbed his rucksack. "Meant to say, this morning I stopped by the station and picked this up."

He was holding something I never thought I see again—my notebook. "Holly's Book of the Best Christmas Ever." Had he really managed to track it down?

"Th...thank you." I couldn't believe he'd found it. Although something about it felt like it was written from another time.

"No problem. Now..." He flicked on the indicator. "Are you coming?"

But I had to say no. Because being around him was just making my head hurt.

I thought me and my book had the perfect Christmas all figured out—but nowhere in my plan had there been anything about meeting a boy like Nick.

CHAPTER TWENTY-TWO

Elle

I was wearing a onesie and looked like a total mess, but Little Marsh was just going to have to deal with it. I'd needed to speak to Nick—in private.

I'd shouted to Sophie that I was taking Colin out, so my disappearance wasn't quite so bizarre. I'd almost tripped on a twin, I ran out the door so fast. Colin-human saw I was upset, and I gave him the "pretend not to notice" look, which, after a discreet double thumbs-up in my direction, he did admirably. He really wasn't anywhere near as bad as Holly had made him out to be. But twenty-five missed calls later, and I'd still had no answer from Nick.

By my thirtieth attempt, I was getting stressed—so stressed, I took desperate measures. I messaged Logan to ask if Nick was with him. But his reply just made me even more confused.

I couldn't believe how wrong my last full day in the UK had

gone. Although one good thing had come of that total fail. I knew Holly was right—about Dove.

I'd asked her why she'd said what she had—and she told me exactly what had happened in Cheeze Pleaze. And it sounded... off. Way off.

And something about Clara's reply had made me feel extra weird.

> Hey Elle. Long time no speak. Honestly? It's not me. Tbh I'd noticed too. I know you might not believe me, but maybe if you speak to someone close to home it'll make more sense? Good luck anyway. But not too much! I don't wanna be the SpillMoreTea of this competition.

She'd even followed up.

> PS, I never really got to say it before... but sorry.

What was niggling at me so much? Was it that Clara was being friendly? Even after everything that had happened? And who did she want me to talk to? Dove?

Even thinking about winning that newbie comp back in Nashton, and beating @SpillMoreTea, made me feel uneasy.

I'd gone back through Clara's comments to try and figure it all out.

Maybe her message was legit. Looking back on her comments, they weren't *that* bad, even if I'd taken them that way. It was only really @tooblessed2bstressedxx that had been causing all the problems. But were they definitely not the same person?

As I searched through, trying to make the pieces fit, Dove posted the daily update. I was on 14,698 new followers to Clara's 13,987.

I was so close—but I didn't feel smug about it.

I think I'd actually felt happier when Clara had been out of my life. Competing with her hadn't made me feel better about what happened, it had just made me sad thinking about it. She'd been the reason I'd stopped trusting people, and even though I thought beating her would be the best revenge, what had really made me happy was finding people I could trust. Who liked me for me. People like Ruby and Fred.

And not like Dove.

Something was going on, and I knew it had something to do with what I'd seen that night in London. If only I could figure it out.

It might backfire in a major way, but I needed to be brave. Ask the one person who might know.

Hey Dove—just a heads-up that I'm not going to have that selfie for you. I also wanted to ask—do you have any idea who's behind tooblessed2bstressedxx?!

I wondered if she was going to kick me out of the competition for not getting her photo? And I wondered if I cared? I couldn't believe what a difference seven days could make.

I marched past the village Christmas tree all lit up and twinkling, to the swings where Fred had given me not-moldy apple juice, and tried Nick again.

On my fiftieth attempt, he finally picked up. "Sorry..." He fiddled with the settings. "I was...driving. You okay?"

"I'm okay." I sniffed. "Cold, but okay."

"Well, I think it's fair to say that didn't go how we'd planned." Nick laughed. That's the thing with my brother—even when things got bad, he knew how to make me laugh.

"Note to self. Never try and do a surprise again."

"You're telling me. I think I tore a ligament, crouching for that long." I laughed, but I knew I needed to be honest, tell him what I'd found out. "Oh, and for the record, I am not *allergic to tinsel.*"

"For the record, you don't need to explain." I paused. It was so long since the two of us had really spoken, and right now hearing his voice felt like being home again. Which is why it sucked that I might be about to ruin it.

"So..." Here goes nothing. "Holly met Grams?"

"Ahhh." Nick said it like he'd known it had been a long time coming. And the timing couldn't have been more perfect, because messages started popping up from Holly—but I swiped them away to read later.

"That's where you've been going, isn't it?" He didn't answer. "Nick?" He moved the camera around—he was parked in the row of stores near the Alpine Peaks Residential Home. "Why didn't you just say?"

"C'mon, Elle." He sighed. "You know what Mom and Dad are like." I did. "Being with the band, doing sports, got them off my back. If they knew I was spending all my time here..." He shrugged. "Well, let's just say I'm not exactly in a hurry to move again either."

I couldn't help but laugh—I had no idea we'd been playing the exact same game.

"Jeez..." I should have figured it out. "I had no idea." Suddenly it all made so much sense.

"And you're not mad?" He looked genuinely concerned I was going to freak out at him.

"Well, I'm mad you didn't tell me. But not mad at what you did."

"Really?" He looked relieved.

"'Course. Do you not think I hate those 'so what plans have you got for the weekend' dinnertime interrogations too?" We smiled at each other. "But do you really think they would have minded that much?"

"Well, I didn't, which is why I tried to tell them once—about a month after Grams's fall. But they sat me down and started asking if I really thought I could be happy in Alpine Peaks."

Whoa—it was like the exact conversations they had with me. "That's when I knew it wasn't worth it. And I didn't want to risk any more drama." I knew what he meant. Grams had been furious with our parents for moving us yet again, and they were only getting things back to how they were. "Grams needs to focus on getting better, not on me." He squirmed. "I had to tell her to keep my visits secret from Mom and Dad, since they were stressed about my 'commitments'... I know, I know..." He shook his head. "Not cool."

"TBH, I'm mainly impressed you managed to pull it off." Getting one past Grams was not easy. "But you could have told me?"

Nick rubbed his face. "I swear, in my dysfunctional little way, I was trying to make things easier for you—not worse..."

And I believed him. That's what had been so hard to understand about the whole thing—I had always thought we looked out for each other, but now it made sense.

"So is that when you 'joined the basketball team'?" I did full air quotes.

Nick shook his head, bemused. "Wow, you really do know it all..."

"Only just." When Logan had replied earlier, he'd been as confused as me—apparently he and Nick weren't even on the team together, they just practiced. That's when I'd realized I really had no idea just how deep Nick had gotten into whatever he was covering up. "But if you'd told me, I might have been able to help? In *my* own dysfunctional little way."

But this time, he didn't smile back. "Seriously, Elle? I didn't want to drag you into it." His voice dropped. "You had enough of your own stuff going on. Y'know..." He waited, like he was trying to figure out what to say. "With what happened."

"You mean back in Nashton?" He nodded slowly—he was the only person who knew how hard the trolling had hit me.

He cleared his throat and stretched back in his car seat. "Look, there's something I haven't told you." He looked out the window and took a deep breath. But nothing came out.

But he'd been honest with me, so it was time for me to repay the favor. Tell him why I'd really been so upset, what had really happened—and what I thought could be happening all over again.

"Nick, there's something I need to say too."

He laughed through his nose. "No, Elle, this one is serious."

He took another deep breath—but I knew mine would be bigger, and if I didn't say it now, I was worried I never would.

"*It's about Clara.*"

We matched each other word for word.

Turns out we both had secrets—and no idea it was the same one.

CHAPTER TWENTY-THREE

Elle

"So let me get this straight." I'd let Nick go first. "You were together? With *Clara*?!" I thought Clara and I had shared everything—I had zero clue that included my twin brother.

I stood up off the swing. And sat back down again. I didn't know what to do with myself. None of this made any sense.

He had his eyes closed but was nodding. "Uh-huh. And can I just say another sorry? To add to the hundred I just did?"

"And you didn't tell me..." He'd explained, but I still wasn't dealing. "Why?"

"I dunno. You guys were just so close—and I didn't want it to get in the way. For it to be weird."

"Weird like this, you mean?"

"Kind of exactly." He was wincing so hard, I wasn't sure if he was ever going to open his eyes. "Look, I'm so sorry, I should have told you. But Clara asked me not to, and I wasn't sure it was going anywhere, but then it did. And then it felt like we should have told you months earlier." *Months?!* "Then when things started to go wrong, it actually felt better that you didn't know—saved you getting dragged into it all."

"Months?! And what do you mean *wrong*?" I had NO idea about any of this. "Excuse me while my head just explodes over here."

"I dunno, Elle. This guy told her I'd gotten together with one of the girls in another band."

"And did you?"

"Never." I knew when Nick was lying—and this wasn't one of those times. "That's not my style. I think he just liked Clara and was trying to cause trouble. But once she had it in her head, it was like she couldn't trust me." I could tell from the way he was squirming, this wasn't the whole story.

"Sooo, what happened?" I swallowed, still in shock. "With my ex–best friend you were seeing behind my back."

"Thanks for clarifying there."

"So..."

"You really want to know?" I nodded even though my mind was already full-on melting. "Well, eventually I told her that she either had to trust me, or it was over. And she chose that. After almost a year."

"A year?!"

"Yup." He scrunched his nose. "That was probably something I should have mentioned too."

"Well, at least I know why you started to disappear—because you were spending time with my ex–best friend you were seeing behind my back."

"And again." But he sighed. Hard. "I really liked her, Elle, I promise..."

I could tell there was more. "But..."

"But she really hurt me. So when she changed her mind and asked to get back together, I said no. I couldn't risk it. She hadn't trusted me, plus I hadn't liked how it had come between us—you and me—either. And that's when she got really mad." Things were rapidly making sense. I kept silent so he'd keep talking. I needed to know everything. "She accused me of never liking her—and told me she was going to get me back." He stopped. "Which I thought meant nothing until..." He chewed his lip. "Until I saw that she was part of this challenge thing. Holly showed me. That's when I knew I had to tell you. I'm so sorry, Elle—all this time I've been trying to stay out of your way so I didn't cause problems after what happened, and now..." He dropped his head in his hand. "Now I feel like I've just made everything even worse."

But I didn't know what to say. All these months, I had no idea why Clara had suddenly turned on me back in Nashton—and now I knew. It wasn't me, or because my old account did well. It was all to do with Nick.

It didn't make what she did any less painful. It still meant she'd never been the real friend I thought I'd had, but at least now I understood.

It was weird. Part of me was raging that Nick hadn't told me. Part was shocked I'd never guessed. But mostly I was relieved. Relieved to finally know and maybe to have my brother back too.

And judging by his face, maybe he felt the same—he looked like he'd been struggling with this for months.

It made what Clara had messaged earlier make a whole lot of sense. She'd wanted me to speak to Nick—get things finally out in the open.

And she'd finally said sorry.

I really did believe that it wasn't her behind whoever was trolling me now. Maybe it was one of the other competitors or a random after all?

"And here was me thinking you thought my account was stupid?" I shook my head.

"Stupid? I think you're the bravest person I know. Putting yourself out there like that."

"You don't even follow me, Nick."

"You really think that? I've always kept an eye on it. And who do you think @betterplayliststhanyou is?!"

So *he'd* been my new follower calling out tooblessed? Despite everything, if he weren't a million miles away, he'd be getting one hell of a hug right now. Well, alongside some major calling out.

But it was my turn to be honest—about what happened in Nashton. So I told Nick everything. That he didn't need to worry—Clara had already gotten her revenge out of her system on my old account. That the trolling hadn't been random comments like I'd told Nick—they'd been personal, mean comments...about him. Clara hadn't been trying to get at me—this had been about Nick. But I'd closed it all down and never told Nick. It was my way of protecting him, so he'd never had any idea. Maybe if I had, things would have been so much simpler for us both.

Nick was furious—more at himself than Clara. He blamed himself for everything, even though no one could have predicted how she would react. I guess, looking back, I had been so involved with my old account that maybe I was partly to blame. Maybe I'd pushed her away just when she needed me the most. And I'd never let her explain either.

As much as I hated hearing it all out loud, admitting how bad things had gotten, I felt so, so much better for it to all be finally out in the open. And to have my brother back on my side.

Which is why I told him the other thing.

The decision I'd made after my call with Holly. That even if I won the challenge, I wasn't joining Dove's crew, however big it made my account. I didn't need a friend like Dove—I never had.

Ever since I'd said yes to her, all she'd done was ask me to do more things, tell me I wasn't doing well enough. And the more I'd tried to impress her, the more I hadn't felt good enough, the more the distance had grown between my online life and my real one. If I hadn't been trying to prove myself to her, none of that stuff with Woody would have happened. And I wouldn't have messed things up so much with Fred.

I'd wanted to win the challenge to feel good about myself, to feel like I fit in. But here, in Little Marsh, I'd felt that without even trying. And I'd loved every second. Because Ruby, Fred, Holly, even @_Beckywiththemediocrehair_, had reminded me how having a friend was meant to feel. That it was okay to just be me.

And now I was leaving in just over a day.

I kicked the ground. Guess we might as well get everything out in the open. "You like her, don't you? Holly?"

"Ermmm, were you not there for the most awkward call in the world?" Nick laughed. "She said it herself, Elle. Flights, not feelings." His dropped his head onto the steering wheel. "And yes, I can't believe I just said that either."

He didn't deny it though. And grilling him further was going to have to wait. Because I'd realized I wasn't alone. Someone was walking across the park. Lit up by the Christmas tree at the edge. Hands in their pockets, head down. Coming straight to me.

Someone I recognized.

I promised to give Nick a call later, said bye, and tried to unscramble my brain. Urgently.

"Twiglet?" Fred held out his open packet.

"Most people call me Elle." Wow, I was getting good at nerdy jokes. Fred smiled at me—his big, warm smile that made me feel like however much I'd messed up, things could be okay. I couldn't believe this was one of the last times I'd ever see him.

"They help with anything...even freezing to death on a child's swing."

Could they help with really liking the nicest guy in the world—just as he got together with his ex? I took one in case. I was such a doofus. I should have just been honest with myself about how I'd felt about him, because now it was too late.

He sat down on the swing next to me. "That's one good thing about living somewhere so small." He looked around. "Nowhere to actually hide."

"I'm not hiding..." I instinctively protested, but my mind didn't have a clue what it thought—did I want to avoid him because of the Eve situation or spend every second with him, because I really, *really* liked him? "I was..."

"Going for a mid-evening swing." Fred smiled, but he wasn't throwing shade. "I do it all the time."

He pushed himself forward. When I first met him, Fred had seemed so awkward. Cold, maybe. And now, in this most awkward of all awkward moments, he seemed to know exactly what to say to make all the weirdness disappear.

Oh hell. I liked him *so* much.

"I didn't message Woody, you know." My words hung in the air. I didn't want to get in the way of him and Eve—but I did want him to know the truth. "Well, I did, but not like that." Fred's swing squeaked, but other than that, nothing. "Holly knows everything. He was just playing it to get at her. I think the whole thing was the final straw she needed to finally get closure."

"So that whole call wasn't a total disaster then?" Fred smiled. "Hol getting over Woody has been a looong time coming."

I took another Twiglet. And another. In fact, I had four more before I built up the confidence to say what came next. But it mattered to me that Fred of all people knew, despite what he'd heard, not everything about this trip had been just for the challenge. Sure, it might have started off like that, but being around Fred and Ruby had made me care less and less about being the Elle that was online—and more about being me.

I really didn't care what *everyone* thought anymore—I cared what *they* did.

"You know what Holly said—about me caring more about follows than I do about you guys?" Deep breath. "You do know... that's not true?"

"Uh-huh." Fred nodded, accepting what I was saying without making me feel even worse.

"Good. 'Cause I wanted to say thank you. For this week... For the introduction to Twiglets..." I didn't know where this was going. "For throwing popcorn. For hanging out with a potential murderer who likes waffles and nails."

"As if you're that." Fred snorted.

"Well, that's what you thought when you met me, right?"

"Maaaybe?"

"Fred, they were your exact words." I nudged him in his ribs, but he didn't notice due to today's extra woolly sweater. "It's just, trust me on this, most people tend to like online Elle way more than this one." I tugged at my onesie. "I mean, who would click follow for this?"

Fred dragged his feet on the ground and brought himself to a standstill. "Can I be honest with you, Elle?" No one ever asked that for anything good, but I nodded anyway. "I literally couldn't give a flying turkey about it. Your OneElle thing. In fact"—he stood in front of me—"if anything, I actually find the whole, 'here's my hot drink, y'all'"—oh jeez, he was *terrible* at American accents—"thing kind of annoying. Like, if you love it THAT much, drink it? And yesterday...yesterday was so *nearly* one of the greatest days ever, but having to do it whilst sprinting really took the shine off. And by the way. These"—he grabbed the metal swing chain—"are one of the biggest reasons kids go to A&E."

"Well, I'm sorry to have been so..." I couldn't think of another word. "Frustrating."

At least I knew why he liked Eve and not me. "You're not!" Fred dropped his head on his hand holding the chain. "But you are now. Do you really not know what I think?"

I think my silence told him the answer.

He stood back up straight. "Okay, fine." He looked me square in the eyes. "What I think is..." He took a deep breath in and out. "You're great, Elle. And even more so at times like this, when you're not trying to be."

"Are...are you joking?" I couldn't tell—I looked down at myself. "I'm wearing pajamas in public."

"And you've got Holly's mum's coat on." Great job, me. I must have grabbed the wrong one. "But that's *exactly* why I'd swap online Elle for real-life you any day."

"Well, I appreciate that." I stood up and started to walk toward the path. I knew Fred was trying to cheer me up, but I was done with today. "But I think you might be the only one who thinks that... The swap thing, not the coat thing."

Fred looked genuinely confused. "Are you kidding me? Holly's told me about all your friends she's met." He must have gotten mixed up. "Don't look at me like that...look." Fred got out his phone and turned it on. "Yes, I'm on three percent battery, but I'm counting this as an emergency, okay?"

After scrolling back through his messages, he held it out. "See...read this."

It was a message Holly had sent him a few days back. "*Wish you were here. But seeing as you're not, I made an AMAZING friend of Elle's. Literally the coolest! She's dressed like a pot roast. And is more obsessed with Elle than me?!* So that's one."

Gosh—that must have been Flo at the party. Maybe that's why she started to follow me a few days ago?

"Oh, and another. *No jokes. Has anyone other than Ruby asked after me? Because I almost couldn't order at this burger bar because the dude has soooo many questions about Elle.*"

Rohan? Was asking about me? I thought his comment the other day was just a fluke? Fred looked up. "Not to mention actual Temi. Who Ruby told me—and I quote 'has made me swear I'll sort a hanging out before Elle leaves." He nodded. "True story. She's got a Christmas card for you. I've seen it."

Well, this was all news to me. I'd always thought the only people who might like me did because of my account? But had focusing on being internet Elle just made me miss what was right in front of me all along?

"Fred...I..." But I didn't know what to say. Maybe today hadn't been a total mess after all. "Thank you. Really. Thank you."

He didn't know it, but he might have changed everything. I felt like a weight had been lifted. Dove or no Dove, I suddenly knew being back home was going to feel way better than it ever had before.

I looked at Fred's phone again and smiled. Which only got bigger when a sudden burst of earlier messages all popped up one after another all from Holly.

ELLE IS NOT WITH LOGAN I REPEAT
ELLE IS NOT WITH LOGAN IGNORE
EVERYTHING WE SAID!!!!

EXCEPT WHAT I JUST SAID, AS THE LOGAN THING IS TRUE.

Weird, but fine—and nowhere near as good as the last one:

ALSO I'M A WET WIPE!! I MEAN YOU KNOW THAT. BUT I TOTALLY GOT THE WRONG END OF THE STICK. AND I'M BUYING YOU SO MANY AIRPORT TOBLERONES IN CELEBRATION OF YOU FINALLY BEING OVER EVE!!!!!!!!!!!!

But then his phone died, and I couldn't be sure Fred had even read them.

But I had.

Fred wasn't with Eve.

So this was it. My last chance.

But with time running out, was I finally going to be brave enough to tell him?

CHAPTER TWENTY-FOUR

Holly

"Hi, Dottie." I put down two hot drinks on the small table by her armchair. The communal breakout area was full of visitors.

She held up her arms for a hug, her massive cardi dangling. "Well, this is a treat. You must have just missed Nick!"

"Oh, well, at least it means I get you to myself." I said, leaning in to give her a big cuddle, hoping she couldn't hear the cover-up in my voice.

"Everyone..." Dottie clapped to get the attention of the room. "Look who's here—my British friend!"

The lovely people in the room actually clapped. I waved like a really cold, damp celebrity who was on the verge of full-on ugly cry.

I'd realized three things in the car park. How I really felt about Nick.

How I really felt about messing it all up.

And that I was probably going to have to have at least three toes amputated.

"You live with total dudes, Dottie."

"I know. They're a good bunch." She picked up the tea and took a sip. "Boy, am I going to miss this when you're gone! *Finally* someone who knows their way around a tea bag." She slowly clinked it back on to the saucer.

Yup. This was a good idea. Dottie was cheering me up already. I pulled out the Christmas card I'd made for her, and she put it up on the table lovingly, like it was a work of art.

"Don't tell anyone"—she pushed her glasses farther up her nose as she looked at it—"but these stopped being useful about a decade ago, but they look *so* good on, I can't bear to part with them." She pursed her lips. "One can never know when a handsome gentleman might appear..." She laughed, her naughty, playful laugh. Wow. When I grew up, I wanted to be like her. "So, have you got any more photos for me?"

With me holding my phone as close as I could without touching her face, I showed her some of the ones from New York. Every one made me feel both tingly with happiness and also really sad. I really had had the best time.

I went further back, showing her my whole week here. Grinning when I met Dominic, laughing as Nick and I flopped into a ball pit, dancing at Dean's party... Some of my best-ever

Christmas moments, and yet none of them had been part of my plan. They'd all been because of saying yes to Nick.

"Are you okay?" Dottie put her hand on my arm, concerned as my voice had started going all tight and wobbly.

"Just some biscuit going down the wrong way."

I opened Elle's account so we could talk about something, or someone, else instead.

"Look at that girl." Dottie zoomed in, very close. Like "here are her nostrils" close. "All around the world on her own two feet."

I felt genuine relief she didn't ask me to explain what "heavenly AF" meant in the comments.

She stopped on the video of Elle singing next to the Christmas tree in Trafalgar Square. I could hear Fred going full opera beside her.

"Now I know you wouldn't break her confidence, but do you think Elle might have found someone special under the Christmas tree?"

I smiled and shrugged. "Who knows? But it would be the best Christmas present for me if she had."

I'd messaged Fred a zillion times in the hope I could tell him about Logan before it was too late. I'd told Elle he wasn't with Eve too in case that helped, but last time I'd checked, neither of them had read anything. "Okay, well, tell me one thing." Dottie delicately tapped her finger on my leg. "Do. You. Approve?"

I nodded. Hard. "What's the biggest way I can say yes?" We both laughed.

"Well, in that case, I can't wait for Elle to come back and tell me all about him or her... And it's not long now." Yup, just over twenty-four hours till Elle was here—but Dottie had a glint in her eye. "And you? Is there anyone special in your life?" She gave my knee a squeeze. "I always think love at Christmas is like no other time of the year. It's when I met my husband, y'know."

I tried to smile, but the timing wasn't exactly great for this one. "It's a big, fat no, I'm afraid."

On the plus side, I *had* definitely moved on from Woody. I couldn't wait to tell him exactly what I thought of him—but I was going to do that in person. Way more enjoyable.

On the not-so-plus side, I had caught both flights and feelings and was fully into Nick. And he thought I was a Christmas-loving, list-making, untrustworthy lunatic and wanted nothing to do with me.

Dottie was looking at me like she thought I had more to say. "Not even someone over here? No one caught your eye?"

I shrugged my shoulders. I wasn't about to explain the Nick situation. "'Fraid not."

"Well, I'm not going to pretend my heart hasn't broken a little." She leaned back in the armchair. "I love love. Always have, always will. But love at Christmas, well, it's just something...magical, isn't it?" I made a noncommittal noise of agreement—that's exactly what I thought. "And far be it from me to put ideas in anyone's head, but..." She paused. "I haven't seen my grandson this happy since... No. I just haven't seen it. Plain and simple."

Sorry, what? Her grandson?

I shook my head. What little was left of my brain wasn't following. "I think there are some crossed wires here, Dottie."

"So you haven't seen Nick with a spring in his step? A big smile on his face?"

"All I've seen is him being very patient with me—hoping for me and my Christmas-obsessed ways to be gone. I think Elle made him my surrogate babysitter as I dragged him around everywhere."

"You really think so?" She took one more sip of tea. "From what I heard from their father, it's been Nick making all the plans. In fact, wasn't Nick the one who made all those calls to pull those strings to get you into that fancy schmancy party in Brooklyn?"

He did what?! I thought that was a fluke?

"But I thought he hated all that stuff?" She must have got mixed up.

"Is that so?" Dottie pushed herself slowly up and out of the chair. I reached over to help, but she brushed me away. "The day I can't get out of this chair is the day I want to be left in it. Now..." She lowered her voice. "Can you keep a secret?"

"I'm not sure I can handle any more." I said it as a joke, but Dottie chose not to listen. Turns out she wanted to sneak me to see something in her room. I already knew what to expect, as I'd seen in some other open doors along the corridors. My main takeaway was, "Who knew brown could come in so many shades?" For a fellow Christmas enthusiast, I had a feeling it might make me a bit sad.

But when Dottie opened the door to her room, it wasn't what I'd expected at all.

It didn't come close.

It. Was. Incredible.

"Dottie?! You live in a...grotto!" She beckoned me to follow as she shuffled in. There was a small tree on her table, lights strung up all around her bed. Her sheets were cute polar bear ones, and there was an actual sack of presents by her drawers.

"Only Charl, and some of the nurses and cleaners, know. Isn't it glorious?"

It really was. Even her walker had been decorated with miniature Rudolphs. They must have blown the budget on this room—maybe that's why they only had enough for five pieces of tinsel for the rest of the building.

"How did you wangle this?" It put my bedroom to shame.

"Wangle?" She looked confused.

"Yes—you know. Make it happen?"

"No, I understand you, dear." But her face hadn't changed. "I just thought you would have worked it out."

"Worked what out?"

And just then I saw the picture in the corner. The picture of Dottie and Elle and Nick and their family all around the tree.

And the yellow bobble hat stuck on her bedpost—that matched the three in my suitcase from Brooklyn.

And the candy cane garland that matched the one Jess had put up yesterday in their kitchen. When she hunted high and low for a second one, she couldn't find it.

Right now I was the one who needed a walker to hold me up.

"Believe you me, he's always been this way." Dottie flicked a button, a "Christmas Is a Feeling" sign lighting up, Santa waving alongside it. "But from the moment he told me about you, I knew you'd be the one to help him get his spark back."

Nick had done all this?!

All this work to give his grandma the Christmas she loved?

"You know." She pulled a thin piece of paper out of her pocket—the strip of photos of Nick and me in the snow globe in Brooklyn. He must have gotten a copy and just given it to her.

"Thanks to you, I don't just think he's fallen back in love with Christmas." She put her soft hand on mine. "I think he's fallen in love with the British girl who made it happen."

CHAPTER TWENTY-FIVE

Elle

I told him.

I told Fred I'd met someone who'd made me laugh till I ugly-cried.

Who made me feel hot even when I was a hot mess.

Who somehow always looked cute even though he only ever wore 3D sweaters.

Who didn't just make me like him—he made me like *me* more.

And all Fred said was, "He must be quite a guy." So I'd had to tell him I meant him.

And then we just stood and stared, neither of us knowing what to say.

Thank goodness Colin was there. If he hadn't tugged to go for a pee, we might still be there.

"I think he needs a wee," Fred said. That was his reply to what I told him. To saying the person I liked was him.

"I think he does," I replied.

"It's snowing," Fred then said.

"It is," I replied. Turns out truth bombs can really mess with good talk.

We then continued to point out things that were happening for at least a minute.

"Colin is still peeing." (Me.)

"It's cold, isn't it?" (Fred.)

"Have we given Colin pee anxiety by watching him?" (Me.)

"Probably." (Fred.)

The pee really did go on for an alarming amount of time—Colin stopped and started at least six times. Then we walked back to the house and dropped Colin off.

But I wasn't ready to say goodbye to Fred. Not now that I'd told him how I'd felt. Not now that I had nothing left to lose.

I was glad I did it though—even though nothing had come of it.

Even though saying goodbye for real in just over fourteen hours was going to be extra hard. In fact, we'd made a pact—whatever happened in the next day, neither of us could use the G-word.

And seeing as we couldn't say it, we'd decided that meant that the evening couldn't be over yet. So we went to see if we could sneak in to see Ruby in the pantomime again.

And we did.

And Fred laughed even louder than before.

And Temi gave us a hidden wave when she was onstage.

And this time I knew the parts where to join in.

And we told Ruby how great she was, and Temi grabbed me after to give me a Christmas card, just like Fred had said. My first real one this year.

And Fred walked me home for the second time in one evening. And he asked me what I wanted for Christmas, even though I had no answer. And we still didn't talk about what I had said.

And it had started snowing again—and I'm not sure why, but it looked way cuter over here. Was I getting romantic over frozen water now? Wow, that boy really must have done something to me.

And despite the walk home being quite long, it took not enough time at all.

And Fred said, "Ta-ra," and, "see you tomorrow," as we couldn't say the other word—plus he knew anything super-British made me smile.

And I had supper with Sophie and Colin and the twins. And it wasn't nuggets, much to their disappointment.

And then I came up to my room to figure out what on earth just happened.

And now I can't stop replaying it. And...

I sat up. This was no good.

I had hardly any time left here. Going over and over it was not going to cut it. Saying not-goodbye to Fred wasn't enough.

I pulled on my coat—checking it wasn't Sophie's—and my scarf. And then took it off, went upstairs, swapped my sweater for one of Holly's that said "Jingle My Bells," and wrapped up all over again.

Not going to lie. It looked cuter than I thought. Even with my hair pulled up.

As I headed out, I looked at my mentions. Ha.

People were losing their minds. Guess I *had* gone slightly off brand.

But who cared if I lost followers? And not just because I hit the fifteen thousand new ones I'd been so desperate for. Yes, technically I'd won the challenge—but I wasn't going to post my winner's post till I was ready.

I needed to word it just right.

And I knew just what to say after Dove had finally replied to my question, just before I'd hit fifteen thousand.

> Sorry babes? No idea? You just keep doing you boo. I'm sure they'll quit—unless you're telling me you want to drop out? (there's no shame in second place) xoxo

That's when I'd realized exactly what was going on. Clara's message had made me put it all together. Reminding me what happened with my old account.

Everything made so much sense.

The last-minute invite from Dove to the competition. But how every day since I'd said yes, she'd only seemed to make things harder. What I'd seen in London. That both her and @thingsthepeakgirlsdo followed an account I recognized. More than one.

That's what Clara had made me think about—how I'd beaten @SpillMoreTea. Or as I knew it now—one of Dove's old accounts. Dove Moore. It was actually @SpillMooreTea. The same account she mentioned in her house—the one about British stuff she loved. How had I not realized sooner?! And that day on her stairs, when I'd told her @NoWayNoelle was me, she must have decided it was payback time. Just what she'd been saying on the phone when Holly overheard her. Dove must have only asked me to compete so she could see me lose and shut my account. But when I'd done better than she thought, that's when she'd stepped things up on her other account: @tooblessed2bstressedxx. The *xoxo* on her message had been the final piece of the puzzle.

I didn't know what I was. Flattered she'd go to all that effort? Pissed I'd gone so far along with it without realizing? I couldn't figure it out. But what I did know was that I wasn't scared—this time my account wasn't going anywhere. I had things to say, and someone like Dove wasn't going to stop me. I'd messaged her to ask to meet when I was back.

And in the meantime, my winner's post was going to say

thanks to all my followers for the support—but no thanks to joining @thingsthepeakgirlsdo. Instead, I was going to use it to tell my followers that if they weren't here to help support each other rather than tear each other down, then they could click unfollow. And that from now on, my account was getting a whole lot more real. Who cared if I was left with three people? They'd be three pretty damn good people.

It was the first time I'd actually felt excited about my account since I'd started it. And I'd already done my first post that felt more like me. From now on, I only cared about the people I cared about. Which is why I was grinning over how happy I'd made @_Beckywiththemediocrehair_. It was a multiple-comment situation—she was freaking out! I told her I'd DM with full details.

I'd come here to the UK to show everyone my take on British Christmas. But all I'd shown them were arty shots of drinks, and twinkling trees, and London in full festive flow. Stuff anyone could have done. But this post, these pictures—they were the real story.

The things I was going to remember, really remember, from this, one of the best weeks of my life, were the things in between.

Hiding in a cupboard with Ruby's knee in my face. Laughing at a bald Father Christmas.

The twins trying—and failing—to put a red nose on Colin (human).

Christmas wrapping with Holly's mom.

Ruby trying to get a paper crown over my freshly zhuzhed hair.

Fred reciting historical facts on the London Eye. Fred clinging to a plastic penguin on the ice rink. Fred being...Fred.

In every single photo with him, I looked happy.

Especially the one I'd just posted, the one of us on the train—I'd put a giant Christmas tree over his face, but if you knew, you'd know.

I pictured Holly's face when she saw it—we'd have to talk about it when I landed tomorrow.

I looked at the caption again and laughed.

Move over, Harry, I found the best one. 🇬🇧🖤

Dove wouldn't approve. And I didn't care one bit.

Fred—he wouldn't even see it. Although that was the point. It wasn't for anyone but me. This wasn't shady. It was about honesty.

And it was time to take it up a notch.

I stepped on Fred's "Merry Christmas" doormat and rang the doorbell.

His mom answered. Time to turn the full charm on. "Sorry to trouble you, Mrs...." Why didn't I know his last name?! "Fred's mom." Great. "Is Fred in?"

She looked kind of shocked. "You want to see Fred? My son, Fred?"

I nodded. "Uh-huh. If that's okay?"

She looked at me very suspiciously. "I'll just go get him." She kept her eyes on me as she backed away, slightly closing the door.

"MUM?" A voice that sounded very much like his little brother was shouting behind the door. "WHY IS THERE A FILM STAR ASKING FOR FRED?"

Hardly, I looked like a melting Popsicle.

Feet thundered down the stairs then there was a shout of "shut up" and what sounded like a door being shut very quickly.

And then the front door opened wide.

And then there was Fred. Even though he didn't have shoes on, just socks, he stepped outside into the snow, and pulled the door behind him.

"Sorry about them."

I shrugged. "Sorry about calling your mom Mrs. Fred's Mom."

He smiled. "Not many people know this, but that was actually her christened name."

"Jackpot, then." I smiled. It was weird how being around him made me feel so comfortable—yet so totally out of my depth all at once.

Fred glanced at my watch. He didn't mean for me to see—but I did. It *was* a strange time for me to be here though.

"Everything okay?"

"Sort of." Boy, I was nervous. "I mean, yes. I just... Well, I just realized I had an answer."

Fred scratched his head. "An answer?"

"To what you asked me earlier." He looked none the wiser. "The best Christmas present thing?" We'd talked about it on the walk back from the pantomime.

"Ohh." He finally remembered. "And?"

"It's like you said..." I laughed. "Well, not the sausage roll part. The part about the best ones being ones that when you think about them, they make you smile again and again." Jeez. I swear I used to think I could be cool. Must add "becoming massive cheeseball" to things that have happened here.

"So?" Fred looked like he was trying to figure it out. "What then? A recording of Carol? Endless supply of Dairy Milk?"

Well, here goes nothing.

"No, Fred." My heart was beating so hard, I swear my voice was wobbling. "I was more thinking this."

And as "Last Christmas" played in his kitchen, and his little brother pushed his face so hard against their front window, his nose went yellow, I leaned forward and kissed Fred.

And he kissed me back—and it felt...brilliant. Despite being terrible at first (through to fifth) impressions, Fred was completely perfect at first kisses.

Christmas rom-coms had *nothing* on this.

And when we finally stopped, we both took a second, as if neither of us could be quite sure that actually just happened.

I wanted to be cool, but my face had other ideas. It was at least 99 percent goofy smile.

"Well, that was something."

Fred nodded. "Yup. Definitely something."

"Want to go for a walk? In the snow?" I pointed at the snow—I don't know why I did that. "For old time's sake?"

"I think I could maybe do that," he said, which would have been a lot more believable if he didn't sprint to grab his shoes in record time.

As we stepped off the doorstep, Fred reached out and took my hand in his.

"That was brilliant, by the way." I felt him squeeze my hand. "A bit like you."

And as we walked, I knew one thing. No disrespect, Santa Claus.

But this amazing boy had just given me the best Christmas present ever.

Happy, happy holidays indeed.

CHAPTER TWENTY-SIX

Holly

On the walk home from Dottie's, I hadn't just looked at photos of my trip. I'd looked back at all the ones I had from Christmases over the years.

I must have looked bizarre—a human ball of wool trudging along the side of a road, who kept sliding into snowy ditches because she was staring at a phone while laughing and crying to herself. Often at the same time.

Christmas really was the best time of the year—which is why it felt so weird to be feeling so sad. And so on my own. It was almost Christmas Eve Eve, and normally I'd be wrapping Naomi's presents with her (/for her) while we watched a film with Mum.

Uh-oh. Danger of a second wave of tears.

I really wanted to tell Mum how much I loved her (maybe Colin too), so I rang the landline, but Colin-human answered. Mum was out, but it was weirdly nice to chat to him and get the updates on the twins. In fact, something about hearing his voice made me tell him slightly more than I meant to. That I was missing home. A lot. They say "a problem shared is a problem halved," but this was more "a problem shared is a problem awkwardly coughed at." At least I managed to not admit that, despite how lovely everyone here was, I was petrified at the thought of not being home for Christmas. But, when I put the phone down, I did feel a tiny bit better—especially as another call came through within minutes.

"I'm sorry, but that face does NOT look okay."

I'd never felt so happy to see Naomi—even though my credit was only going to last a few minutes. I adjusted my headphones and deployed an emergency smile.

"Honestly, I'm fine."

Naomi pulled her hair up. She looked so tanned and happy—and there was my face in the corner. Blotchy, cry-y and potentially slightly blue—rushing out the house to try and find Nick was one thing, forgetting it was minus twenty was another.

"Honestly, you're not." She lifted her sunglasses, squinted at the screen, and put them down. "Where are you anyway? It looks like...a blizzard."

"It kind of is."

Naomi sipped something that looked like a green coconut with a straw in it. How could a drink make me feel worse?! Still, at least she was having a good time. That was the main thing.

"Jelz."

"Hardly." If she was jealous of bad weather, she could have come home and not decided to spend Christmas on a beach. "So?"

"So what? I can't just ring my sister for a catch-up?"

"Not at seven a.m., I mean, I didn't even know you could do words at that time?"

She shrugged. "Couldn't sleep." She fiddled with one of her curls that had popped out of her ponytail. I knew her well enough to know this fidget meant there was more.

"And?"

"Fine." One of the best things about my sister was how easily she caved. "Colin might have messaged me." Ah. "Human, not dog. And I might have decided that a dorm with six other people wasn't where I wanted to make this call. He's worried about you, Hol."

Cringe.

"Well, he doesn't need to be."

"'Course. And in unrelated news, waterproof mascara is a thing, you know."

IGNORE.

"So how is Koh Samui?"

"Excellent." I could see the sea behind her, so I already knew that was the answer. "As is the subject change."

But I didn't want go into the details of how much I'd messed everything up on this end.

"Aren't you missing out on having breakfast with turtles or something?"

Naomi sat up, taking off her sunglasses as she moved into the shade.

"No, Holly. I'm not. And believe it or not, talking to my little sister who is on her own and having a tough time is exactly the one thing I want to be doing right now."

And something about the way she said it, and knowing that she meant it, made me miss her more than ever.

Oh, great. Wave three of intense tears. At least my mittens were incredibly absorbent.

But it was like the tears took off my mouth brakes, and without meaning to, I told Naomi everything. About how everyone had been right about Woody. About how scared I'd been about the move. About how I'd gotten Nick all wrong. And jumped to conclusions about Elle. And told Fred all the wrong stuff about Logan. Let alone being rubbish to Ruby. About how I'd come here for the perfect Christmas, but right now I felt miserable, not magical, and couldn't figure out how to get it all back on plan.

"So." Naomi listened to it all, not interrupting me once. "There's a lot to unpack here..." She paused. "But let's take a moment to celebrate that when you're back, you're finally going to tell Woody to do one. That has been a LONG time coming."

Between the sobs that were still popping out when I didn't expect them, I high-fived her back at the screen.

"Good." Naomi smiled. "Can my Christmas present be watching out the window?"

I nodded, trying to smile, but she could see right through it.

"C'mon, Hol, I *hate* seeing you like this. We all make mistakes, admittedly some more than others, and actually...not me so much..." She laughed. "But you were trying to help in your weird little way. And now you've apologized to everyone, so *please* stop beating yourself up."

I semi-nodded. I knew she had a point, but until I saw Ruby and Fred, even Elle, in person, I was going to feel rubbish. "And looking on the bright-normal-Holly-Isn't-Christmas-Magical side—doesn't all this drama mean you're actually in the running for one of the best things about Christmas?"

"Chocolate?"

I felt Nay roll her eyes even behind her sunglasses. "Nope—a holiday romance."

This time I properly laughed. Well, it was that or cry even more. As if that could happen.

"Bit late for that, Nay. It's almost Christmas." Naomi waved her hand in front of the screen.

"*Details!* The ball's in your court, Hol. If you like Nick, you've got to at least tell him."

"We'll see." Which meant no way.

"Of course. 'Cause you'll be so much happier kicking yourself about it for, what...oh yeah. FOREVER." She had a point, but I didn't want her to know it.

"Mooooving on. Any ideas what I can wear for the Snow Ball?"

Her mouth dropped so far open, I could see at least three fillings. "Sorry, what?!"

How had I not told her?

"Uh-huh. I know Twenty One Pilots is playing and everything." Her face didn't move. "Christmas Eve. We've got backstage tickets. That's why I'm not back till Boxing Day like you. Didn't Mum say?"

"Nope." Naomi looked genuinely impressed. "I mean, I knew you were staying longer, but Mum failed to mention it was because you'd decided to go break the internet."

I shook my head. "Enough of the guilt trip already. I checked first, obvs. Maybe the real question is why you're choosing a turtle over her turkey?"

Naomi wrinkled her nose. "Well, it's not exactly like that, is it?" She picked up some sand and let it spill through her fingers.

Oh no. *No way*. She wasn't going to try and make me feel bad when she was the one who started it. "Isn't it? You're away till the twenty-sixth too, don't forget."

"Yes, Hol. And Mum gave me all that 'exciting times at Colin's' speech as well." Speech? "But there's no way I'd not be home if I could."

"But I thought you were having pigs in beach blankets?" Or whatever she'd called her sunny Christmas Day plan.

Naomi lifted her sunglasses. Her eyebrows were down, and she was squinting, but not because of the sun—because of me. "No, Hol. None of my friends are going to be here. As in NONE. I'm not going to know anyone. *A-ny-one.* I ABSOLUTELY want to be home—I just couldn't afford the connecting flight until then." So it wasn't a choice? "I messed up my booking, and I'm gutted."

"So...you don't want to be there?"

Naomi laughed. "I mean, it's not exactly a hardship." She smiled. "But no. Give me hanging up our stockings with you guys, leaving out a half-pint of Baileys for 'Father Christmas' and your terrible charade of David Beckham any day."

Oh. I'd really got that wrong. "So. Mum?"

"What? You think she's going to tell us to come home 'cause she's missing us?" Awkward. That's *exactly* what I'd thought. "Hol." Naomi actually laughed at me. "She knew full well you were worried about Christmas being crap this year. And how much it means to you—so of course she wanted you to go to America. But do you *really* not think she would have loved a Christmas at home together maybe even more?"

And that's when it hit me. Full on in the chest.

That's when I finally got it. What Nick had been saying all along.

I'd come here for the best Christmas, but no matter what I

did, I was never going to cross "Having the Perfect Christmas" off my list.

Because having the perfect Christmas wasn't the one with the coolest lights or biggest parties—it wasn't about exactly following my traditions and making sure everything was perfect.

It was about hanging out with the people you love.

Ruby, Fred, Mum, Naomi and Colin. Both Colins.

Getting to do all the small, funny, chocolate-filled, pajama-wearing, normally-too-ridiculous stuff you didn't get to do year-round.

Saying yes to things you never would. With the people you loved the most.

Having Christmas Day at Colin's wasn't what would make or break it. Nor was seeing Central Park in the snow, or even going to the Snow Ball—it was having my amazing friends and family around.

And as I stopped still, taking in what Naomi said, my feet wet, freezing, and a mile away from Elle's house, I realized something.

I could spend the rest of this holiday doing all the things that I thought *should* make me happy. Sticking to my plan.

Or I could try and actually make the best Christmas happen. For everyone.

I told Naomi she was a genius, said bye, and allowed myself one last list.

It was time to make it up to my friends.

Tell Nick I was sorry—he'd been right all along.

And hope the magic of Christmas could help me pull off something really special.

CHAPTER TWENTY-SEVEN

Holly

Two Days till Christmas

The hall had filled up, but Dottie and Nick were nowhere to be seen.

Elle had done amazing work talking Charl into convincing Nick that Dottie had been asking to see the band play outside Peakstown City Hall tonight. So Nick, being Nick, had dropped his plans to take her there.

All Dottie knew was that I'd asked her to get Nick out of the way for a few hours. She had no idea why, but she loved being part of anything she thought could be a bit of an adventure. I'd clocked her putting on her sexy glasses before she left—she was a permanent mood.

"Have you got everything you need?" I looked behind Dean at the makeshift setup we'd pulled together.

"Think we're good." Dean looked pretty impressed with what we'd managed. "Although cut us some slack on whatever comes out..."

I'd cut Au Revoir Hairs all the slack in the world—despite their big gig tomorrow, they'd pulled out all the stops to be here. Dean had been incredible from the moment Elle had put us in touch. Blake too. It was the first time a band had ever played in Alpine Peaks Senior Living hall, and we were a bit worried it might blow the power—but, well, that was part of the fun.

And it looked amazing. With Pete's permission, I'd raided their spare decorations—when I'd told him why, he was confused but into it. He'd even made a comment about hoping Nick hadn't been keeping anything from him, as for such smart people, him and his sister really could miss that all they wanted was for him to be happy. I nodded vaguely and made a note to try and tell Nick if I got the chance.

It was such a shame Pete and Jess wouldn't get to see what I had planned—but it was the Snow Ball tomorrow, so they were pulling an all-nighter. Pete offered that whatever I took, I didn't need to bring back, meaning the decorations could be here for keeps—they wouldn't just brighten up the home this year, they could do it every year. I was going to leave the ball in Nick's court about whether he told them why I'd done what I'd done. But I couldn't help but feel if they were all honest and didn't try to second-guess each other, they might all have some surprises.

Nice ones. Like the five-year lease I'd seen Jess reading this morning, for new premises for their business.

I hadn't just tackled the hall—Charl and some of the staff had helped me decorate the reception area, the corridor, the bathroom, anywhere we could get access to. I'd even helped some of the residents put up bits in their rooms. The whole atmosphere felt so different—like something special really was in the air. The only thing I hadn't found was someone to put on the Father Christmas costume to give out the presents. They were only little dollar things I'd picked up from the shop in town earlier, but I'd wrapped them all and, hey, a present is a present. I looked around the room, everyone chatting and taking in their new-look home. This wasn't how I imagined spending today. I was meant to have gone to my first parade and worked my way through anything else I'd missed—but I already knew this was way better.

I couldn't wait to see Dottie's face. Or Nick's.

I'd thought long and hard and figured this was the best possible apology I could think of for Nick. Showing him I finally understood what he'd been saying—and giving him the best Christmas by giving his gran one.

"SHHHHHHH."

Charl was peeping out of the curtain, her finger to her lips.

"They're coming!"

Was this sick feeling adrenaline—or terror? Nick and I

hadn't spoken since the car park yesterday. He had no idea what I'd been up to all last night, or that after about ten minutes' sleep, I'd spent today rushing about on a total mission. And he had no idea how much my plans had changed either. I hurried over to the big double door, flattened myself against the wall—which was quite hard in a full, 3D pumpkin costume. Not exactly festive, but it was the only one available two days before Christmas.

I flicked the main lights off, leaving the hundreds of lights I'd strung up twinkling away.

An *oooooooooooooohhhhhhh* rolled up from the room, even some claps.

My heart was thudding so hard, I couldn't tell what was circulation and what was the sound of Nick's footsteps.

I heard him chatting to Dottie about their trip before he stopped to read out the sign.

"One second, Grams... Have you seen this? 'Could all residents come to the breakout area for a mandatory...Christmas Sip and Share, four p.m. December twenty-third'? That's today? Now?!"

He sounded confused—excellent.

I really hoped this worked. If it didn't—well, it would be the most awkward taking down of decorations ever. Crying while dressed as a pumpkin would be a new level of tragic.

But they were heading in!

I looked over at Dean, my hand up, ready to give him the sign. Everyone shut up, except Max, who was ninety-eight, couldn't really see anything, and was chatting loudly about how if he had his time again, he'd love to try and be on *Drag Race*.

I saw the light under the door change.

It was now or never. I dropped my hand. Right on cue, the band started playing.

"Dorothy Miller," Dean purred into the mic in his smoothest voice as the door opened. The room broke into applause. Dottie and Nick both froze. "Please, could you come and join me onstage...?" Dottie looked up at Nick as if he knew what was going on, but Nick shook his head, his mouth hanging open. "We would like to start the Alpine Peaks Senior Living Christmas party in style. Would you do us the honor?" They were playing "White Christmas," Dottie's favorite. Her face was a picture—she looked eight years old, not eighty.

Nick whispered, "Better give the people what they want, Grams..." Great, he hadn't seen me. Being in the shadow of the door behind him, and dressed as a food, definitely made me less recognizable.

Hand in hand, they walked up to the stage.

"And no excuse for you, Nicholas." Dean was keeping the lead guitar line going on loop. He nodded over at where Nick's bass was propped up. "Figure it out as we go."

I was worried that although she'd told me she used to love

singing, maybe when faced with it, this would be too much for Dottie, but as Nick helped her up to the mic, her face lit up almost as much as the room. Phew, we didn't have to resort to emergency plan B. No one wanted a warbling pumpkin.

Dottie steadied herself with a deep breath, leaned into the mic, and...started to sing. "White Christmas."

Wow. I knew she would be good, but I didn't expect her to give Adele a run for her money. Dottie's body might have gotten small and frail, but hearing her sing was like getting a glimpse of her when she was my age. And as she got more into the song, waltzing around the stage, her fragile arms and legs suddenly a lot surer of themselves, it was like the clock had been rewound.

I couldn't take my eyes off her. Well, I could, but only because Nick looked so drop-dead gorgeous next to her. He was smiling, laughing, even joining in with her dancing. And he wasn't the only one—the normally quiet, calm hall was full of everyone who could, getting up to dance, and those who couldn't were swaying in their seats.

It was even better than I'd hoped, and when they got to the end of the song, it was fair to say the room went wild, even people I'd never seen stand were on their feet.

"Well..." Dottie looked around. "I really don't know what to say."

Nick leaned into the mic. "How about, what's next?"

Charl whooped a loud, "Hell yeah!"

"But..." Dottie had a hand up and was trying to look into the dark of the room. "But who did all this? Who are we thanking here? Charl? Was it you?!"

Charl shouted back, "Guess again..." She laughed, enjoying how well this evening was going down.

But she'd promised, so her lips were sealed. There was no way I wanted credit, that wasn't what tonight was about. Tonight was about Dottie getting the Christmas surprise she deserved. It had taken me a while, but I finally got that Christmas wasn't about doing things perfectly, it was about having the perfect people to do them with.

With Dottie's friends and the staff clapping a chant of "one more song," the band launched into "Winter Wonderland."

And as they played, and the party notched up another level, that's when Nick finally saw me. He did a double take, probably because of my bright-orange face, but then grinned.

Was this you? he mouthed from the stage, trying not to lose his place in the song.

I shrugged innocently, but who knows what that looked like when I was fully round, my arms only just sticking out.

When the next song finished, and Dottie took a quick break, Nick slipped off stage.

He walked straight over. "This *was* all you, wasn't it?!"

"I couldn't possibly say."

"And I couldn't possibly say what an awesome job it is." It was so good to see him smile—especially after yesterday.

"I knew Au Revoir Hairs was going to be epic, but *seriously*?!"

"Thank you...I mean, not the band thing, even though obviously I'm biased." He looked over at Dottie, already back up dueting, shaking her shoulders, loving every second. "I mean thank you for—" But I didn't let him finish.

"Don't. It was the least I could do. My way of saying thanks. For everything. And sorry. And...well, I get it. A little late, but I get it." I held out a piece of gingerbread house I'd been stress nibbling on. It was Dottie's favorite, so we had a massive one for all the residents. "No more Grinch chat. I promise."

"But this must have taken you forever?"

"It's been a busy day, put it that way. And I don't know if Dottie will ever find the stocking I hid in her room. But Elle's been amazing. And Charl, Dean, Blake, your parents—everyone." A new song cut in, and we stood and clapped as Dottie led the room in what I think was the start of "YMCA." Guess they were branching out. "I just thought why carol sing when you could Christmas karaoke, right? Miller style."

"Well, it's amazing. What you've done..." We watched Dottie and her friends pulling some serious shapes. "I mean, tomorrow when you're at the Snow Ball, remember how it absolutely doesn't compare to this."

Guess it was time to tell him.

"I'm not going..." Truth was, I was going home—tonight. Elle had helped me swap the flights but, despite missing out on time here, missing out on meeting her properly, I knew it was the right thing to do. As amazing as tomorrow would be, being home for Christmas, being there with Mum, was more important—whatever house we were in.

"You were right, Nick. A hundred percent right. The perfect Christmas never had anything to do with making sure it all went to plan, did it?" Nick was too kind to say anything. He just smiled. "And I get it. Seeing what happens doesn't make it less special. Doesn't make someone love Christmas any less. In fact, thanks to you, I've had some of the best times ever." I laughed. Why was being honest so cringe? "I mean, not many people could have made me break onto a rooftop...or do the double of bacon and pumpkin costumes in one week."

Nick laughed softly. "Hey, it's not like I haven't been putting in the work too—never have I ever drunk so much hot chocolate. Or hid under a desk for so long. Let alone had my photo taken while a woman yelled at me to 'be more reindeer.'"

"Well, I've had the best time. Thanks to you..." But I had to tell him the thing. "But I need to go home." That wasn't quite right. "Well, not home—I just need, want, to be with Mum. My plane's in a few hours."

It meant tonight would be the last time I saw Dottie, that I would only have a few hours left with their whole family, with Nick.

"Wow." Nick slumped back next to me against the wall. "I wasn't expecting that."

Neither was I—it all happened so quickly. "Look, I'm not going to pretend that I don't wish I could have more time here, or I dunno, be in two places at once. Three, if you count your gig..."

"Hey..." He gestured toward the corridor. "Can I tell you something? Something I should have said yesterday?" Ominous, but I followed him. It took two attempts to fit me through the door, and when I made it through, Nick looked uncomfortable. Not as much as when I'd attacked him with a singing dog, but up there.

He exhaled so hard, his fringe fluttered up.

"Glad I chose the brightest lit, most echoey place to do this." He cleared his throat. "Yesterday...." Uh-oh, here we go. "One of the reasons I got so mad in the car was because...well, I just thought you knew me better than that."

"Sorry about that."

"No, don't apologize. That's not what I mean." He rubbed his forehead, as if this were just as painful for him. It really wasn't. Was I going to get a lecture on just how many things I'd gotten wrong this week?

"I just thought you hated Christmas." I shrugged. "Hated me." Nick shook his head—and almost laughed.

"You really have no idea, do you?" He looked back up at me, but this time there was a tiny smile. A tiny, gorgeous smile. "You go to all this effort for Christmas, all these things to make it special, but you have no idea it's you... *You're* what has made this Christmas special."

"Me?" I couldn't believe what I was hearing.

"Yes, you. It's you being here that's made everyone so happy this year. Mom, Dad, Dottie...me. That's what's changed. And yes, I know you said you were all about 'catch flights, not feelings.'" He rolled his eyes and laughed. "And, no, I still can't make that sound okay, but I need you to know... Whether it's on the list or not, it's too late for me—my feelings have been well and truly caught."

Oh. Wow. Nick liked me?

Nick liked *me.*

I hadn't left it all too late?!

"Even though I do things like this?"

I looked down my giant orange body, wishing I wasn't at least three quarters of a meter in depth. And width.

"*Especially* because you do things like that." Nick looked up. I looked up.

How had Charl managed to put the one piece of mistletoe here?!

Was Nick going to kiss me?!

Were we going to kiss? He raised his eyebrows. "Little twig dung, huh?"

I raised mine back. "What's that doing there?" is what I wanted to say but all I managed was "dwig tung" instead.

The gap between us was getting smaller—even with a giant foam fruit between us.

But that's when we both heard it. The little glockenspiel noise playing out.

The international signal for Christmas. Could we pretend we hadn't heard it?

"Hollllly." Charl burst the door open. "This is your request, right?"

Yup, it was. My brilliant, stupid, terrible-timed request.

"All I Want for Christmas Is You" was playing next door, but all I wanted was right here.

And as much as I would have traded every Malteser Reindeer in the world to stay and see what might have happened under the mistletoe with Nick, we both knew that Elle's challenge to have a kiss under the mistletoe was the one thing left I was now never going to accomplish.

I smiled at Charl and thanked her for letting me know. Which was better than breaking down in tears, grabbing her ankles, and asking why she couldn't have just given me sixty seconds to have the Christmas kiss of my dreams.

But a rule's a rule—so grabbing Nick's hand, I pulled him into the hall, and onto the stage.

And together, we did a word-perfect, tune-definitely-very-far-from-perfect, rendition of "All I Want for Christmas Is You," top notes and all.

Dottie had her camera out for the whole thing, taking as many photos as she could between massively unsubtle winks.

Nick and I laughed, we screeched, we potentially caused some damage to Max's hearing aid.

Nick twirled me—I twirled him straight back.

Nick pulled on the Father Christmas outfit he'd spotted beside the stage. I dealt with the moral quandary of seriously crushing hard on Father Christmas. With arms around each other—as much as you can when one of you is spherical—Nick and I sang the last line, laughing, smiling—at Dottie, at the crowd, at each other.

And as Mariah crooned, we ended by giving the crowd what they were cheering for.

Me giving Nick the tiniest kiss on the cheek.

I hadn't exactly managed my mistletoe kiss, but feeling as happy as I did right now, I really had made my Christmas wish come true.

And as I looked at Nick, I knew. *All I want for Christmas is you.*

CHAPTER TWENTY-EIGHT

Holly

"Flight BV197—gate seven now open. Could all passengers make their way to the gate."

I looked around nervously. I couldn't go, not yet. Not until they said it was the last second was I going to budge.

I couldn't believe this was the end. Saying goodbye to Jess and Pete sucked, but they had to drop me and race off to the Snow Ball. It was amazing they even offered to give me a lift when they had the biggest event of their working lives starting in a few hours. They were incredible. I knew they'd smash it—I told them I'd be watching everything online.

I shouldn't worry though—they seemed to have extra energy for it now that they'd had a big chat with Nick and Elle. They'd caught Elle at the airport before her flight, and they'd all finally come clean about what had been going on. All this time, Nick and Elle had been worried that their parents had been figuring out if they should move again, when the truth was, they'd been loving life in Alpine Peaks and had only been asking all those questions because this time, they really thought they should all stay. Pete and Jess knew they had the option of signing a long-term lease for the business here and had been trying to make sure it was the right thing for Elle and Nick. It had never been about them trying to make Elle and Nick leave—all they'd wanted was to be doing whatever they could to make them be happy here. Even if that was spending more time with Grams. But now with Elle and Nick both feeling better than they had done in years, Dottie too, and the business doing so well, they'd all come to an agreement. They all wanted to sign the new lease, to properly commit to staying. And to commit to honesty being the best policy if they wanted to make it work.

But I'd already told them a white lie. None of them had any idea I'd left them presents under the tree. As well as the onesies, I'd made a printed photo book for Jess, full of all the old photos Mum had managed to dig out of Little Marsh back in the day.

For Pete, I'd written up the Christmas Treefle recipe in a handmade recipe book. The front cover just said "Pete Miller: King of Waffles (and probably Treefles too)." And Nick—well, we'd agreed not to do presents, but I couldn't not leave him *anything*. So I'd printed out the photos from our trip to New York—mainly the ones of me messing up the poses at the Top of the Rock—and put them in a copy of a *Gremlins* DVD that I'd picked up at a thrift store. ARGH. I mean charity shop. This place was getting to me!

Thinking about leaving them all made my breath catch in my chest—uh-oh...like I might cry again.

It happened every time I thought about the goodbyes. Especially the one with Nick. It had been so rushed—but he'd had to go straight from Dottie's to squeezing in a gig rehearsal. I really hoped someone would film it tomorrow. That would be my January entertainment sorted.

"Flight BV197—gate seven now open. Could all passengers please make their way to the gate."

I hoisted my massive hand luggage off the floor and tried to get a grip. It didn't help that I was lugging around the massive sign I'd bought for Mum and Colin in Manhattan. It weighed a ton but wouldn't squash into my suitcase. I pulled back the Bubble Wrap to check it was surviving. "Welcome to the home of Sophie, Colin, Naomi, Holly, Zai, Kai, and Colin." I'd wanted to put "Colin x2" but had resisted—it was going to look great outside our new home.

Being away had really made me realize that home wasn't about the postcode, it was about being where Mum and Naomi are—if Mum wanted to add more people into the mix, well, it just meant more pressies...and more chance of multiple tins of Quality Street.

My phone buzzed.

Literally. Cannot. Wait. One and a half more sleeps till Christmas. And one more till YOU.

It was the early morning there—she should be asleep!

I set my alarm to wave you offffffff

She was the actual best. She never normally woke up for anything!

Remind me to never be apart from you for this long ever again. Genuinely have developed an eye twitch it's been so stressful without you.

LOVE YOU SLEEP NOW SEE YOU SOON LOVE YOU SLEEP LOVE WAVE FROM THE SKYYYY.

But it already said she was off-line—I think she'd fallen back asleep already. She was worse than Colin. When Ruby woke up, I would have landed. I'd arranged to meet her at That Little Café at two p.m. after I'd had a shower. I said I had film on my disposable camera to use up, so she should look extra HAWT. What Ruby didn't know was I'd also asked Temi to meet me—same place same time. It was a setup so they could finally have their date. I was dying to see Ruby, but I could wait, as I was dying to make it up to her even more.

I looked around again and checked the arrivals and departure boards for any hint mine and Elle's last-minute idea might work. But nothing.

"Flight BV197—gate seven now open. Could all passengers make their way to the gate. Boarding will begin shortly."

Guess I better start walking then. Oh well—we knew it needed a miracle to have worked.

BANG.

Ouch?! A human ran at me at full pelt.

THUD.

I only stayed standing as my massive bag balanced me out.

"I can't believe we did it!" Elle threw her luggage down and went in for round two of the biggest hug. "I swear I was about to bribe the cabin crew with Twiglets to make the pilots get a move on. I even had Ruby do a lucky pebble spell thing."

I stepped back, looked at Elle, and hugged her all over again. "I can't believe you're real?!" And that we'd pulled it off. We'd actually gotten to meet?!

I also couldn't believe that, even after an all-day flight, she still looked like a goddess.

"Sweaty, puffy, and probably stinky but yup, very real. Oh..." She dug in her pocket and threw something in my bag. "This is for the plane." It was very much Toblerone shaped—she'd done well. I didn't ruin the surprise by telling her I had something for her too—a thank-you package under her pillow (specially wrapped in tinsel, as I knew she was secretly into it). Fred's sausage roll T-shirt that I'd been sleeping in since he left it at mine. I knew she'd love it and, well...it felt right that a bit of Fred should be waiting for her too. Fred loved the idea. I'd also left the details of something Pot Roast had passed on via Dean last night—details of her Boxing Day party that Elle and I were both invited to. I had a feeling Elle might be up for it.

"I can't believe I only get, what"—I looked up at the clock—"two minutes with you. There's so much to cover. Starting with THANK YOU FOR THE MOST BONKERS HARD BRILLIANT thing I've ever done in my life." I realized I was holding her hands—I just didn't want to let her go, let any of this go. "Honestly, Elle, I've had the most amazing week ever—all thanks to you."

"DITTO. Like a million times ditto." She kept looking at me if she also couldn't believe I was real. "I'm missing everyone so much already! Who KNEW a bad idea could lead to all this?"

"Bad ideas are the best. Oh, congrats on the win, by the way. Well, the post, I mean..." Elle had made the official announcement just before she took off. It was my favorite post of hers EVER. Along with more photos from her trip, she'd announced that she wasn't claiming the prize, wished everyone luck, and told everyone that her account was changing to be a whole load more honest. Starting with her telling everyone about how she'd shut down her old account because of trolls, and if anyone was going through the same, her DMs were open. I couldn't help but notice she'd unfollowed Dove too.

After reading it, I was definitely leaving here a bigger fan of hers than ever.

Elle just shrugged. "Yeah, cool, whatever. It was probably something I should have done months ago." She smiled. "Oh, I didn't tell you the best part, did I? Or did you see what Clara wrote?" I shook my head. "Well, have a look yourself. Basically she liked it—and commented to tell everyone she was going to be more honest too. Starting with admitting to what she'd done on my old account. The full thing!" Elle had filled me in on what went down. "She really went there, Hol?! It was a real apology. And then said she was pulling out of the challenge too—and instead she's going to be supporting me in whatever I do next. Which is, y'know." Elle shrugged again, but she had a massive smile. "Kind of cool I guess."

"Nice." I could tell how much that meant to her. "And any word from Dove?" Elle hadn't just messaged her to call her out—she'd asked to meet to talk it out. It was a big move, but Elle said she'd rather face up to it than pretend it was all okay.

"Still waiting. But...I'd like to hear her out. Is that weird? I mean, we're not going to be friends anytime soon, but if anyone should know that things online aren't always what they seem, it should probably be me."

Well, or me—I'd always thought Elle's life was perfect too, until I got to see behind the scenes.

"And youuuu." She prodded me. "Get you, finishing all your lists?"

"Well, almost." I winced. "Can we agree that even without the mistletoe kiss"—I did a fake sick noise—"you do the surprise for our mums anyway?"

"Well, that was one—"

"*Flight BV197 is now boarding. Could all passengers report to the gate.*"

Elle got cut off. We both knew what that announcement meant. This was it.

"I'm going to miss you." I gave her another hug—as someone who hated physical contact, I was surprising myself. "Which makes no sense, as I've only just met you, but I will."

She wasn't letting me go either. "You too."

If the Holly of two months ago could see this—me hugging @OneElleOfATime in an airport in the States, after switching all my plans super last minute—I would have assumed it was a weird Christmas cheese dream.

"And you're going to be okay waiting for Nick?" He was coming to pick her up after rehearsal.

Elle grinned. "You know it." She dropped her head on my shoulder. "And sister-in-law has a nice ring to it." She'd made me tell her everything just before she took off. Although it turned out Nick had beaten me to it. Guess those two really were back on track.

I shook her off, but I was laughing. "And so does friend-in-law."

Elle smiled—her big, perfect smile. "Watch this space."

Fred hadn't told me what was happening next with them, but I knew neither of them were in any hurry for this to be the last time they saw each other.

I scooped up my bags... "Send my love to everyone!" I started to half jog, sideways-walk away. "And happy Christmas! The real one and the family one in January. THANKS FOR ONE ABSOLUTE JINGLE BELL OF A TIME."

And as we both blew kisses, tears spilled down my face as I hurried to not miss my plane. I couldn't figure out if the tears were sad to say bye or so happy for everything that had happened.

I sprinted for what felt like a mile, but I got through final security checks and made it to the gate in time—there were still people boarding, so I joined the back of the queue, trying not to sniff too loudly. Just hearing British accents around me suddenly made me feel nearer to home.

My stomach twisted—an excited twist. Mum had no idea what was going to happen when I landed. My final surprise that Elle had helped me pull off. Her travel contact hadn't just changed my flight—they found one for Naomi too. And an hour after I landed in Heathrow, Naomi would be landing too. The three of us were all going to be home for Christmas after all. And thinking about my mum's face when I told her was going to be... NOPE, ABOUT TO CRY AGAIN.

"Ma'am..." An attendant was standing in front of me. "Ma'am?"

Uh-oh.

"Yes?!" Everyone in airports had a knack of making me feel like I was going to somehow end up in prison.

"I think this gentleman is trying to get your attention."

"Erm, I think you might have the wrong person." But she shook her head and pointed behind me, to the barrier I'd just walked through.

"Something to do with... poop?"

I didn't see anyone I knew. Just people dragging cases and someone in a terrible Christmas comedy hat. There was always someone who took it too far—which, coming from someone who had polar bear socks with sticky-out ears on, was a lot.

But the person in the massive, green dangly hat was waving.

Was it...

In the middle of everyone racing about, there he was—standing still in all the chaos, waving straight at me.

Nick.

What. Was. Happening?

I walked over, the edges of anything that wasn't Nick blurring. I couldn't actually be sure if my feet moved or if I floated there.

"W...what are you doing here?"

"I ducked out of the last few songs." He was still trying to catch his breath. "The guys understood. I thought I'd missed you!" He bent double for a second before standing back up. "But I couldn't not at least try."

He'd done all that for me?! I was almost speechless.

Brain—focus. BE USEFUL.

"You've got a hat on." Out of all the things, you went for that?!

"Well, after all the effort you put in, I couldn't let you leave without completing your final thing." He suddenly looked shy. "Only if you wanted to, of course."

And that's when I realized what his hat was. A big green foam cap, yes, but the thing sticking off wasn't a fake tree.

It was a bunch of fake mistletoe. Dung twigs.

Dangling right above his face. "It was the best I could do!"

He'd never looked more ridiculous. He'd never looked more nervous. He'd never looked more gorgeous.

And right there, with less than a minute left of my holiday, at gate seven, Newark Airport, Nick and I crossed off the final thing on my final Christmas list.

A kiss under the mistletoe.

And out of all the magical Christmas things that had happened in the last week, it managed to be the very best.

JANUARY 5

Happy Christmas, Future Holly!

Well! Where to start with this one?

Oh, yes. If you're not holding a hot drink, go get one. And make sure you're wearing a jumper. The one Mum got you of the New York skyline with light-up windows HAS to be first. IT'S A WORK OF ART. Woolly art.

Oh, and do me a favour. Message Mum and Nay and tell them you can't wait to spend Christmas with them. Hug them when you next see them—unless Naomi is back off being reunited with an octopus. Or at uni, or whatever.

Tell Ruby and Fred too.

And it's Christmas, so what the heck. Get Colin x 2 in on the action.

IN FACT, STOP EVERYTHING. Most, MOST crucial

thing is IMMEDIATELY put on the playlist Nick sent you to wake up to on Christmas Day. It's audio perfection.

Sooooo...where to start with this year?! It's hard to know. I thought the year before might have been the best ever, but then BOOM. After a shaky start, this year snuck up and blew it out of the gingerbread-flavoured water.

I set out to have the most perfect Christmas ever—and guess what? I did!

Mum cried her eyes out when Naomi turned up at the airport on Christmas Eve. But then so did Naomi and so did I—so no judgment. The drive home was almost two hours, but Mum played "Driving Home for Christmas" on repeat the whole way, and we sang along every time and it honestly didn't ever get boring.

Colin was so excited to see me, he ran into a door. And Mum's Colin was really sweet—he'd made a welcome-home banner for us when we got back. Sure, it was black-and-white and looked like a hipster coffee shop sign, but it was the thought that counted. And, oh my Christmas puddings—did he and Mum love their present?!? When they opened the sign for the new house, they kept holding each other's hands and giving each other weird misty looks before hugging me and telling me how special I was. Obvs the even better thing was that Naomi's present of a wood carving of an elephant was nowhere near as good, even if it was for charity.

(I shouldn't have enjoyed that so much—but then again, I shouldn't eat my whole selection box before 10 a.m. on Christmas Day. And I still do. Every year.)

They've already taken the sign to Col's—apparently it will be the first thing they decorate with. All we need is an offer on the house, but someone's interested, so fingers crossed.

Oh, and the twins LOVED their present even more.

Top tip-off from Elle.

Naomi looked a little confused at the two defrosting soggy bags under Jenny-Fir Lopez (this year's tree who overachieved in every aspect), but when they opened them, it all made sense. Well, as much sense as chicken nuggets could.

After dinner (OMG, Colin does mashed potato AND roasties AND totally off-piste Yorkshire puddings—I've seen a new side to him), we FaceTimed the Millers. Pete and Jess had rushed back so they could be together on the 25th and, even better, Dottie was home with them too! The old people's home had had a change of heart and residents had been allowed to leave for Christmas Day after all—maybe Charl had just had too much mulled wine at the party?!

They all loved the presents I'd left and had on the onesies, so we all matched each other on the call. Except Nick, as obviously I'd made it back in the day, when I thought he was a six-year-old. He had it on his arm though. High-five us on a new tradition, two sides of the Atlantic! I'd stayed on after to speak to Elle—and then Nick.

Even though I'd only been gone just over a day, it was still the best seeing them. Nick and I had one of those conversations which is a lot of smiling and not many words, and if I weren't me I'd think we were gross. But I am me, so I can confirm it was amazing, and I'm still as into him two weeks after I left. Maybe even more. He'd watched Elf in my honour. Twice!! When I closed my laptop, I actually licked it. TELL NO ONE.

Elle did go and hang out with Pot Roast—and from her feed, they've been hanging out loads.

What else, what else? RUBY AND TEMI. Are together!!! Their date on Christmas Eve led to them snogging after their final panto performance. OH NO THEY DIDN'T! OH YES THEY DID!

Fred was a bit of a sad sack, cos he said he'd packed his heart in Elle's suitcase and it may never return. Still, I told him I'd help save for a trip back. Evil cackle. If only he knew?!

Funny. I really thought all the changes meant Christmas would be ruined, but this year everything was different, totally off plan, and it was my best yet. Although, Mum has promised, wherever we live, we can always come back for Carol's singing. That's one thing I'm not missing out on.

AND BEST BIT? It's the fifth of January today and

for the first time ever, our decorations are still UP. But how could we take anything down? Because when Jess said they'd planned something big for their "proper" Christmas in January, I'd had no idea what she was planning.

Elle's sponsors were so impressed with her new style of posts, they offered her loads more travel. So that was her last surprise for our mums. She'd been working on it the whole time. Helping fix something Jess had wanted to do for ages... coming to visit where she had Christmas as a child. Elle, Pete, and Colin had worked out the details, and the big reveal was on Christmas Day on our video call. Elle totally played it down and said it was only fair as I'd done all of her list after all. WHAT A LEGEND (especially as I'd already got the best thing ever from that, a.k.a. snogging her brother in the airport OMGHOWHOT). Anyway, it means any second, we're leaving to pick them up. ALL OF THEM—Nick and Elle too. I couldn't BE more excited.

It's going to be the BEST SURPRISE ever for Fred.

ULTIMATE CHRISTMAS CRACKER!! I can't believe Elle and I managed to keep it quiet!

Ruby's coming to the airport with us, and Naomi's staying behind to make the thank-you Christmas Treefle as she wants Elle to know what a star she is for sorting her flights. Imagine, two months ago, I was panicking about Christmas not just being the three of us—and now

I'm buzzing we're having one two weeks late and with ten people?!

If this is a yearly tradition—I'm INTO it.

HAPPY HOLIDAYS & MERRY CHRISTMAS & MAY ALL YOUR DAYS BE FILLED WITH MALTESER REINDEERS.

Hol xxxx

CHRISTMAS DAY PLAYLIST FOR CHRISTINE P. BACON

and Remember Mariah Is Watching (Listening) Xxx

1. **"I Wish It Could Be Christmas" by Wizzard**
   I will never NEVER forget the sight of you clutching that singing dog. (Especially as I'd never heard this song IN MY LIFE before). A true classic Christmas (crime) scene.
2. **"White Christmas" by Bing Crosby**
   Sorry I couldn't find the jazz version from the market, but don't mess with perfection, I say. Obviously nowhere good as Dottie's version though (this was her choice for the list btw). Also Bing wasn't his real name. It's Harry. I know you love a Christmas fact. You're welcome.
3. **"Little Donkey" by The Beverley Sisters**
   Dominic will never be okay that you've left. Please continue to spread his reindonkey fame across the land (Little Marsh).

4. **"Last Christmas" by Wham!**

   Elle's choice. She said it always makes her smile when Fred sings that she gave away her heart "the very next Dave." And it was playing when we had our first real chat. I've put it on ALTHOUGH I FUNDAMENTALLY DO NOT BUY INTO THE LYRICS. OKAY?

5. **"Christmas Time (Don't Let the Bells End)" by The Darkness**

   You put this on in my car, and I haven't been able to get it out of my head since (just like you). (Oh God, I can't believe I just wrote that. In pen.)

6. **"Candy Cane Lane" by Sia**

   Your face when you came to yell at me for waking you up with this was somehow both terrifying and incredibly cute.

7. **"It's Beginning to Look a Lot Like Christmas" by The Bublé**

   Full disclosure, this was Mom and Dad's choice. Well, Mom's. They send their love. Perfect song for you to put on in...October? (JOKE.)

8. **"Driving Home for Christmas" by Chris Rea**

   It's your mom's favorite (clearly a woman of excellent taste), and it reminds me of the best day I've ever had in New York. They didn't have a "flying home" version, so this will have to do. Monster Elsa says hi btw.

9. **"Blue Christmas" by Elvis**

Remember that time when we had a really awkward convo in my car, and you were dripping snow everywhere and I was bummed out because I thought you hated me? But weirdly it somehow made everything get really good? Well, you do now.

10. **"Winter Wonderland" by Anna Kendrick & Snoop Dogg**

Honestly, the Alpine Peaks Senior Living crowd was the most lit audience ever. I will never forget this. And neither will the rest of the band. New York will have nothing on this. I went for the Pitch Perfect (and yes, I've seen it, so don't even ask) version, as there are too many dudes on this list.

11. **"One More Sleep" by Leona Lewis**

I didn't know this one, but I tried to find songs about wishing this random girl wasn't about to fly around the world and you weren't going to completely miss her, until whenever it was that you got to see her again. But this was the nearest I could do. And it's—as you would say—a bop.

12. **"Once Upon a Christmas Time (The Girl in the Turkey Slippers)" by the Au Revoir Hairs**

NOT YET HEARD SOON-TO-BE CLASSIC. Written by the hottest band in the States, soon to be world. It's about a very special someone (you). (I know how bad you are at hints.) #wattle

13. **"All I Want for Christmas Is You" by Mariah Carey**

Too many reasons to mention but the main one is… I couldn't have said it better myself.

ACKNOWLEDGMENTS

Okay, I'm going to make a wild guess that you're reading this somewhere in the vicinity of December 25? In which case, HAPPY CHRISTMAS!

I love this time of year, so a massive, extravagantly gift-wrapped thank you to the awesome team at Sourcebooks for giving me the best Christmas present ever—bringing Holly and Elle (and Colin) to America. Thank you! With an extra special big thanks to Steve, Zeina, and Cassie for all the amazing editorial-ness, Kelly and Nicole for the gorgeous new cover, and Beth for the marketing and publicity.

Back in the UK, thank you to Lauren at Scholastic for giving me the chance to write about all things festive and to Yasmin for jumping straight in and being a Christmas guru. Pete—what can I say? Dead poinsettias, sandwiches, sausage rolls, spreadsheets.

Just the biggest thank you (and to your mum too). Big thanks also to Jessica, the proofreader of dreams, and to the rest of team at Scholastic, especially Harriet and the awesome publicity team, Emily and the brilliant rights team, and Ruth too—thank you all for your support. Gemma, as always thank you for being the very, very best (and for the commitment to incredibly strong festive accessories for Charlie).

Like Holly in the book, I love all things Christmassy—and the reason I love it all so much is because of my wonderful family. Daddles and Moomin—thank you for making every Christmas so very special, and thank you for being you. I can't tell you how much I'm looking forward to this one. Becca, you're the best co-present-giver-out-er there is, and well, Ian, your jumpers really raised the game. Rose, you are pure Christmas magic all year 'round—you brighten up any day you're in with your sparkle.

Chris, thank you for everything, always. And to fellow elves Babs and Kev—thank you for all the inspo (shout-out to turkey-eating Chester), and thank you Phil and Ashlee (my paper-crown-wearing American guru).

Molly and Mikey, thanks for the photo poses; Jess, thanks for...everything; Ro, you couldn't have been more supportive; my London friends, let's have many more Christmas adventures (James, fingers crossed no more Christmas trees fall over); and Julie, Jackie, the New York power women, I owe you many pickle-backs for making my time there so great. Tina, I can't believe you go to the beach for Christmas now (but I still love you). And finally, a big stuffed stocking of thank-yous to Team Cooper, all the bloggers who've been so supportive, Dan, Temi, Laura, Matt & East 17—that was a lights switch-on to remember.

And lastly to everyone who has been in touch, your messages are like mini Christmas presents all of their own. Thank you. Hope you liked this one.

So all that's left to say is a very VERY happy Christmas.

And next time you hear Mariah, please sing along.

ABOUT THE AUTHOR

Beth Garrod lives in East London with her husband, Chris, and when she's not writing books, she works with charities and broadcasters around the world to make content that helps empower young people. Beth really loves Christmas. Like really, really loves Christmas.

OTHER VOLUMES IN THIS SERIES

John Ashbery, editor, *The Best American Poetry 1988*

Donald Hall, editor, *The Best American Poetry 1989*

Jorie Graham, editor, *The Best American Poetry 1990*

Mark Strand, editor, *The Best American Poetry 1991*

Charles Simic, editor, *The Best American Poetry 1992*

Louise Glück, editor, *The Best American Poetry 1993*

A. R. Ammons, editor, *The Best American Poetry 1994*

Richard Howard, editor, *The Best American Poetry 1995*

Adrienne Rich, editor, *The Best American Poetry 1996*

James Tate, editor, *The Best American Poetry 1997*

Harold Bloom, editor, *The Best of the Best American Poetry 1988–1997*

John Hollander, editor, *The Best American Poetry 1998*